VANITY AND VENGEANCE

A Sequel Inspired by <u>Pride and Prejudice</u>, *by Jane Austen*

Linda Mako Kendrick

Risky Venture Publishing Company

LAKEWOOD, OHIO

VANITY AND VENGEANCE

Copyright © 2017 by **LINDA MARIE MAKO KENDRICK**

All rights reserved. No part of this publication may be reproduced, distributed or transmitted in any form or by any means, without prior written permission.

Risky Venture Publishing Company
www.riskyventure.org

Publisher's Note: This is a work of fiction. Names, characters, places, and incidents are a product of the author's imagination. Locales and public names are sometimes used for atmospheric purposes. Any resemblance to actual people, living or dead, or to businesses, companies, events, institutions, or locales is completely coincidental.

Book Layout © 2017 BookDesignTemplates.com

Book Cover Design by EverpageDesigns.com

Vanity and Vengeance/Linda Mako Kendrick. -- 1st edition
ISBN 978-0-9989861-0-4
Vanity and Vengeance/Linda Mako Kendrick. – 2d edition; Large Print
ISBN 978-0-9989861-1-1
Vanity and Vengeance/Linda Mako Kendrick. – 3d edition; e-Book cf
ISBN 978-0-9989861-2-8

In loving memory of
Martha Alma Deering Wolf Mako
because she bought me comic books when I was a kid
so I'd learn to love reading as much as she did.
Thanks, Mom.

CONTENTS
in the Language of Flowers

1. "New Beginnings"..1
2. "Esteem, But Not Love"..11
3. "I Declare Against You"...17
4. "Resolved to Win"..25
5. "Deception"..29
6. "Your Temper is Too Hasty"..................................33
7. "Your Presence Soothes Me"................................39
8. "Wit"...45
9. "Beloved Child"..51
10. "You Are Too Bold"..57
11. "Let's Take a Chance"...61
12. "Play!"..67
13. "Revenge"..73
14. "Jealousy"..79
15. "The Variety of Your Conversation Delights Me"........85
16. "Sorrowful Remembrance"....................................89
17. "My Regrets Follow You to the Grave"..................95
18. "You Have Disappointed Me"...............................103

19. "I Engage You for the Next Dance" 107
20. "Keep Your Promise" 117
21. "Baseness" 123
22. "Bravery and Humanity" 129
23. "Assignation" 133
24. "Worth Beyond Beauty" 141
25. "If You Love Me, You Will Discover It" 149
26. "The Witching Soul of Music" 153
27. "Do Not Refuse Me" 159
28. "Let Me Tempt You" 163
29. "Beware of a False Friend" 169
30. "Hopelessness" 175
31. "I Have Lost All" 181
32. "I Am Sensible to Your Kindness" 185
33. "A Deadly Foe is Near" 189
34. "Wishes Will Come True" 195
35. "Bitter Truth" 203
36. "Thank You for Understanding" 213
37. "Counterfeit" 217
38. "I Burn!" 223
39. "I Have a Message for You" 233
40. "Flee Away!" 243

41. "I Fall a Victim" 251

42. "I Am Your Captive" 259

43. "Never Despair" 267

44. "Justice Shall Be Done to Thee" 273

45. "Return of Happiness" 283

46. "My Destiny is In Your Hands" 289

47. "You Puzzle Me" 295

<u>A BONUS FOR MY READERS!</u>

*References to flowers are scattered throughout
VANITY AND VENGEANCE, and I enjoyed "matching" their
numerous traditional meanings to the various situations.
If you would like a complete list of all the floriographic references,
please send an e-mail request to:*
<u>LMMK201213@gmail.com</u>
And be sure to INCLUDE "FLOWERS" in the SUBJECT LINE!

CHAPTER ONE

Daffodil

It is a truth universally acknowledged, that a man possessed of a sister of marriageable age and independent fortune must be in want of a healthy bachelor born of a good family.

"*She will not have him, either,*" Fitzwilliam Darcy told himself, as he watched another young man hover about his sweet, reserved, lovely, sister. "*He will flatter, he will smile, he will cajole. Then, one of two things will happen: If he is sincere, her disinterest will drive him away. If he seeks her fortune of thirty thousand pounds, he will persist until I drive him away.*" Darcy shook his head. "*All these years of disdain, and I find myself in rapt admiration of my wife's ridiculous mother and her gift for marrying off four of five impoverished daughters, all of them at a younger age than my one wealthy sister.*" Darcy thought for a moment about his use of the adjective 'ridiculous' in describing his mother-in-law and resolved to expunge that word from his vocabulary. His wife was too dear to him; he had never known any other woman and never would. Such was the nature of Fitzwilliam Darcy – to love only once.

He frowned. Was that Georgiana's fate, too? To love only one man? Is that why this business of receiving suitors had proven so fruitless? Darcy kept his posture of mild disinterest, but colored a little at the unwelcome idea. *"Blast him! It cannot have been love! I should have killed the rabid cur when I had him by the tail. I could have saved myself an ocean of recrimination and my wife's family an equal amount of scandal and humiliation."*

Although it was imperceptible to all others, Elizabeth Darcy had noticed the change in her husband's mood and swept to his side. As he turned to acknowledge her presence, he once again felt a pleasant rush of desire. It amused him to realize how little she had to do in order to capture his full attention. When he was a young man, he took great pride in his disdain for the petty flatteries and alluring devices of women. As a man married ten years, with a son aged almost eight years, he was paying the price for that youthful invulnerability. He whispered into her ear. Now, Elizabeth colored a little and smiled just enough to indicate her pleasure.

Just then, a perfidious twinge of envy crawled into Darcy's breast, and he worked to beat it back. Yes, Rosings was a far more elegant estate than his own Pemberley. The floor of Rosings' ballroom, for example, was Italian marble, while Pemberley's room was half its size and with a hardwood parquet floor. Pemberley's room had tapestry wall hangings, where Rosings' ballroom walls were lined with oil paintings. Darcy sniffed. *"Tapestries better control the sound. Too much echoing in this room. The music and conversation collide here, where at Pemberley they blend. Pemberley has the atmosphere more conducive to..."*

He stopped himself. Since becoming a father, Darcy found that he yearned for things for his wife and his child (and yes, for his sister, too) that he had never wanted for himself. To all of his acquaintance, Fitzwilliam Darcy was a man to be envied, but in this past eight years, his vision had focused on his limitations. Wealth was not enough because he already had wealth. Being welcomed at court, being addressed by a title, these were all just beyond his fingertips and so they were what he desired.

Aloud, Darcy remarked that this ball at Rosings was "quite delightful" and the society "elegant, yet all of pleasant acquaintance."

Elizabeth nodded but watched Georgiana carefully. "No," she concluded, "*she is not interested in him. She will be twenty-eight in the summertime, and she will be unmarried. Is the girl determined to turn Pemberley into a cloister?*" Elizabeth collected herself. She was unhappy for Georgiana. The girl is miserable in large companies like this! Yet, how else would she make acquaintance with an appropriate suitor? Miss Darcy is so solitary in her daily life, seeking only to study music and read and draw. She will ride to the hounds only when pressed by her brother, and she engages in candid conversation only when no stranger is present. "*So sweet-tempered, patient and gentle. Will no man ever know her goodness?*" But then, Elizabeth recalled that there might be one man who knew her too well.

"There they are!" rang out a cheerful, enthusiastic greeting.

Darcy smiled. He would recognize Charles Bingley's voice anywhere.

"We have been here for an hour, Darcy! Why are you hiding in this corner?"

Darcy nodded toward Georgiana and the persistent, buoyant, doomed suitor. "I am trying to be invisible. I do not want to frighten any young men away, but if I do not watch her closely, she will do what she has done at every other social occasion. She will find the library, then a book, then a nook."

Bingley laughed. His wife covered her smile with her fan and looked to Elizabeth, who concealed her smile with a cough. Few words are needed by sisters, particularly sisters as close as these two. They had shared all confidences when growing up, and their bond was still strong, even after the separation required by their marriages. Jane took Elizabeth's arm and led her to the punchbowl.

"You should not let Darcy bully Georgiana. She is very intelligent, and she knows her own mind. These balls do not allow a man to demonstrate the worthiness she seeks in a husband. They are a waste of her time."

Elizabeth pouted a bit at the criticism of her husband, even though its source was her dearest older sister. "My husband is not bullying her! He thinks constantly of her happiness." Elizabeth glanced at the retreating figure of this night's unlucky swain. Tall. Handsome. Dashing. A junior officer in the dragoons. No doubt a second or third son of some titled family who had purchased his officer's commission for him. The eldest son would inherit everything: Title, properties, income from the properties leased to others, the family mansion, its furniture, any jewelry, any collections of value (such as paintings or statuary), the power to distribute patronages to ensure profitable friendships – everything. Georgiana, who had her own fortune (which could comfortably support a large house in the country, a stable and a carriage, a full staff of servants both inside and out, and a house in London for the winter months) lured dozens of such socially wealthy but monetarily indigent young men. In theory, she needed merely to select the one she would have. But she made no selection. "She is too shy," sighed Elizabeth.

"Perhaps it is not that she is shy. Perhaps she knows too much," replied Jane.

"Whatever do you mean?" Elizabeth snapped.

Jane was surprised by the sharp edge in her sister's voice. She was completely unaware of Georgiana's unfortunate liaison, so she did not realize that both Elizabeth and Darcy were extremely sensitive to the possibility that some other person might learn of it. If that were to happen, there was a very real danger that Georgiana's reputation and opportunity for a good marriage could be forever ruined.

"I meant only that, while our three younger sisters gossip and chatter and flirt, Georgiana observes. While we are interpreting her prolonged silences as indifference, she may be making an active decision that her best interest lies elsewhere. Surely you know your husband too well, Elizabeth, to think that any sister of his could be oblivious to her surroundings, or ignorant of her own advantage!"

Elizabeth could not conceal her smile as she thought of her husband's public façade of dignity, gentlemanliness, and self-control. She well knew his capacity for passion, both in anger and in love. Elizabeth felt her cheeks redden. *"Married ten years and still like a bride! When will I become truly a wife, bored and indifferent? Will I be mooning over him until the day that I die?"* To Jane, she said, "Perhaps you are right. If the sister is only one-part-in-ten of the brother, then may the heavens help anyone who would stand between her and the object of her desire."

Wait one moment...where was Georgiana? Elizabeth searched for her husband and found him locked deep in conversation with her energetic brother-in-law. Bingley was smiling charmingly at every lady in the company, all the while maintaining on a subject that Elizabeth could tell, even from across the room, was a request for a favor from her husband. *"Has Darcy not done enough for you?"* she asked, but not so that Jane could hear. *"You very nearly destroyed my marriage with the last promise you extracted from my husband."*

Just then, Darcy saw his wife was eyeing him. Elizabeth glanced in the direction where she had last seen Georgiana and raised one eyebrow. He followed her glance and saw a puzzled young officer holding two punch glasses and standing all alone. Darcy's shoulders sagged, and he shook his head in mild disgust.

"What is it, Darcy? What is wrong?" asked Bingley.

"Nothing, except that I am grateful that I have but one son and no daughters."

Bingley understood immediately and laughed. "So, the fawn eludes the predators one more day. Clever fawn! Oh, take heart, Darcy! Do not put on the long face! We both know that Cupid is a relentless hunter, and he will not be denied."

This made Darcy laugh, and he clapped his friend on the back and said, "Send for your cousin, Bingley. Have him visit at Pemberley, so I may come to know him. If he is as humble and decent as you say he is poor, then I will find something for him. Perhaps, a small parsonage if one comes open. Or, I may press my aunt to give him one in her county."

"What is this, Darcy?" Lady Catherine de Bourgh peered at her nephew through her pince-nez and down her nose at a taller man, which necessitated that she tilt back her head and arch her back even more dramatically than was her custom. "Are you disbursing my patronages for me, now?"

Darcy grinned, the little boy caught in the act by his mother's elder sister. He winked at Bingley. "I thought you would appreciate an opportunity to be freed of some of the burdens of your wealth, Aunt Catherine. I understand that the Hunsford parsonage is still without a Rector."

Bingley suppressed a playmate's giggle.

Lady Catherine was definitely not amused. "I was most grievously deceived by that odious little pop-in-jay. Gretna Green, indeed! An elopement is entirely improper for a man of the cloth."

"So true, Aunt. But...for the man to be without a living when he needs it most..."

"Oh, Darcy!" she waved a lace handkerchief as if to dismiss him. "Let me have my temper. He is not suited to religious life. I have told the girl's father that there will be something else for him. Perhaps in the stable, where he can roll in the hay without having to leave his place of employment."

Bingley exploded with laughter. Darcy's cheeks puffed out like a chipmunk who had just found his first corn crib, while air was escaping through Darcy's tightly clasped lips in tiny high-pitched burps. Lady Catherine, who was well known to be absolutely humorless, asked the suffering Darcy, "What is he laughing about?" Darcy's effort to maintain his dignity brought unsympathetic tears to Bingley's eyes, while Lady Catherine merely looked from one to the other with perfect aplomb and one raised eyebrow. Never a chuckle. Never a sly pursing of the lips. Never so much as a conspiratorial wink. Lady Catherine appeared as imposing and as dignified as Gibraltar…if one is mindful of the fact that Gibraltar is the sanctuary of monkeys.

Jane came to her husband's side and touched his arm, in the hope that she could recall him to his proper social behavior. Elizabeth trailed after her sister, acknowledging her husband's aunt with the respect due her hostess. Then, Elizabeth innocently inquired after the whereabouts of the great lady's daughter, Anne de Bourgh.

Darcy scolded his wife with his eyes, and Elizabeth almost felt a pang of regret, as Lady Catherine proudly informed the company that "Anne's health is far too delicate to grace every ball at Rosings." Had Darcy not intervened, Elizabeth would have said something sympathetic, which would have required further comment from her hostess. As it was, the otherwise perfectly behaved Mrs. Darcy had done enough damage to suit her, and so she abandoned the subject.

Thankfully, a gentleman presented himself to the party, thereby relieving both Lady Catherine and Elizabeth from having to continue their pretense of mutual regard.

Lady Catherine introduced the newcomer, who turned out to be the Baron of Coxcroft. The Baron was quite affable and, over the course of the evening, told several tales of his experiences as a merchant seaman. Apparently, he had just received his Captain's papers when he was notified that his ancient great-uncle had passed without a direct male heir.

"From sailor to peer in one minute of time!" proclaimed the Baron, joyfully.

Elizabeth was warmed by the manly tone of his laughter and quite fascinated by his physical appearance. He was not as tall as her husband and not as slim. He looked to be at least a dozen years her husband's senior, and he had immense shoulders and huge hands. A man like this could crush a woman, force her to his will, if he wanted to do it. His skin was leathered, undoubtedly from the workings of sun, sea spray, and hard labor. There was a glint that caught the light – Yes! He wore a single golden earring in one ear, nestled deep in the untamed mane that engulfed his head and shoulders. And, of course, there was the matter of the Baron's facial hair. The current fashion called for a gentleman to be clean-shaven, which was the way Darcy and Bingley groomed themselves. The Baron, however, had a full beard, more than two inches of silken red-gold hair, parted and combed to the sides just below his chin.

When he asked her to dance, Elizabeth could not speak. Darcy nudged her, and she intended to refuse, but the Baron took her elbow and they joined in a quadrille. At the Baron's side, Elizabeth felt an energy and a helplessness that she had never experienced before. The tip of his beard lightly brushed against her cheek, and she blushed. Even before the dance ended, Elizabeth resolved that she must never be alone with this man again.

"Ho, Darcy! When are you going to dance with your wife, man?" called the Baron, as he returned Mrs. Darcy to her husband's care.

Darcy smiled and began to escort Elizabeth back to the dance floor for *"Miss Moore's Rant"*. Then, the Baron asked if the young Miss Darcy was any relation.

"She is my sister, sir."

"I gather she was feeling poorly. I have not seen her just lately, and I had intended to ask for a dance after the young men tired her out a bit." His smile was just sheepish enough, as he added, "I was hoping that as the evening wore on, she might develop a tolerance for an older, more sedate companion. Do you know, sir, if she will return to the ball?"

Sensing that her husband would volunteer to locate Georgiana and leave Elizabeth again in the Baron's care, she quickly offered to locate her sister-in-law and ascertain the condition of her health.

The rest of the evening passed pleasantly enough, with Georgiana spending the balance of the night dancing and conversing with the Baron of Coxcroft. (Actually, Georgiana did not converse, but she feigned sufficient interest in his sea-stories to keep other potential suitors away.)

Elizabeth's sole remaining joy of the evening arose from the realization that Lady Catherine had hoped to ally the Baron with her own daughter, the morose and steadily aging Lady Anne de Bourgh. Instead, there he was – every moment monopolized by the younger and prettier Georgiana Darcy. What a triumph!

Of course, it would never cross Elizabeth's mind that her contempt for Lady Anne as a romantic rival might have sprung, not so much from Elizabeth's affectionate wishes for Georgiana, as from a prick of jealousy in the bosom of a woman now past thirty – one who might herself have been the object of so splendid a catch, had she not already been married.

CHAPTER TWO

Moses in the Bulrushes

The next morning was filled with preparations for the Darcy family's return to Pemberley. The ball had been the last event of their two-week stay at Rosings. Darcy huddled with his aunt on family business, while Georgiana and Anne found a nondescript corner in which they could converse privately and finalize their plans for Anne's summer visit to Pemberley. Elizabeth gave instructions to her maid and joined her husband's Cousin Fitzwilliam for a walk of the grounds.

"I am reminded," observed the Colonel after several minutes of silence, "of our first becoming acquainted, here at Rosings." He smiled, but did he betray a note of sadness?

"Does he regret that he did not pursue me?" she wondered. *"Had he done so, he most certainly would have won my hand, for I had no affection for Darcy at that time!"* Elizabeth dwelled for a moment in her past, the time before she came to know her husband as an honorable man, a loyal friend, and…she blushed…an enthusiastic lover. At that time, it had seemed as though the Colonel considered making an offer. In the end, however, he contented himself with a very polite dissertation on the relative impoverishment of certain children of wealthy men.

"I recall, Colonel Fitzwilliam, that you spoke of marrying a wealthy widow. I am surprised to find you still a bachelor!"

He smiled but did not laugh. "A wealthy, well-born, proper Englishwoman. Yes." He contemplated the horizon for a moment, then he resumed their conversation. "I have always been too practical in the matter of marriage." He looked at her very earnestly. "You were wise to marry for love."

Elizabeth laughed. "Yes, love! And it was just a coincidence that your cousin happens to be quite rich!"

"Cousin Elizabeth!" Now, he laughed with her.

"Oh, you are not mistaken, Colonel! It was love! And it remains love." She smiled and dropped her eyes. "I have been very fortunate. As has my sister, Jane. She adores Bingley! If only…" She stopped. She had been on the verge of remarking on the unfortunate situation of her sister, Lydia Wickham.

They walked in silence for some time. Then Colonel Fitzwilliam sighed deeply and told her that, "He has damaged more lives than you can imagine. You think you know him?" He turned and looked her full in the face. "You do not have any idea! I have indulged a dislike for a few men, but I allow myself to wholly despise only one. His name is George Wickham, and I pray he rots in Hell." He looked again towards the horizon. "I take great comfort in knowing that he will."

Elizabeth thought it best to mention the ball of the previous night and the fox hunt of the previous week. The Colonel's melancholy persisted, but he marched on. "The Baron of Coxcroft," he said carefully, "took the fox. Have you met the Baron?"

"I have met him. He is a very charming man. What is your measure of him?"

The Colonel paused just a moment, and then said, "I am certain I liked him better than the fox did."

Elizabeth laughed and shook her head. Men can take such odd turns. She changed the subject by remarking that she had looked for him at the last night's ball and had hoped for a dance, but she did not see him there.

"Miss de Bourgh was indisposed, so I tried in some small way to entertain her."

"Poor Miss de Bourgh!" commiserated Elizabeth. "Forced to surrender the pleasure of a crowded dance floor (even though she does not dance) and the fascinating conversation of so many old and new acquaintances (even though she does not converse), so that she might be privately entertained by one of the most eligible bachelors in the county. How did she bear up, Colonel Fitzwilliam?"

"Prodigiously well, Mrs. Darcy!" laughed the Colonel. Then he became a little gentler in his speech. "She is very fondly thought of by your sister."

"What sister is that, Colonel? They all run from her company at the first opportunity!"

"I speak of your sister, Georgiana Darcy."

Elizabeth came back to herself and acknowledged the alliance between her and her husband's family was complete, except for one element. "You do understand my feelings, do you not? Lady Catherine's insulting dismissal of me and my nearest relations still remains a rift unrepaired. My disregard for Anne de Bourgh has nothing to do with Anne, herself. It is merely a response to the action of her mother."

The Colonel took a very deep breath, then sighed. "I ask you to mend with Lady Anne, even if you cannot mend with her parent. I ask it because I anticipate that our friendship will depend upon it."

Elizabeth understood his meaning. He intended to make Anne his wife.

She was very sad for him. That such a man would limit himself to that sickly, reticent, colorless shell of a girl. *"Girl! Eight years Georgiana's senior! So wealthy! She will herself inherit all of Rosings when her mother dies. Has she ever had even one suitor?"*

"I know your thoughts," he smiled ruefully. "I remind you that I have the power of asking, but her power is limited to mere reply. If you must pity one of us, pity the one that cannot choose. She has the worst of it. Besides, it is not settled yet, and it may be some time before such settlement comes. I confess I am in no hurry, for I take no pride in my part."

"Keep in mind," Elizabeth counseled, "that she is without other suitors, and she has long admired you. Your offer will bring her every happiness. If an equal portion of wealth is not there, what of it? If youth's first blush is not there, what of that? You are kind and honorable. She can rely on your integrity. For a solitary woman with the responsibility of financial health for more than a hundred families, your devotion and character mean much more than flowery declarations. She could not design a more worthy husband and partner."

They returned from their walk just before the noon meal. Since Mr. Darcy intended to depart in the early afternoon, Elizabeth went to their rooms to confirm that all was ready. As she passed Georgiana's room, she heard weeping.

"Georgiana?" she called. "Are you alright?"

After a moment, a reply came. "Miss Darcy is not here, Mrs. Darcy."

It was the voice of Mrs. Annesley, Georgiana's Companion.

"Is there anything you need? Do you require the assistance of one of the maids? Perhaps Hannah could…"

"I am here, Mrs. Darcy. Mrs. Annesley is, she is…"

That voice belonged to Hannah Hill, the youngest Darcy maid.

"Hannah was a little unwell, what with the excitement of the ball and the difference in surroundings, and...just...I was just helping her with the packing," interrupted Mrs. Annesley.

"Very unusual for a Lady's Companion to help with a maid's work," thought Elizabeth. Usually, the women servants resent paid Companions because of their more elevated status within the household and because Companions designate their payment as an allowance, instead of as wages. *"Perhaps because Hannah is so young, those resentments have not yet had the opportunity to fester."* Aloud, through the closed door, Elizabeth asked if they required the assistance of one of the de Bourgh maids.

"Oh, no! Please, no! I have the packing done, Mrs. Darcy. Thank you! Please!" responded Hannah.

"Yes, Mrs. Darcy," added Mrs. Annesley. "Hannah has done all of her work. I was merely assisting her with...something."

This exchange, through a closed door, troubled Elizabeth more than a little. Elizabeth felt a responsibility for the girl. Hannah was the granddaughter of one of the Bennets' long-time servants. Just sixteen, she was very fortunate to enter service at an estate as grand as Pemberley. Perhaps she had encountered jealousy from someone who aspired to such a placement. Or, perhaps she was overwhelmed by the even more august surroundings of Rosings. Elizabeth chided herself for insisting that Hannah accompany the party. Although it was appropriate for Mrs. Darcy to bring a personal maid (to alleviate some of the extra demands that would be placed on the Rosings' staff during the Darcys' stay), the choice of so inexperienced a girl may have been the result of a certain tendency toward headstrong behavior on Elizabeth's part.

Elizabeth went downstairs, assuring herself that her intentions had been good. Still and all, the girl was in tears.

When Elizabeth entered the dining room, she found Georgiana and Anne locked in whispered conversation, while Mr. Darcy and Colonel Fitzwilliam were planning some kind of hunt for early autumn. Since Lady Catherine and Elizabeth had an unspoken agreement to converse with each other as little as possible, Elizabeth's preoccupied silence was not too noticeable.

CHAPTER THREE

Wild Liquorice Flower

Almost immediately upon his return to Pemberley, Mr. Darcy learned that a Fox had entered the chicken coop. Specifically, one Etienne Foucauld had taken a room at the Red Onion Inn at Lambton, had accosted Darcy's servants in the stores, had initiated conversations with townspeople in the streets, and had gossiped with the local tradesmen.

Consequently, the next day after his return to Pemberley, Mr. Darcy sat behind his desk and waited. He had invited the Fox to his home and had instructed the butler to show Monsieur Foucauld into the library immediately upon arrival. A little over an hour later, Darcy heard a sound in the hallway, so he set aside his book. The door opened, and Monsieur Foucauld was announced. He was a man close to fifty, Darcy judged, with eyes that did not smile. He had curly black hair, very fair skin, and a waxed mustache whose twirled ends jutted forward like the horns of a bull. *"I wonder,"* thought Darcy, *"if he is much like his sister?"*

As Foucauld bowed and tipped his hat, Darcy glanced at the man's cane. It had a counterweight at the base of its handle and a brass ring encircling the shaft not fifteen centimeters above that counterweight. Darcy remained seated for a moment, pursed his lips, and then rose to his feet. "You have been a long time seeking the whereabouts of your sister, Monsieur."

"There has been a war between our countries, Monsieur. Perhaps you heard? This area is remote, but I would expect that almost a quarter-century of death and destruction would…"

"Your humor is not appreciated, sir. Many good men have died."

"And a few English, also, I hear."

They stared at each other, neither blinking, neither breaking a smile. The war was over, but the hostilities remained.

"Magdeleigne left France twenty years ago, in the company of an English smuggler who slinked between England and France under the protection of the night and whoever would accept his bribes. He promised to make her his wife. I have learned that he debased her and then discarded her when they reached England. She either could not or would not return to France…" Foucauld spread his hands and shrugged his shoulders, "much has changed, since the Revolution."

"Are you referring to the Reign of Terror, Monsieur, or Bonaparte?" Darcy stabbed. "There was the Treaty of Amiens, sir. An entire year of peace. Why did you not come to England then?"

"I had no money. Napoleon…my fortunes improved."

"How do soldiers in a losing army acquire enough money to travel abroad, purchase fine clothes, grease palms, and buy kegs of mustache wax, I wonder?"

One side of Foucauld's mouth smiled. The other side did not. "I was not a soldier, Monsieur. I was a teacher. It has taken years for me to acquire the funds to support my search for her."

Darcy sighed. He regretted that his resentment of the French had boiled to the surface. It was not the war that was the issue between them. "Monsieur Foucauld, it grieves me to inform you…"

Foucauld waved his hand. "I know she is dead, Englishman. And I know she left a child, Pierre. But he is not in Lambton. Is he here?"

"No." Darcy held up his finger to signal a pause in the conversation and walked to the other side of the room. He opened the liquor cabinet and selected two glasses.

"I will not drink with you, seducer!" Having said that, Foucauld whipped his blade from its concealment in the cane and lunged at Darcy.

"*Yes,*" confirmed Darcy to himself, "*he is just exactly like his sister.*"

Had the Frenchman been as observant as his host, he would have realized that Darcy had positioned himself directly underneath his family's coat of arms, which covered two crossed sabers. In one motion, Darcy freed one of the sabers and parried Foucauld's thrust. The force of the blow was so great that the Frenchman's blade broke into two pieces. Foucauld, having come to this house for one purpose, would not yield. He raised his blade again. But, now his blade was less than half its original length, and Darcy's straightened arm placed the point of his saber directly against Foucauld's throat. With what was left of his sword, Foucauld could not possibly reach Darcy's heart.

"I am not a seducer, sir. I was your sister's friend when she was sick and alone and with child. For her sake, I am your friend."

Foucauld laughed. With the point of Darcy's saber at his throat, he sneered. Leaning backward, off balance, helpless and at the mercy of an enemy, he spat out his hatred of all things English.

Darcy shook his head. "When you are calm, I will tell you everything that you do not know. But, before I lower my weapon, you will return yours to its sheath and promise me that you will not dishonor the hospitality of my home ever again. I have a wife and child here."

Foucauld's eyes glowed with hatred.

"Would it not be your sister's wish, that you place her child's well-being above your revenge?"

Foucauld lowered and sheathed his weapon. "I will not kill you in your own house." With Darcy's saber still at his throat, he added, "I will kill you elsewhere."

Darcy shook his head and returned to his desk, laying the saber across it. "In that case, I shall keep this close."

Darcy told his visitor of a young girl who came to Lambton via Cambridge "in the company of an acquaintance of mine. My acquaintance asked that I find some sort of employment for her because...he wished to disentangle himself from her acquaintance."

"The man's name, Monsieur Darcy?"

"Oh, Monsieur Foucauld, there were so many. He could have simply abandoned her, as others had done. He was good enough to find her a placement. Give him that."

Foucauld tightened his grip on the handle of his cane, but he did not draw the remnant blade from its sheath.

Darcy bowed his head. "Sir, I know this man. Had he made a promise, he would have honored it." Now Darcy looked directly into the eyes of the Frenchman. "He told me the offer came from her, and there was no hint of marriage in it."

"And you believe that, Monsieur!"

"Monsieur Foucauld, I take no pleasure in this account! I, too, have a sister I love! Mademoiselle Foucauld was already cynical and bitter when she was brought to me. She was using the name 'Madelyn Fox,' undoubtedly to protect your family honor. She spoke little English, and she had no skills by which to earn a respectable living. My head of housekeeping, Mrs. Reynolds, took her on as a maid. Had she applied herself, your sister's French accent would have made her extremely desirable as a Lady's Maid and Companion in any wealthy household, and she would have been treated almost like a member of the family. But she was not amenable to the work. Sir, within days of being hired, she entered my room after midnight. Undressed. Unbidden. I sent her out of my house at once."

Darcy wearily seated himself behind his desk. "In Lambton, she found a sponsor. A rabid cur. He provided her a room at an inn on the edge of town and arranged a number of introductions. All the while, he encouraged her resentment of me, for reasons of his own. When she became obvious with child, she declared it was mine."

"When I heard she would give birth, I rejoiced because I thought that she would return to France, invent a recently deceased English husband, and have her baby there. Had she done so, no one would ever have known that her child was not born within wedlock. But she did not leave Lambton. It pains me to tell you this, Monsieur, but by this time, she was beyond rational thinking. She lived in the streets. She did not bathe. She did not eat. She wailed at all hours of the day and night. She was desperate, sir, yet she vilified anyone who tried to help her, man or woman. Finally, her health declined to the point that she became manageable. I placed her in a cottage and obtained a midwife. The child's birth had an astonishing effect. She took in washing to support herself and her son and regained a modicum of her self-respect. She put her true name on the child's birth register, although she continued to go by Madelyn Fox. Sadly, the dissolute years, which were at this point behind her, had a pernicious effect on her physical health. Five years she lingered, but then she was gone."

Foucauld's expression did not change, even though teardrops glistened on the ruffles of his shirt.

Etienne Foucauld stood up and looked Darcy directly in the eye. "Because I knew my sister, I know that you have told me the truth about how she lived and how she died. Except for one item: I have been told that the father is known and that you are he."

"Many people think so. I tell you, Monsieur, on my word, I never dishonored your sister."

"On your word as an English gentleman?"

"Yes."

"I spit on your word. I challenge you to a duel, Monsieur Darcy. Name your weapon."

"No."

"You refuse?"

"Certainly."

"Then, you are a coward, Monsieur Darcy!"

"I am not a coward. But I am an accomplished marksman and an accomplished fencer. You, sir, are a schoolteacher, are you not? It would be the same as murder. I will not do it. Really, Monsieur, there is no point! I am not your sister's seducer! I am not the father of her child! What complaint could you have against me?"

Foucauld sneered at the Englishman's display of rectitude. "You admit that you cast out a young woman of your employ, a girl you knew to be in a foreign land, unfamiliar with the language, without friends, without family, without access to funds, and in a fragile state of physical and mental health. You do admit these things, do you not, Monsieur Darcy?"

Darcy winced. He had not previously examined his behavior in such a light. He had thought that he had behaved properly, even nobly. But, now confronted by a less friendly point-of-view, his sense of honor demanded that he be brutal in self-assessment. "Your analysis is accurate enough, Monsieur Foucauld."

"I, and my nephew, are all that remains of our ancient family. As long as I live, I will not tolerate insult. You must answer for your actions. There must be a duel."

Darcy hesitated. "There were kindnesses to your sister. Do they not answer, in part?"

Foucauld paused. After a few moments of thought, he agreed that when things were darkest for his sister, Darcy provided for her care, and that was some atonement.

"Would a contest, in place of a duel, satisfy your family's honor, Monsieur?"

Foucauld nodded. "To settle your shortcomings as an employer, yes. You have a fine stable, Monsieur. We shall race horses to settle your debt. I will select and ride a horse from your stock. If I win, I take the horse as your penance. If you win, the debt is discharged."

Relieved, Darcy offered, "your pick of any animal in my stable, Monsieur. We will race and settle our differences tomorrow!"

"Good. That is done." Foucauld, too, was relieved. "Now, where is Pierre? Is he here, in your house?"

"No. Peter now lives with two people who treasure him." Darcy assured the Frenchman that they were good parents and that "they truly love Peter. They treat him as if he is their own child."

Foucauld stiffened. "*Pierre* is not their child. He is my sister's child. I will be here tomorrow, Monsieur Darcy, to settle our account. But, let me be clear: Do not believe that I will not re-open this matter, if I come upon facts that establish absolutely that you are the man who despoiled my sister and made her child a bastard." He then picked up his cane and hat, threw his flaming red cape over his shoulder, bowed, and left the house.

CHAPTER FOUR

Purple Columbine

Etienne Foucauld stood impatiently at the side door of the Darcy mansion and looked out across the lawn. It was a beautiful setting, but so English. The gardens were groomed but arranged in a haphazard manner that was disturbing to a taste accustomed to the French standard of horticultural beauty. French garden paths were straight lines with precise border plantings all of the same color and same kind. English garden paths meandered, curved this way and then that way, a splash of red here, a daub of blue there. Flowers of different types and blooms of different sizes. Pretty, yes, but so undisciplined! In Monsieur Foucauld's world, a garden is a haven of serenity and repose. In the English world, a garden is an adventure, a place for children to frolic and adults to explore.

When the butler answered the bell and indicated that Monsieur Foucauld should enter, Foucauld politely refused. "Please inform Monsieur Darcy that I am waiting for him at the stable entrance," he replied.

"But, sir," said the surprised butler, who was just buttoning his vest, "it is dawn! Mr. Darcy will not rise for several hours!"

"At his leisure, please inform Monsieur Darcy that, in France, we settle our disputes at sunrise, not at sunset."

With that, Foucauld turned on his heel and proceeded to the stable, where he busied himself evaluating the horses in the stalls and in the paddock.

After about one-half hour, Mr. Darcy appeared, adjusting his tie. "I beg you to excuse my lateness, Monsieur. I should have informed my servant to wake me at the appropriate hour, but I was remiss."

Etienne waved him off. "You are precisely on time, Monsieur Darcy! I was foolish not to realize that I would require this space of time to select my mount." Foucauld patted the neck of a magnificent stallion with a luxuriant mane and an angora tail. It looked to be part English Saddlebred, part Friesian, and all Pegasus. Entirely black, he had a long nose and feathered hooves. "I will ride the black, no?"

"But that's Mr. Darcy's horse!" cried the groom. "Mr. Darcy, that's your horse, sir!"

Darcy smiled and told the groom to saddle Dark-of-the-Moon for Monsieur Foucauld and the bay for himself. By this time, Elizabeth had joined the party. She did not like it when a servant approached her husband while he was still in her bed, and she liked it even less when Darcy left her side in a manner that would allow her sleep to continue undisturbed. The master of Pemberley quite obviously did not wish her presence at this event, which of course made her attendance mandatory. In order to avoid any suggestion that she return to the house, she eschewed all conversation and went directly to the paddock fence. There, she was eagerly greeted by a scrawny grey stallion with skinny legs and a wispy mane and tail. It nickered and pawed the ground, shook its mane, and nuzzled her cheek. She rewarded him by tickling his upper lip and scratching him behind his ear.

"They are in love!" chuckled Foucauld.

As the men conversed, Elizabeth realized that there was to be a contest of some kind and that the Frenchman was going to be riding Dark-of-the-Moon. She was aghast! The Dark could outrun any other horse in the county, save one. She immediately went to a stableboy and gave him precise instructions.

When the horses were brought out, Darcy's jaw dropped. The Dark was readied, but in place of Bay Rum stood Arabian Moonlight, Elizabeth's horse.

"I said, bring me the bay!" snapped Darcy. "Take Moonlight back to the paddock at once!"

"But, Mr. Darcy," stammered the stableboy, "Mrs. Darcy ordered me to release Bay Rum to the pasture! She says that if the Frenchman is to take your horse, then you must take hers."

Elizabeth favored her husband with a satisfied smile.

Etienne Foucauld threw back his head and laughed. "Your wife is quite the judge of horseflesh, Monsieur Darcy. Except, it is not a horse – it is a housepet!" And he laughed some more.

The amusement of the Frenchman, which amounted to ridicule of his wife's discernment, angered Darcy to reddening. He turned to the stablehand.

"Take the bridle off him. I will not risk harming his mouth, which might harden it to my wife's gentle touch. I will ride him with a halter." Darcy unfastened his spurs.

Foucauld now became indignant. "Do you think the honor of my family will be satisfied, if you intentionally lose the race, Monsieur?"

Darcy swung into the saddle and took up the reins. "Mount, sir! And, if you are still offended at the conclusion of this race, there are sabers in the library."

At this, Elizabeth became alarmed. What was this talk of sabers? She had thought that this was sport, a gambling wager. What was going on?

Foucauld mounted, the groom dropped a handkerchief, and the horses ran. As they crossed the meadow, Foucauld was a little surprised to hear hooves pounding just behind. As they topped the hill, Foucauld was even more surprised that the puny grey was almost even. As they rounded the stand of beech trees, Foucauld's mount started breathing heavy, while that wretched grey stallion seemed to be loping along at his side. Racing back down the hill, Foucauld's black giant was giving its all, while Darcy seemed...was he reining back his mount? The horses were side by side, crossing the meadow on their way back to the stable, the finish line, when Foucauld caught sight of Elizabeth Darcy, tossing an apple into the air and catching it. The grey stretched his neck, flattened his ears, and showed Etienne Foucauld what a horse's tail looks like from an ever-increasing distance. Foucauld reined in The Dark, about half-way back across the meadow, as Darcy dismounted by the stable door, and the little grey housepet claimed its reward. Arabian Moonlight was happily munching on his apple as Foucauld trotted into the stableyard, alit in front of Elizabeth Darcy, dropped to one knee, and lifted the hem of her skirt to his lips.

"Madame," he said, "I yield."

CHAPTER FIVE

Snapdragon

Breakfast was being put on the table as the Darcys re-entered their home. There were framed eggs, breads, steak, fruits, sausages, and jellies. Obviously, the cook had been unprepared to accommodate such an early meal. Since the Darcys prided themselves on their kindness to their servants, they gave every indication of complete satisfaction with the morning repast. Still and all, the cook would remain disconsolate for several days thereafter, and the Darcys would be faced with several exotic dishes that had not previously been their normal fare.

On this particular morning, however, Elizabeth was primarily concerned with the import of the race and the purpose Darcy had in concealing its occurrence. Georgiana and her Companion, Mrs. Annesley, were in and out, searching for this thing or the other, gossiping about this neighbor or that one. There never seemed to be a private moment for a direct question. So, Elizabeth tried hinting, she tried pouting, and she tried an irritable tone, but her husband would speak only of other subjects. It was not until the late afternoon, when all of the servants were busy elsewhere in the house, and Georgiana was ensconced in the privacy of the music room, that her husband firmly took her elbow and directed her into his library.

"Mrs. Darcy," he told her sternly, "you are to say nothing more about the horse race. Is that clear?"

Her response came back, flat and distinct. There was no smile on her lips when she said, "It is perfectly clear, Mr. Darcy. May I go now?"

Receiving no reply, she turned and walked to the door.

"He is…he says he is Peter's uncle."

Elizabeth stopped dead. Darcy poured a small glass of sherry and brought it to her, placing his left hand in the small of her back as he stood by her side. "He is mad with hatred for the man who seduced and abandoned his sister. He is absolutely determined to find him and obsessed with the idea of killing him."

Elizabeth felt all of her thoughts rush to the back of her head. The light in the library dimmed, as though the sun had gone behind a cloud. She felt quite tired, and her eyes closed so that she might sleep. Had her husband not been at her side, she would have fallen to the floor. But Darcy was there, and he held her and poured the wine down her throat and helped her to the sofa.

After she recovered her senses, she plied her husband with questions and grew ever more fearful with every answer he gave.

"Does he suspect any part of the truth?"

Darcy furrowed his brow. "No. Absolutely not."

"I have never told Jane…"

"I have never told Bingley!"

Elizabeth resigned herself to the main point: "He plans to remove Peter to France, does he not?"

Darcy took a step toward her and brimmed over with emotion. "Blast his plans! Peter stays here!"

"Does Foucauld have a name? For Peter's father. Does he have a name?"

"Yes. Yes. The town gossip has identified me. I denied it, of course, but the suspicion remains intact."

Elizabeth nodded, for that was the rumor that she and Darcy had encouraged, by haughtily denying it at every mention. "Do you think he might seek to harm you?"

Darcy glanced at the saber still laying across the top of his desk. "No," he lied. "The horse race settled things between us. Except," he paused, "he now has another reason to want me dead."

To Elizabeth's frightened inquiry, he replied, "Why, you, my dear. Did you not notice how he worshiped the hem of your garment, even though it had swept over the mud of a stableyard?"

She reddened, which only encouraged him.

"Do you not remember his confession of complete surrender, even in the presence of your husband? 'Madame, I yield'? What a heartless wench you are, Eliza." Darcy placed his hand over his heart. "I, myself, was deeply moved."

Elizabeth blushed. She had been flattered, and a bit more than that, by the Frenchman's declaration. But Darcy's teasing was very irksome. *"He could make some little show of jealousy, simply as a matter of courtesy,"* she thought. *"He could behave as though he believes it possible that another man might desire me. Or,"* she glared at him, *"he could just stop laughing about it!"*

At that moment, Darcy did indeed abandon the jest. "I have made arrangements to escort Monsieur Foucauld to GanderGlen on this coming Wednesday."

"What? You cannot take him there!"

"Elizabeth, he crossed the Channel for two purposes: First, to ferret out his sister's seducer and, second, to see this boy. The meeting cannot be avoided. But, see here, Elizabeth: You must go along, and indicate a desperate wish to speak privately with your sister for some foolish reason. I rely on you to convey the facts to Jane and to caution her to be on guard. Then, she must warn Bingley. I dare not send a written message, for I am certain that Foucauld has already bribed at least one of our servants."

"But how have you explained Peter's presence at GanderGlen? Might not Foucauld come to believe that Charles…"

Darcy interrupted her. "The child lives with the family of my wife's eldest sister. Who else would I entrust him to, if I were, in fact, the boy's father? Foucauld will not suspect Charles, because no wife would take her husband's illegitimate child into her home and treat him as lovingly as she would treat her own. It is your sister's goodness that is Bingley's shield."

"And the most damning evidence of your guilt," said Elizabeth.

"Wife, I told you that the horse race settled all things between us."

"I know what you told me, Husband, and you were lying."

Darcy straightened. *"This must be the reason why I do not lie to Elizabeth,"* he told himself. *"It is because it is a waste of my time."*

CHAPTER SIX

Grammanthes Flower

Darcy and Elizabeth had just returned from their morning ride when the de Bourgh carriage pulled up before the doors of Pemberley.

"You did not tell me *she* was coming," whispered Elizabeth, reproachfully. Her husband flinched a little. He was forever caught between his uncompromising aunt and his treasured wife.

Lady Catherine espied her nephew (and his unsuitable wife) and ordered her driver to go to the paddock area. "Darcy," his aunt called (giving no greeting whatsoever to Elizabeth), "our plans have been amended."

When the carriage stopped, Elizabeth caught her breath. Lady Catherine's carriage contained not just her daughter, but the compelling Baron of Coxcroft. As he dismounted from the carriage, his eyes fixed on the face of Mrs. Darcy. Lady Anne remained seated with her mother.

The Baron explained that he had convinced Lady Catherine to summer in Blackpool instead of Bath. As Lady Anne had plans to travel north anyway, this alteration allowed all three to travel together. "I will go as far as Liverpool and ship out from there to Cornwall. My castle is there." The Baron's words addressed Mr. Darcy, but the Baron's eyes rested elsewhere. Elizabeth stepped backward, into her husband's shadow. "Mrs. Darcy, are you faint?"

When the Baron reached to take Elizabeth's hand, Moonlight charged him. Darcy went to the horse's head immediately, taking the bridle in both hands and pulling Moonlight's nose into his own chest. Had the groom attempted that maneuver, the horse would have reared and kicked. But the horse sensed that this one man was valued by his Friend above all others, so with this one man, Moonlight was cooperative.

"He is unaccustomed to strangers, sir," said Darcy.

"Still got his wind up from the race, I expect," said Tom, Pemberley's stablemaster.

"Gambling, Darcy?" asked the Baron.

"In a way, Baron. There is a foreign visitor to the nearby town, a Frenchman. He imagined some slight and demanded a settlement. Hence, the horserace."

Coxcroft studied the departing grey. It was smaller than Darcy's mount and seemed a bit ragged about the edges. "And you rode that horse, instead of your own?"

Darcy smiled. "I had intended to make a brave attempt, and then courteously lose. But, Mrs. Darcy," he shook his head at a suddenly very discomfited Elizabeth, "Mrs. Darcy does not often consult with her husband before launching her own plans. The Frenchman took my horse, and I was maneuvered into taking hers. Naturally, the Frenchman lost."

"Naturally, Mr. Darcy? The grey is smaller, with a shorter stride. It would seem your black…"

"But the grey is an Arab, sir! Moonlight is a direct descendant of the original Barb!" Darcy suddenly realized that the Baron had been a sailor for most of his life and, therefore, was unfamiliar with the bloodlines of fine horses, so he went on. "The story goes that Lord Godolphin found an Arabian horse pulling a tradesman's wagon. His friends ridiculed it as the ugliest animal they had ever seen! But Godolphin felt sorry for the horse, and he bought it. As it turned out, the horse could run, fast and forever! Its lung capacity and physical strength were amazing, not to mention its intelligence. Godolphin bred the Barb to his best mares. By an odd turn, this ugly and unadmired stallion managed to sire magnificently beautiful colts and fillies! And they inherited the stamina and the heart of their parent. These offspring now prevail in almost every race they enter."

The horses had been taken by the grooms, and Lady Catherine's carriage had returned to the mansion entrance. The Darcys, accompanied by the Baron, strolled toward the house.

Coxcroft looked back over his shoulder. Moonlight was challenging the groom for every step. Finally, the groom let the grey into the pasture without a cool-down walk. "Spirited animal," the Baron remarked, wetting his lower lip with his tongue. "I should think you would not allow your wife to go near him. He seems very," the Baron licked his lips again and savored the word "defiant." He rushed on. "You should get rid of him, Darcy, before he harms her! I will buy him! I will take him far from here. Name your price!"

Darcy stopped and stared at him. Elizabeth had been silent this whole time, and she stayed silent. Arabian Moonlight was Elizabeth's horse only in the sense that she was its rider; Darcy actually held ownership to everything at Pemberley. He had absolute power to do as he wished with "her" horse or anything else that was "hers." For a moment, she feared that her husband's ever-growing eagerness to ingratiate himself with his social betters would tempt him to consider this very generous offer. She had been walking at her husband's side, bashfully apart from the magnetic Baron, but now she drew closer to both men and touched Darcy's shoulder.

Without looking at her, Darcy replied, "You are very generous, Baron, and if we were discussing any other horse in my stable, I would not deny your request. But my wife is not comfortable with most horses. Despite his temperament with everyone else, Moonlight is gentle and obedient when he is with her. In fact, today's ill manner came when you approached my wife too quickly. The animal believed you to be a danger to her!" Now, Darcy laid his hand comfortingly on Elizabeth's hand, which she had wrapped around his arm as he spoke. "There is no possible inducement that could convince me to part with Mrs. Darcy's friend and protector."

The Baron nodded in silence and seemed disappointed for a moment. Then, he smiled charmingly, and Darcy mentioned that each year Pemberley hosted a ball during the summer months. It was a shame that the Baron was returning so soon to Cornwall.

"A ball, you say? I thoroughly enjoyed the ball at Rosings. I hope to host one, well, actually several! At the castle. It would certainly be a great benefit if I could attend another, before I attempt it myself!"

The invitation was quickly extended, and the Baron promised that he would return to Derbyshire specifically to be their guest. Darcy was delighted. Elizabeth gave every evidence of equal delight, but stole a glance back at the pasture and the little grey horse.

The Baron and Lady Catherine would stay the night and continue on their journey the next morning. Anne de Bourgh had been invited for the entire summer, being as how the seaside air (which was so beneficial to the wellness of others) might not agree with her delicate health. In the past, Elizabeth had noticed that Miss de Bourgh's multiple health issues, as enumerated by Lady Catherine, always seemed in remission during the summer months she visited Pemberley, but unfortunately reasserted themselves immediately upon Lady Catherine's return from her travels. Remembering her conversation with Colonel Fitzwilliam, Elizabeth resolved to express every kindness to her husband's cousin during this visit.

That evening, Georgiana played her piano for the company, and Elizabeth played, also. Darcy watched the Baron carefully, hoping for a sign that he had taken more than a casual interest in Georgiana. The Baron made no sign, except that he seemed to listen to Elizabeth Darcy's every word and seemed to smile invitingly to her and to admire her figure when she rose to go to the piano.

"Curse me," Darcy scolded himself. *"Since that Frenchman flattered her, I am wild with jealousy! There is nothing wrong here. The Baron merely attempts to become friends with his hostess so that he may visit frequently without alarming Georgiana. He knows my sister is shy! He is being a wise and considerate suitor. That is all!"* Darcy ordered his watchful tension to leave his body. Soon, his sister would be happily married to a titled peer. All was progressing as he had always hoped.

CHAPTER SEVEN

Petunia

Foucauld arrived early. Darcy had promised to take him to meet his nephew, and Foucauld was eager to get on with it. Darcy, however, was in no hurry to inflict this foreigner on the Bingley household, for he could imagine no scenario that did not culminate in disaster. Moreover, Lady Catherine and the Baron of Coxcroft were late in their departure. Darcy was forced to make introductions.

Monsieur Foucauld bowed deep to the mistress of Rosings and said something flattering. He had learned early on that because he was French, all Englishwomen expected him to be somewhat randy, and they would be disappointed if they could not boast of having rebuffed at least one brazen impertinence.

Lady Catherine, however, had been attempting to conceal a gradual loss of hearing and could not catch his accent-thickened words. She had to ask him to repeat himself, which (after the second attempt) he declined to do. Instead, he said something inconsequential, which inspired the Baron to make a rather coarse remark concerning the stupidity of Frogs.

Foucauld harbored a deep-seated resentment of the English for many reasons, but in part because of their inclination to ridicule the French peoples by focusing on a single delicacy of

French cuisine, specifically frog legs. Foucauld bowed slightly and smiled at the man to whom he had just been introduced and said with a very soft yet very clear voice, "At your leisure, Monsieur."

"That is a safe offer, sir," growled the Baron, "since it is obvious that I am to continue my journey, and any delay would inconvenience my hostess."

Darcy saw Foucauld's fingers tighten about the handle of his cane and wondered if this schoolteacher was determined to challenge every man in England.

Anne de Bourgh could contain her curiosity no longer. "Cousin, does this gentleman come to us from Europe? Belgium, perhaps? Or France?"

Foucauld turned his attention to a tiny woman Darcy had not yet introduced. She was somewhat like Lady Catherine in appearance, but younger. Instead of an air of hauteur, this younger lady was natural in her manner, serene and sincere. He amended his attitude and confirmed his nationality.

Darcy hoped to be able to complete the introduction of "Lady Catherine's daughter, Lady Anne de Bourgh" before the Frenchman could manufacture a reason to take offense and demand that one – or both – of the ladies meet him on a field of honor.

Anne was delighted to have encountered someone who knew the French language. She spoke to Etienne in his native tongue and spoke it almost as fluently as a native, prattling on about her trip to the continent almost eleven years past, during "that short bit of time our countries were at peace," and her appreciation of French culture in general. For a few moments, Foucauld forgot his resentment of the English and basked in the pleasure of being able to converse casually in his own tongue. But the mother disapproved of her daughter's unseemly affability with a foreigner and eventually silenced Anne with several throat clearings and one stern look that persisted through all of them.

The introductions complete, Foucauld withdrew and went into the house. The family turned to the business of bidding their farewells. Soon enough, Lady Catherine and the Baron had gone, and Anne began her search for the Frenchman's hiding place.

Anne wanted very much to resume her conversation with Foucauld, but she knew it would be improper to approach him alone. So, she tried to persuade Georgiana to leave the music room and go with her to the library.

"No, Anne!"

"But he is French, Georgiana! Did you not love France, when we were there? The food, the music, the art…"

"I was not in a mood to love much of anything at that time."

Anne chided herself for bringing up a painful memory. Still, "France was so beautiful. And the language itself was music. I have so few opportunities to practice speaking it, I am afraid I will lose all that I have learned."

"Were you completely blind to my brother's posture? The coolness in his tone? The absence of any information with which a conversation could be initiated? Darcy displays me to every unmarried man he meets, yet with this one, nothing! Clearly, Monsieur Foucauld is unsuitable as a social acquaintance."

Anne gazed longingly at the music room's door.

"Anne! Try to remember that you are frail and weak!"

Anne de Bourgh stuck out her tongue, which made Georgiana laugh out loud.

"So, Georgiana. When will you marry the Baron?"

Miss Darcy rolled her eyes heavenward, which made Anne laugh. "He seemed more interested in Elizabeth. Did you see my brother foam at the mouth, each time the Baron complimented her?"

They giggled in unison. Anne's kindness during those wretched months on the continent, and her unwavering confidentiality in the years since, had created a bond that made the difference in their ages seem as nothing. Their summers at Pemberley were a special joy to them both.

"Seriously, dearest cousin," said Anne, breaking the mood and returning to an oft-discussed subject, "you should not continue to delay the matter."

"Oh, they are all the same. They talk of hunting, fishing, and riding, as though I should have an interest in discussing those things. They stand as close to me as they can, they lean over me, they look down on me, and then they rhapsodize about how they will use my income from my inheritance to finance their own diversions."

"Yes, but that is not their doing. It is English law, and English society. Once a woman marries, her husband takes control of her assets. Only an unmarried woman (a widow, or a divorced woman, or a woman never married)..."

"Or a woman whose marriage has been annulled. You must not forget that category in your litany, Anne."

"I said, 'never married,' which is what annulment means. The point is that a woman must be single if she wishes to retain ownership of anything of value."

Georgiana sighed. "All of these men presume..."

Anne became indignant. "Who cares what they presume? If they are so foolish that they believe any human being is without a single blemish, then they merit the fruit of their foolishness! Along with, I might add, the benefit of the comfortable life your fortune will provide for them. These impoverished second sons get no sympathy from me, my girl!"

Georgiana turned away. "I do not want to be united for life with a man who feels he was deceived."

"Do you think any one of these men has told you the absolute truth about his past activities? Do you think any one of them will admit to his indiscretions even after the banns are put up, or even after the vows are spoken? Georgiana, you are trying my patience!"

"You have not married," Georgiana said.

"I was to marry your brother, remember? He preferred Elizabeth."

"Anne! I...I never realized..."

"Oh, do not exercise your imagination over it. He would have been the best of the lot, that is all. Your brother is...was...a very good catch! Exactly the sort of man you should marry: Tall, handsome, accomplished in every manly pursuit, educated in business. A man that would gain you envy from every other woman of our acquaintance...including me!"

"Yes, yes, I imagine so. But what girl wants to marry her brother?" Georgiana shrugged.

"Very well, then. Is not the Baron strikingly different from all other men you have known?"

"If you think so highly of him, Anne, you marry him."

Anne de Bourgh furrowed her brow. "I am too old. I am thirty-five, Georgiana. I shall never marry." Her breast heaved a little, and a single tear attempted to wander out of a corner of an eye. It would have done so, had Anne allowed it. She did not.

"I know you had to have suitors!" Georgiana said with exasperation. "My fortune is nothing compared to yours, and these second sons seem to be everywhere!" Georgiana was almost indignant. "There must have been offers!"

"There were...applicants. I was too solemn. I saw no value in trivial conversation, which (I now realize) most men find comforting when they try to initiate an acquaintance. So, most of them went directly to my mother." Anne peered meaningfully at Georgiana. "My health declined with each importune." Anne paused, reviewing her memories, and found them disappointing. "Still, it would have been nice to have had a man pledge his undying love to me. Once."

Georgiana straightened her music sheets. "Being loved once is not a fate I would wish on anyone, Anne."

Anne clasped Georgiana's hands in hers. "He is married, and you see the kind of husband he makes."

"If you think I pine for George Wickham, then you must think me a fool. Lydia Wickham is welcome to him, and she has all my pity as well." Georgiana shook her head and walked to the door. "How many times have we promised each other that we would no longer discuss this subject? Let us go into Lambton for our noon meal. For the rest of today, we will discuss art and music and fashion. For one day, we shall not discuss marriage, or romance, or men." Anne nodded her agreement.

As they walked to the carriage that would take them into town, Georgiana repeated, "No marriage, no romance, no men." Then she quickly added, "Unless they are French men and near at hand!"

Miss de Bourgh smiled. This summer would pass as had all previous summers. It would be lazy and generally routine and mildly pleasant. There would be nothing memorable about it.

CHAPTER EIGHT

Ragged Robin

Darcy intended that only he, Elizabeth, and Foucauld would visit the Bingleys this day. So, when he heard that Georgiana and Anne had taken the Barouche Box into town for shopping and luncheon, he estimated their time in Lambton and planned the departure for at least an hour prior to the ladies' return. But he estimated wrongly, and when the two ladies learned that a visit to GanderGlen was in the offing, they insisted that they be included.

Darcy demurred. "We are taking the coach. It seats only four, not five. The larger carriage…" he eyed his stablemaster, "requires repair. Is that not so, Tom?"

Tom hung his head in apparent guilt and dutifully replied, "It won't happen again, Mr. Darcy. I'm sorry, sir."

Anne was determined. If Monsieur Foucauld was going to GanderGlen, then Anne de Bourgh would go to GanderGlen. But, of course, she said no such thing to her cousin! Instead…"Will the Bingleys and the Wickhams not think it odd if they learn I am at Pemberley and declined an opportunity to visit them? Will they not think that Georgiana's absence came at my insistence? Really, Cousin Elizabeth," she turned to her hostess, "I would not want your family to think me indifferent to their acquaintance."

It was slight and sly, but it was enough. After Anne's mother's sharp dismissal of the entire Bennet family, Anne's avowed desire to encourage their acquaintance was an olive branch that could not be politely declined. Darcy knew he had been out-maneuvered: Elizabeth had no choice but to insist that the ladies join them.

Elizabeth caught her husband's eye and pondered aloud, "But the Barouche Box! It is an open carriage! It is one thing on a warm day, quite another in the night air. No, Anne, your health is too fragile…"

Darcy seized at it and knew once again that he had found his perfect partner in life. "Lady Catherine would never forgive me if anything…"

Elizabeth said the final word. "No one expects you to sacrifice your health, Anne."

"So," Anne began, "there is room for four in the Coach and room for four in the Box. We cannot ask a guest to tolerate the discomfort of an open-air ride in the nighttime, so he must ride in the Coach. With two others…" Anne paused and smiled innocently at Elizabeth. Then, she went on. "Two must ride separately in the open carriage. I mean, otherwise, one would have to ride alone. And, again, we cannot ask a guest to ride alone." She first turned her placid gaze on Darcy, then dipped the brim of her bonnet in Elizabeth's direction. "Is that not your thinking as well, Cousin Elizabeth?"

Elizabeth turned to Darcy, her posture clear: Anne and Georgiana were going, and they would be in the carriage alone with Foucauld, while the Darcys traveled in the Barouche Box, if Darcy did not think of something.

Darcy being Darcy, he had his next move at the ready. "Tom, please bring out the Brougham." He then smiled charmingly at

Anne and Georgiana. "I am sorry, ladies, it is a small vehicle, a mere two-seater, but it is enclosed, which is the main thing. I hope you will find it not too uncomfortable."

Foucauld smiled. It had been quite entertaining to watch this chess game, even though draws are never as satisfying as victories. There is one thing that can be said for stalemates over checkmates, however: Checkmates produce arrogant winners and resentful losers; stalemates produce a cheerful willingness on both sides to play the game again.

Darcy did, indeed, begin again.

Ordinarily, the larger carriage would follow the smaller one. But not this night! Darcy had been outflanked and forced to include his sister and his cousin in the afternoon and evening activities, but Darcy now had new pawns on the board. The Darcy coach would arrive at its destination before the Brougham. Once inside the Bingley house, Darcy planned to move his group quickly to a separate room with a closed door. Georgiana and Anne would simply have to entertain themselves, as they were having to do now. How they would entertain each other, he did not know. If asked, he would have probably guessed that they would discuss hats, or dresses, or symphonies. Knowing them as he did, he would not have said that they would share bawdy witticisms, or comment on common laborers seen shirtless, or speculate about women suspected to be of questionable repute.

Georgiana and Anne were three kilometers into their journey and there was yet to be a single mention of symphonies, or hats, or dresses. There had been a sizable quantity of laughter, but it had not reached the few hundred yards forward to the carriage containing the Darcys (thankfully, for there would have been questions later).

Anne's brow furrowed. "Georgiana, why is Monsieur Foucauld visiting the Bingleys?"

"I have no idea," she shrugged.

"Your brother has said nothing about the Monsieur's visits to Pemberley? A foreigner's reason for being in a town as remote and small as Lambton?"

Georgiana shook her head and shrugged again.

"Let me approach the matter by a different path. Monsieur Foucauld is French."

Georgiana laughed and said something clever about the nose on Anne's face.

But Anne did not laugh. "Who else do we know, or more to the point, who did your brother know that was French?"

Georgiana's eyes widened. "But her name was Fox! Madelyn Fox!"

Anne frowned. "Georgiana, if you had debased yourself, would you continue to use your family's name? Or would you take on a false name? The word for 'false' in the French language, by the way, is pronounced 'foe,' but it is spelled 'f-a-u-x.' If an Englishman were to see the written word, he could easily mispronounce it as…"

"Fox." Georgiana stared at…nothing. "After all these years."

"Sometimes your brother infuriates me. How dare he keep this from us?"

"And you would have me marry a man just like him!"

"That is really quite far from the instant point, Georgiana."

"The instant point is that we must find out what we can on our own. That means, dear Cousin, that you must enter into lengthy conversation with the Monsieur. Try to get him alone. Try to encourage him to confide in you." Georgiana glanced sideways at Anne. "I hope your health does not fail at a crucial juncture."

Anne did not rise to that baited hook. "What will you do?"

"I do not know. Seize an opportunity, should one arise."

After a few minutes of shared silence, Georgiana said one word. "Peter."

Anne replied, "Pierre."

Their eyes met for a moment, then they both looked away. They did not speak again until they alit from their carriage.

At various times during the five-kilometer carriage ride to GanderGlen, Elizabeth remarked on the elegance of the ball at Rosings and her eagerness to share with her elder sister "certain information" about "certain persons of our acquaintance, one of whom is married" and their disappearance from the ballroom "while the husband was discussing the finer points of lawn croquet!" Elizabeth giggled and chattered about the newest fashions.

Darcy sat in satisfied approval. Her display of empty-headed silliness put him in mind of his mother-in-law. He pictured Elizabeth flouncing into Bingley's house, throwing off her bonnet, hurrying Jane into a corner, and whispering her cautions right under Foucauld's oblivious nose!

Foucauld gazed out the window as she rattled on. *"A very nice performance, Madame Darcy,"* he said to himself. *"But your husband admires you, and he is not the sort of man who would tolerate, let alone admire, a foolish woman. No, this is all for me."* He looked at Elizabeth and smiled. *"Thank you for telling me that there is something more to this matter that Darcy does not want me to learn."* His smile widened, she returned it, and he made a show of adoring the scenery throughout the rest of the journey.

CHAPTER NINE

Cinquefoil

"Thank heaven, you have come!" Jane Bingley laughed. Then, she half-whispered to Elizabeth, "Mother is here."

Monsieur Foucauld stepped forward and beamed. Jane, married ten years, was still the loveliest woman that most men would ever see in their entire lifetime.

"Mademoiselle, this Englishman is too slow to introduce me. So, I introduce myself! I am Etienne Foucauld, and from this day forward, I shall be your slave." He bowed. He kissed her hand. Jane lifted an eyebrow in her sister's direction, but was surprised to see that Elizabeth did not smile.

Darcy spoke. Very formally, he introduced Foucauld and paused politely while the Frenchman expressed his devastation upon learning that the beautiful Mademoiselle was, in fact, the beautiful Madame Bingley.

"So many wives! No wonder your English boys must importune our French ladies in search of love, eh, Monsieur?"

Jane stiffened. Bingley's youthful indiscretion was not common knowledge in this neighborhood. Was this man merely making a coarse remark, or did he know something? Elizabeth was terrified that Jane's reaction might lead Foucauld to think that Bingley is the man he had been seeking.

However, Darcy was prepared. He stepped between Jane Bingley and Foucauld and leaned into the Frenchman and spoke with unveiled hostility. "It is not our custom to make such jokes in the presence of ladies."

"You are offended, Monsieur?" Foucauld hissed. "Do you demand satisfaction?"

"This is my wife's sister's home, sir. In her husband's absence, I will speak for him. You will be civil, or you will leave."

Foucauld most certainly did not want to leave! "Monsieur Darcy, I shall refrain from the humor of my country and adopt the mantle of gloom that you English wear so comfortably." He glanced about the room. "Where is Pierre?"

Jane's head jerked up. *"He means Peter!"* she thought. *"This man is French! And, Darcy is not friendly to him, not at all! Yet he brought him into my home. Why?"* She looked to Elizabeth, but Darcy had so completely blocked Foucauld's view of Jane, that Jane herself could see nothing but the back of Darcy's coat.

Tight-lipped and tense, Darcy commanded Foucauld's full attention. "We have not yet acquainted our host with the purpose of our visit, Monsieur. You will wait." Then, Darcy directed Foucauld to the study and told a servant to locate Mr. Bingley at once. While this was being done, Elizabeth and Jane retreated to Jane's sewing room.

"Who is he?" cried Jane.

"He is Peter's uncle, just arrived from France."

"Lizzie! Is your husband mad? Why did he bring him here?

"Because he does not want him poking about the county, asking any more questions than he already has." Then Elizabeth explained all that Darcy had said, finally telling Jane about Foucauld's bitterness toward Peter's natural father. "Listen to me, sister. He will bribe your servants, as he has ours. He will flatter you, as he has flattered me. He will seek to enrage your husband, as you have witnessed tonight with mine. In the sight of all this, you must remain silent and serene. Give him nothing to work with, for he will use it against us."

Then, she saw Elizabeth nod toward the window and heard a noise, and Jane realized that the Frenchman had already hired a spy. Jane was no longer safe in her own home! She surrendered to tears, sought refuge in her sister's loving embrace, and cried until she heard her mother's voice.

Then, her courage returned. "Oh!" she said, quickly wiping her tears, "Mother!" Elizabeth rolled her eyes. "And, Lydia and Wickham and their children!" Jane put her hand to her forehead. "This is the worst possible time! What more could happen?"

At that moment, Bingley flung open the door and threw himself into the room. "There you are, my dear! And, Mrs. Darcy! Welcome!" He was grinning like a loon.

"*Sometimes,*" mused Elizabeth, "*I wonder how Jane avoids choking him.*"

"Look who is with me!" bobbed Bingley, as he pulled a younger man out of the hallway and into Jane's sanctuary. "It is my third cousin twice removed, Mr. Ambrose Terwilliger. Will you do the introductions, Mrs. Bingley? I am told that Darcy is wild to see me!" Then, he burst out of the room as suddenly as he had burst in, leaving Mr. Terwilliger in the care of his wife and her sister. Wife and sister stared at the door where Bingley had been, and when they became quite convinced that he was not returning, they stared in unison at the man he had called his cousin.

Well, he was not like Bingley. Where Bingley was a roiling whirlpool tossing water outside its edges at every moment, this young man was not too much more than a puddle, but a puddle complete with cattails waving in the breeze and the sound of crickets. Where Bingley was the height of London fashion, Terwilliger was...presentable, in what appeared to be a re-cut ancient Sunday-only coat and britches. And, there was Cousin Ambrose himself. He was not as tall as Elizabeth, which made him shorter than Jane (but, although he was shorter than she, he could not be said to be short). He was not slender, although he was not husky, either. His hair was not quite red, but it was not quite brown or blond. His eyes were not brown and not blue, green perhaps, or maybe hazel. He was not athletic, not buoyant, not charming. And he certainly was not handsome! With most people, one can select some item of appearance (a bulbous nose, fine eyes, a golden ring in just one ear...something!) or personality (a shimmering laugh, a crooked smile...again, something!) to describe them to others. Ambrose Terwilliger, however, presented nothing of note and could only be described by what he was not.

They stared at him, and he stared at them.

Finally, Jane introduced herself and her sister. His shoulder twitched. They realized that they could not hint for him to leave because he had only newly arrived and knew nothing of the house. So, they led him about, with Jane explaining the household schedule, and Elizabeth describing the shops in nearby Lambton. As they strolled, the ladies were able to simply enjoy each other's company. Ambrose Terwilliger was present all the while, and although he did speak occasionally, they did not much notice his presence. For some reason, they felt swaddled in a soft blanket of serenity that comforted them and let them forget the Frenchman and remember each other as when they were children together.

When the men emerged from the study, Bingley was much subdued. He did not even smile. He sent the servant to fetch Peter and introduced the boy to his "Uncle Etienne." Foucauld went down on one knee and embraced the boy. He asked if Pierre (for he insisted that the boy's name was Pierre and not

Peter) remembered his mother and learned that she had made her son a toy that he still had – a wooden ball attached by a leather thong to a pedestal that the ball could be made to balance upon. Foucauld knew the toy without having to see it: He had one as a child, and it taught him patience, coordination, and economy of movement. He had played with it constantly. She must have remembered how he treasured it. While an expatriate in England, she had made no effort to contact him, no letters, no message left behind. But this toy for her son, this gift of love…she had remembered her brother.

The rest of the afternoon was spent pleasantly enough. Foucauld went the entire rest of the day without challenging anyone to a duel. Peter liked him.

Anne seized her opportunity to practice her conversational French while she and Etienne watched the children play on the lawn. At first, their conversation was tentative, for each was trying to elicit information from the other by a pretense of confidentiality. But they proved to be equally devious and equally fair-minded, so they quickly tired of that charade and progressed to a companionable tete-a-tete in a mix of French and English. She reveled in her memories of her eleven-year's-past visit to France; he spoke of his school in Boulogne.

"An encampment of over 150,000 soldiers, Mademoiselle. All with nothing to do!"

"Nothing, Monsieur? Were they not daily in preparation for an invasion of England?"

"I was not a soldier, Mademoiselle, merely a poor businessman presented with a huge quantity of consumers in search of diversion during their endless days of boredom. I began by offering lessons in the English tongue, and then in other subjects that the soldiers identified, such as the value of English money pieces relative to the Franc. Practical things that…visitors…might benefit from knowing."

"Invaders, you mean. The troops gathered just across the English Channel bred fear throughout England for many years. I would not mention your role in their preparations too freely, sir. You will find few sympathetic listeners. Indeed, you are treading a bit upon *my* sympathies."

The focus of their conversation deftly shifted, and they found themselves laughing at the confusion that arose when an English word sounded like a French word (or vice versa). Foucauld mentioned that Darcy said Wickham had a faulty heart – Did he mean that Wickham's health was bad, or that Wickham was evil? Upon questioning, Foucauld remembered Darcy's exact phrase – that Wickham was "a rapid coeur." Anne giggled and said, "Not 'rapid' – 'rabid'! Not coeur! C-U-R! He called him a dirty dog!" They laughed first at Etienne's error, then at Darcy's remark, then at how (even though the words themselves had such different meanings) both interpretations meant essentially the same thing.

Her children being safely watched, her husband nowhere to be found, Lydia took up her sketching pad and occupied herself in the garden. The Darcys and Bingleys strolled the grounds, out of earshot of anyone else, and alternated their conversation between what steps they should take next, and what they thought Etienne Foucauld might do, and of course, how much they all hated him. Georgiana went to the Bingley's music room: Since everyone was outside, she knew she could rely on having their grand piano entirely to herself.

CHAPTER TEN

Trumpet Vine

There was only one servant at the GanderGlen door, and he had not realized that there was a second carriage.

"Give me your wrap, Anne. Now!"

Lady Anne de Bourgh was not accustomed to receiving orders, so she did exactly as she was told. When she saw Georgiana carrying their two capes and following the butler, only her scandalized shock prevented her from calling out. Georgiana admonished her in a severe whisper: "You want to know what is going on, do you not? Visit the nursery and talk to the Governess! I will visit the kitchen!"

While Ambrose Terwilliger waited for his cousin at the top of the stairs, he witnessed the arrival of a party of three visitors, then two more. He could not hear what was being said, but he saw a vision of a girl taking an older woman's cape and following a Bingley houseservant towards the back of the house. *"How typical,"* mused Ambrose. *"The most beautiful creature on earth's face is a lady's maid, and the plain one is rich. When will there be justice in this world?"*

"Cousin Ambrose?"

"Yes! Cousin Charles! Thank you for inviting me to your home, sir!"

"I look forward to becoming acquainted with you, Cousin, but I must ask your indulgence. A friend and his family have arrived unexpectedly, bringing one other person. I must attend them. Will you permit me to give you to my wife for introductions and diversion, until I can free myself?"

Ambrose nodded agreement and allowed himself to be led to a sewing room. The ladies there – Bingley's wife and a Mrs. Darcy – were kindly and thoughtful. After a while, he managed to disengage himself and wander the house without impediment. Eventually, he found the music room, which held a magnificent instrument. He ran the scales. The piano was in perfect tune, a treat he not often was able to enjoy. He played a phrase of his own creation, then embellished it. Absorbed in his own creativity, he did not hear the door open and did not see the young woman approach.

Propriety required Georgiana to withdraw at once – she had never been introduced to this man! Whether it was because he was so indistinct he was almost invisible, or whether it was because she had heard his music, one cannot say...but what *she* said was "Oh!"

He knocked over the piano bench and then fell over it.

"Are you alright?" Georgiana gently inquired of the young man who was sprawled so clumsily at her feet.

He looked up and saw poise personified. Her features were even, her eyes infinite. Her hair fell in relaxed curls around her face. But, despite the kindness in her voice, he knew she had to be laughing at him. He got to his feet, returned the humiliated piano bench to its previous position of dignity, and assessed his attacker. She was at least six inches taller than he. *"A few years older, too,"* he guessed. He apologized profusely for entering the room and for playing the piano too loudly, and he apologized even more for "abusing Mr. Bingley's hospitality."

"You are forgiven under one condition. You must teach me that melody."

Ordinarily, Georgiana would be the one desperately searching for an escape route. However, since this young man was not leaning over her, or flinging witty banter haphazardly about the room, or spouting poetry he had memorized just this morning, she felt very much at ease.

He, on the other hand, was extremely ill at ease, and he began to nurse a mild resentment of the cause of his embarrassment: This annoyingly self-assured woman.

"I am sorry," he apologized, "but I really do not know the melody."

She cocked her eyebrow and looked him straight in the eye. If she had called him a liar to his face, she could not have achieved a more dramatic effect.

"Truly! No!" cried the visually impaled Mr. Terwilliger, pleading for mercy. "I was just playing. I often…just…play! I almost never write anything down. I could not repeat it now, not if my life depended upon it!"

He was so sincere and so desperate, Georgiana had to fight to control her merriment. She affected an angry tone and demanded, "Sir, do I understand you to say that you create such music often, and you make no effort whatsoever to preserve its beauty? Unconscionable!" She put her hands on her hips, stamped her foot, and leaned over him. She was within a moment of laughing out loud, so she turned her back to him and haughtily concluded, "I am afraid I shall have to ask my brother to thrash you!"

Ambrose suddenly remembered where he had seen her before. She had arrived in the party of his cousin's visitors. She was a maid! A servant! Ambrose had his footing now! "Young lady, you are the boldest girl imaginable! Do you speak to all of Mr. Bingley's guests this way?"

Georgiana turned and faced him. She was speechless. She had never before heard anyone describe her as "bold." She rather liked it! And this time, she could not keep her most dazzling smile from her lips. Ambrose Terwilliger noted that when she did not smile, she was beautiful; but when she did smile, time stopped, the air did not move, and sound faded to nothing.

It was then that Bingley himself appeared, surrounded by an entourage of friends and relations. "There you are, Miss Darcy! In the music room, of course. And I see you have found our wandering Terwilliger."

Instantly, Georgiana's manner went from taunting to timid. When she allowed that introductions had not actually occurred, Bingley corrected the oversight at once. Ambrose, of course, flushed red upon realizing that he had just affronted his potential patron's sister.

Georgiana mentioned that Mr. Terwilliger had consented to share his musical expertise with her on the very next day. Ambrose opened his mouth, but could think of no response that did not begin with *"She is lying!"* so he closed it up again. Darcy thanked him at once for his thoughtfulness, Bingley slapped him on the back, and Jane whispered in his ear, "You must be extremely gentle with her. She is painfully shy, you know."

Ambrose noted the almost imperceptible smile on Georgiana's lips as they all went in to partake of the evening meal. *"You cunning vixen,"* he thought to himself. *"You are a spoiled brat!"*

CHAPTER ELEVEN

White Violet

When he heard that one of the Bingley servants would be going into Lambton, Ambrose asked if he could ride along. Her husband's cousin seemed eager to familiarize himself with the local community and its inhabitants, which in Jane Bingley's mind confirmed him as a young man well-suited to a quiet religious life in the countryside. The true reason for Mr. Terwilliger's explorations was much less admirable: He desired to visit a diversity of taverns.

Tavern-hopping was a dangerous business for a man in Ambrose Terwilliger's position. Charles Bingley's letter inviting Ambrose to visit GanderGlen had explained that Mr. Darcy had substantial patronage in the church. So, if Mr. Darcy were to be sufficiently impressed by a young man's character and behavior, then Mr. Darcy might be willing to entrust a parsonage (and the income from its tithes) to that deserving young paragon. Consequently, Mr. Terwilliger was determined to be convincing as a suitable candidate for the cloth (and the money), by refusing liquor of every kind and feigning a discreet ignorance of feminine charm.

The truth was, Mr. Terwilliger was not averse to an occasional glass, nor even an occasional lass. On this afternoon, as the servant obtained the supplies needed for barn roof repairs at GanderGlen, Ambrose meandered into The Bent Twig. The locals sized him up easily, a foolish boy if ever there was one. They overcame his shyness (this was the first time, he sheepishly admitted, that he ever dared enter a den of sin), bought him his very first pint of ale, and then persuaded him to engage in a friendly wager. He lost the bet, of course. He was so sad at losing his farthing! But they convinced him that if he tried another wager and doubled his bet, he would surely win, eventually. For doubling the bet and redoubling it if necessary (and so on, ad infinitum) they explained patiently, ensures that you will get all your money back with your first success. This strategy is foolproof! Presuming, of course, that success comes before your pockets are completely emptied.

Already slurring his words from just one pint and happy with the knowledge that the return of his farthing was absolutely guaranteed, they had little difficulty convincing Ambrose Terwilliger that he could down a glass of whiskey without actually touching the glass. How they arrived at the exact terms and wording of this wager was unclear, but it had something to do with Ambrose's boastfulness and his clearly apparent lack of coordination. There was a great deal of laughter and joyous camaraderie as Ambrose wantonly agreed to side bets. The Publican shook his head and looked at his customers with a disapproving eye as he poured Ambrose the glass of whiskey. Of course, his reproof would not have prevented him from joining in the wagers! It was only his skepticism that Ambrose had sufficient funds to pay off that kept the Publican from betting.

Ambrose stared at the little glass. He tilted his head one way, and then another. He put his chin on the bar and slid it toward the rim of the glass.

"You can't touch it, boy-o! That means, the drink must go down your throat without touching your lips!"

Ambrose lifted his chin off the bar, looked at the speaker, and blinked his eyes.

The bar was full of rough and raucous men, and they were saying unkind things and laughing. Ambrose looked at the barmaid with eyes filling with innocent tears. She came close, put her hand on his shoulder, and told him not to make wagers in bars with men that were not his friends. He nodded. His lip trembled. He lifted her apron to dry his eyes and, in one smooth motion, used the apron to pick up the glass, hold it a foot above his head, then cock his head back and pour the whiskey straight down his throat. He pounded the empty glass onto the bar, rim down, and called in his bets (for it was the apron, and not his hand, that touched the glass).

The bar was silent. Ambrose, sober and neither frowning nor smiling, waited. A particularly large man leaned over him. "Do you think we are fools?"

"Did you think I was?" Ambrose replied. With one elbow resting on the bar and one foot hooked on the rung of his barstool, he appeared to be completely at ease. Nothing in his tone of voice was offensive, but his manner was plain: He expected to be paid.

Another man spoke. "We thought you were..."

"Drunk," said a third.

"On one pint?" asked Ambrose with good-natured innocence and an open smile.

The first man spoke again with undisguised hostility. "How do you think you are going to make us pay?"

"It has nothing to do with me," Ambrose said matter-of-factly. "Either a man pays his debts of honor, or he does not. The men in this bar think they already know whose word is good and whose is not. Each will stay and watch, just to see that their opinion of each of the others is confirmed." Ambrose turned his attention to the second man who spoke, who he deemed early on to be the one most likely to gossip. "You, sir, will you leave before knowing?"

The man looked about the bar, dug into his pocket and produced his wager. Then he stood to the side as the others, almost all of them, left a couple of farthings each on the bar near where Ambrose sat. Even the large, hostile man paid over his loss.

Ambrose winked placidly at the barmaid, and at her come-hither (and after pocketing the farthings), he followed her up the staircase to a broom closet on the second floor. She laughed so merrily at his limericks and whimsy that she did not bother to mention her usual fee for private entertainments.

His workday completed, Ambrose sat alone at a table with a view of the street and of the Bingley wagon, waiting for the servant to finish his business. The sun was still high, so he knew it was not yet much past noon. He would leave the wagon as it passed the turn-off to Pemberley, still in the early afternoon, and fulfill his obligation of a single music lesson to that devious little vixen, Georgiana Darcy.

At the bar, he overheard a stranger whine about his misfortunes and mention the name, "Darcy." Ambrose recognized that this man was one of the few that had not paid his wager. He offered to buy the man a drink.

"Why?" the stranger replied warily. "I would not buy a drink for you unless I had a reason. What do you want from me?"

"Tell me about your friend. Tell me about Darcy."

"Darcy is not my friend. He is my brother-in-law," the man said.

Having found an audience and being quite thick with ale, the man talked much. Particularly, about "Darcy the Pure" and how they had played together as boys until Darcy usurped the parsonage at Kympton. "Promised to me it was, by Darcy's own father, who could not have loved me more if I had been his own son. But Darcy was jealous, and once his father passed, he found an escape in the will's writing and used it against my interest. So, my wife suffers. My children suffer. God bless Charles Bingley! Or they would starve." The stranger drained his glass and held it out for more, but Ambrose would not pay for a second pint.

It did occur to Mr. Terwilliger that a man with a wife and three children (for he now knew that this stranger was, in fact, the heretofore missing George Wickham) might abandon the status of a gentleman and stoop to clerking in a store or even manual labor, as demeaning as that would be. But Wickham did not lower himself (as he was undoubtedly afflicted with too much self-respect). Instead, he pursued one of the few money-making endeavors permitted a gentleman: Wagering. Ambrose suppressed his snort, for he knew already that George Wickham had no gift for a gentleman's game.

Then another thought presented: Wickham had to know Miss Darcy. Wickham was well thought of by her father. It would have been natural for Wickham to court her (perhaps even, expected that he would court her!) and win her hand. Such a beneficial marriage would have ensured his life of gentlemanly leisure. Yet, Wickham had not wanted Miss Darcy. Wickham married Lydia, who was without wealth. Quite a slap in the face to Miss Darcy, that! Was this the reason Darcy withheld Kympton? What kind of man was this Darcy, to reduce a boyhood playmate to poverty simply because that friend had chosen true love instead of a wealthy wife? What kind of a woman was Darcy's wife, to allow her own sister to be punished for loving and being loved? Ambrose wished he had thought of some way to decline Miss Darcy's invitation –

invitation! – (her manipulation, he meant) yesterday, when it was issued. He consoled himself with the thought that he would tarry for the merest hour, and then never see her again.

Having just tied down the last of the load, the servant began to wonder where he might find Mr. Terwilliger. Lo, Mr. Terwilliger miraculously appeared (for Ambrose certainly did not wish to be found in a tavern, nor did he wish to be found in the company of the disfavored Mr. Wickham)! The servant, a sensitive soul, detected the sound of clinking coins where there had been silence before, but he asked no questions.

CHAPTER TWELVE

Pink Hyacinth

When Ambrose reached Pemberley, Miss Darcy was entertaining a visitor in the garden. Naturally, the butler ushered Ambrose into the music room to wait for her – out of sight, but not out of hearing. Her swain was obsessed with the color brown. Copper, tan, liver, chestnut, dun, and so on. Dun! He was talking about horses! The coloration of horses! How vain does a woman have to be, Ambrose wondered, to be willing to listen to a recital of horse colors! Just so she can crow to her friends and family about the number of suitors begging for an audience with glorious her! Well, he was in the music room, so he was going to play the piano. If she did not like it, she could send him on his way. Which, come to think of it, was what he really wanted.

He played a ditty from Cromwell's time: Raucous, carefree, and loud. Had he sung the words, the servants would have thrown him out of the house. But then, he remembered that Mr. Darcy had patronages he could bestow, so he segued into a hymn.

"What was the name of the first song?"

It was her. And her Lady's Companion, who had already seated herself in an overstuffed leather chair and was busying herself with knitting needles and balls of yarn.

"Nankee Doodle. Our soldiers in the Americas changed the first word to 'Yankee' to ridicule the colonists, but the colonists loved it and actually took it for their own." Ambrose turned to see if the horse lover was with her. He was not. "Some people cannot be insulted. Too vain." He gazed at her, smiling inoffensively.

He had presumed that her self-centeredness would protect him. He was mistaken.

"Vanity. Is it solely the province of women, do you think? Or, is it possible that men with glib tongues share in that vice?"

Ambrose pressed his lips together and lowered his head. Caught!

She laughed.

"And the second song, Mr. Terwilliger. I have heard it, but..."

" 'Amazing Grace,' written about thirty, thirty-five years ago by a man who regretted mistakes he made in his youth. But you did not ask me here to entertain you with my playing, Miss Darcy. You asked for a music lesson. So, let me hear you play."

She took his seat at the piano, arranged her music, positioned her fingers on the keys, took a deep breath, stared at the opening bars on the first page, confirmed that the pedals were still attached to the piano, paced her breathing...

"Oh, for heaven's sake, Miss Darcy. Play!"

She stared at him, then looked down at the keys, set her shoulders, and forced the piano to make sounds.

"Miss Darcy." He stopped. He was not being fair to her, and he knew it. He resented her wealth and her beauty. He resented being kept waiting while she entertained another man. Most of all, he resented himself because he was so clearly inferior to everything in her life. He cleared his throat. "You have had excellent instruction. Your music is…precise." He stopped. He made ready to leave.

Georgiana regretted inviting him into her music room. She had thought him amusing when she met him, but today he was sharp and impatient. Rude. He was rude.

"Why do you occupy yourself with music? You do not enjoy it," he asked, although he made his disinterest in her reply quite plain.

She had never thought about "why." "I suppose…because… it envelops me. When I am playing, I think only of the music, nothing else. I do enjoy it! I enjoyed your playing, very much."

" 'When you are playing.' That is what you said. But you are not playing, Miss Darcy. You are working. Arranging, positioning, concentrating on ink blobs. When have you ever heard anyone say they are going to work a piano, Miss Darcy?"

She looked bewildered.

His voice became very gentle. "Most people play an instrument to entertain others. Who enjoys watching someone work? Do you?"

In a very small voice, she said, "No."

Ambrose looked about the room. There was a harpsichord, a violin, the piano, a harp, a viola, a cello, and a small organ. "So many beautiful musical instruments, each with a unique voice. Do you limit yourself to the piano, Miss Darcy?"

"Yes. Mostly. The harpsichord on occasion. The harp, rarely." She straightened her shoulders. "Do you not think that it is better to master one instrument than to flit from one to another?"

"I think it is best to realize that the instrument is the master, and we are fortunate that they allow us to play with them. I think no one enjoys being ignored, Miss Darcy. Not even a small organ."

Georgiana was thinking about what he had just said. She had not been looking at him and was not going to look at him now. Sacrificing an hour of her day to sit with another second son of another fine old family had bored her to tears. Now, suddenly, she was awake. She started to smile. Then, she swallowed a laugh.

"So. You think the organ itself desires to be played with?" She tried to not display her amusement too plainly.

When Ambrose said it, he thought Miss Darcy too naïve and sheltered to understand his reference. She understood it, alright! Uh Oh. What about her Companion? Still knitting. Totally oblivious.

"I think, Miss Darcy, that I need to hear you play. Will you try?"

She did, with absolute precision. He asked how many times she had practiced that piece. Dozens. He took the sheet music away. "Play."

"But..."

"Blobs of ink are not music, Miss Darcy. They are signposts on a path to a destination. You have seen enough of what was written. The composer has had his chance. Now the performer must step forward. Stop working on it, and start playing with it."

She did play. Her fingering relaxed, and the music became more fluid. Before today, music was her armor, hard and close. But now she saw that it could become a garden enjoyed by others, if she would only invite them in.

She was just beginning to plant a few pink hyacinths when Ambrose announced that the lesson was over. She pouted.

"You can practice without an audience, Miss Darcy."

Georgiana bristled. "Mr. Terwilliger, you have made it plain that you believe me to be spoiled. I believe you to be disrespectful. That said, you are an effective teacher. Am I an apt pupil?"

Ambrose was embarrassed. She was correct about what he thought of her. She was also correct about how he had behaved this day and he was ashamed of his behavior. "Yes, Miss Darcy. You accept criticism gracefully and you embrace adjustments." He paused. He had presumed she was shallow, susceptible to flattery, and indifferent to the effort of improvement. But this formidable young lady had not let him get away with a thing. His attitude shifted, and his voice reflected the change in his demeanor. "I think I may have learned something, too. I enjoyed this afternoon."

"Really, Mr. Terwilliger? Has this been how you express enjoyment? You, sir, need to learn how to…play."

She smiled.

He dropped his head and he nodded. She had been setting him up for that one, the whole afternoon. She had her revenge, for the quick-witted and impudent Mr. Terwilliger could not think of a single riposte.

He was half-way to GanderGlen when he realized that he had left his heart behind. Actually, he had not left it; she had taken it from him.

CHAPTER THIRTEEN

Bird's Foot Trefoil

George Wickham was asleep. Blessed with a silly wife and her sympathetic sisters, he managed sufficient pocket money to be able, occasionally, to indulge his predilection for bawd. There was a stirring in the room, but he did not bother to awaken much. He knew it had to be Mrs. Duckworth, the divorced lady of the village, to whom he owed so much and paid so little. But, with the needle-prick of what felt like a dagger in a location that shall not be divulged, Wickham found himself full awake, frozen in terror, and staring wide-eyed at a stranger.

"Good morning, Monsieur!" the stranger said.

Wickham saw his hostess cowering in the corner of the room, trying to cover herself with a single lace doily

"For heaven's sake, Mrs. Duckworth, do not be afraid of him! He will not hurt you! Run and get a constable!"

Foucauld smiled, but not pleasantly. "You are very brave, with the lady's life." Over his shoulder, he asked, "Do you intend to annoy me, Madame? Or, do you intend to remain unharmed?"

"Am I safe, here?" she asked.

"Perfectly."

"Quit talking to him and scream for the police!" pressed Wickham.

"That could cause you some measure of discomfort, Madame," the stranger advised.

As she adjusted the strategic placement of the doily, she remarked that she was quite comfortable and that she would prefer not to engage in further conversation of any kind, with either party.

Foucauld nodded and gave his full attention to Mr. George Wickham. "Do you know who I am, Monsieur?"

"Yes, you are Madelyn Fox's mentally deficient brother. She told me that you were always playing with knives, even when you were a small child."

"Did she also mention that I lack the gift of forgiveness?" Foucauld applied a slight amount of pressure, just enough to cause Mr. Wickham to yelp and open his eyes wide. "The reason I am here is because I know who you are. You are the man who seduced and abandoned my sister, once she became pregnant with your child."

"No! That is not true!" Wickham coughed. "May I sit up?"

"Of course, Monsieur!" Foucauld smiled, even more broadly than when he threatened Mrs. Duckworth's well-being, and, between clenched teeth, whispered, "The loss will be yours."

Wickham did not sit up.

"Now, see here, Foucauld. I admit I knew your sister, but she was already using the name Madelyn Fox. I assisted her in making beneficial acquaintances, that is all."

"For money," spat Foucauld.

"Well, she had to live! Darcy had thrown her out of his house. And for what? Generosity! That was your sister's flaw, Foucauld. She was generous! Was it wrong for her to accept an equal measure…no, actually, a lesser amount…of generosity from those men she so kindly favored? And, I was her friend.

Was it wrong for her to share her bounty with me when I was the one who facilitated her in forming new friendships?"

"The more you speak, Monsieur, the more I want to kill you." Foucauld jabbed the tip of his broken sword forward just a bit, and Wickham satisfyingly yipped. "I have asked in the town about you, Monsieur. Your history. Your comings and goings. Your interests and activities. Never have I encountered so much assistance! Tell me, Monsieur, have you betrayed all your friends? Everyone who has known you? Because I found no one who was reluctant to give me the information I sought, and not one asked so much as a sou in payment!"

The tip went in a little farther than Foucauld may have intended, causing Wickham to cry out and babble quickly in a high-pitched voice. "Did you not hear what I said? I gave her shelter after Darcy threw her out. Do you want to kill me for that? I was merely one in a long line. Look to the first, if you want the man who seduced and ruined her. Look to the last, if you want the man who made her child a bastard. I was not the first, and I was not the last! I was her friend, I tell you!"

Foucauld cocked his head to one side, studied his prey for a moment, then opened a new conversational gambit. "I have met your wife and children, Monsieur Wickham. Delightful!"

"Delightful, yes! And, mine until I die, for she will not give me grounds for divorce. Even if she did, she would not give me money for the lawyers."

Foucauld laughed. "I have heard of your English laws. The only legal grounds for divorce is the infidelity of the wife." Foucauld half-looked back over his shoulder at Mrs. Duckworth, who readjusted the placement of her doily. "So, you are unhappy in your marriage, Monsieur? How fortunate for you! A lifetime of misery is a much better vengeance than can be granted by a mere moment of death. Your life is spared." The Frenchman grandly swept his free hand across the landscape of the room, but his blade remained firmly at attention.

"I am so grateful," said Wickham. "So, why have you not removed your dagger?"

"I am thinking." After a few anxious minutes – all the anxiety being on Wickham's part, of course – Foucauld said, "You have neglected to provide the name of the last man who knew my sister. Do you have compunctions, Monsieur?"

Wickham laughed. "I do not know why I would sprout them now! I have never had them before!" Wickham told him of Mademoiselle Foucauld's final lover, the one who "visits her grave every day when he is in Lambton," and who is "expected there within the week."

Still, Foucauld's hand remained steady, and the broken blade did not waver. "And…who was the first man?"

"A wharf-rat named Jammin Hard. Now, he was a real bounder! He used to boast that he would murder his own grandmother if he had a buyer for her wedding ring!"

"He can be found…where?"

"He used to frequent the docks of Dover, south of London, but he dropped out of sight some time ago." Wickham frowned. "If you do find him, there is no need to mention my name. We were once friends, so…"

"I am sure he would be devastated to learn that you turned on him at your first opportunity." Foucauld sheathed what was left of his sword. "Devastated certainly, but I doubt he would be surprised."

With the blade safely away, Wickham gathered his courage and his indignation. "You know, Foucauld, you owe me your gratitude. I was kinder to your sister than anyone else. Had I not given her a room at the inn, she would have been forced to ply her trade in the streets!"

"Yes. Yes, I know. She was surrounded by kind Englishmen, all tripping over each other to provide for her well-being. I am an ungrateful dog to resent such selfless generosity." Foucauld studied Wickham for a moment, then laughed once and turned toward Mrs. Duckworth. He bowed prettily and favored her hand with the breath of a kiss. "Madame," he whispered in her ear, "I caution you. This man serves up his friends without a murmur and describes his basest crimes as innocent kindnesses."

"If you have what you came for, get out of my house!" shouted Mrs. Duckworth, her doily now clutched just under her chin and, therefore, totally ineffective. "I do not need a Frog's advice on the worth of good English stock!"

When the Frenchman was gone, Wickham appealed to his hostess to warm the bedding. But Mrs. Duckworth stated that she had lost her interest in bedding. In so doing, she reminded him, in a most impolite way, that a married woman has all the honors but only one choice, while a divorced woman commands no honors but has every choice. "And," she concluded, "I do not choose you."

CHAPTER FOURTEEN

Serpent's Tongue

Georgiana Darcy was accustomed to the attentions of several suitors at any given time. Currently, there was Sir James Culpepper's oldest son Jeremy, who would invite her to stroll through Pemberley's gardens and woods and pathways and sought to enchant her by recognizing every bird by its call; and, there was the red-coated officer with the thin black ink-line of a mustache and pursed lips, who preferred horseback riding to walking and presumed that Miss Darcy shared his fascination with discussing the various colors of horses.

On such excursions, Mrs. Annesley would more or less join the couple, but at a tactful distance. Mrs. Annesley was Georgiana's Lady's Companion, paid to accompany her when she wished to shop in town, or visit friends, or engage in a game of lawn tennis, or any other diversion that might require a second participant. Included in her duties was the role of chaperone. Miss Darcy valued Mrs. Annesley as the ideal Lady's Companion: She spoke when she was spoken to and kept her silence at all other times. Best of all, she was oblivious. She never saw anything, she never heard anything, and she never repeated anything to Fitzwilliam or Elizabeth. Georgiana knew this to be true because, if her brother had ever learned of her diligent efforts to discourage all of these tedious, pompous, fortune-hunting men, there would have been a lecture, followed by a plea, and then another sigh of frustrated resignation.

Valuable as Mrs. Annesley's inattentiveness was, her best quality was that she took no offense when her presence was not required. So, on this day, when Jeremy Culpepper had brought a basket of food and had invited both Miss Darcy and the ever-present Mrs. Annesley for a noon-day picnic, Georgiana's spontaneous (meticulously plotted) suggestion (demand) that her cousin (old maid houseguest) join them was greeted with delight (horror) by Mr. Culpepper, as Mrs. Annesley voluntarily and discreetly withdrew to the music room. Miss Darcy's design was to interest Mr. Culpepper in the very wealthy Lady Anne. Mr. Culpepper's initial target was the beautiful Miss Darcy, but as Rosings was described to him in detail (to explain Lady Anne's overpowering homesickness, which heretofore had been unknown to Lady Anne), he began to recognize the delightful charms of Miss Darcy's more mature cousin. As far as Miss Darcy and Mr. Culpepper were concerned, the matter was quite settled. Sadly, however, Lady Anne had an opinion of her own, and Jeremy Culpepper took his empty picnic basket with him when he left.

It was not uncommon for Ambrose to arrive at Pemberley at the time designated by Miss Darcy, only to find the lady occupied with the attentions of a suitor. Usually, while being kept waiting yet again, Ambrose would seize the opportunity to practice on the Darcy piano, or the harpsichord, or occasionally the violin, until Miss Darcy deigned to remember the appointment that she herself had specified.

Today, however, Mrs. Annesley was not trailing behind Miss Darcy and whatever suitor happened to be in her web. Mrs. Annesley was in the music room, knitting. So, Ambrose asked her about her knitting, which led to a conversation about what she thought about when she was knitting, which brought them to a subject that truly interested him: Mrs. Annesley had been writing a novel for the past sixteen years. Aha!

"Is it a novel with pirates, a mysterious foreigner, a bearded villain?"

Mrs. Annesley shook her head, *"No."*

"Are there swordfights and abductions and ladies that require rescue?"

"No."

"A princess?"

"No."

"A castle?"

"No."

"Nefarious goings-on in pubs?"

"No"

"Backstairs intrigues among the servants?"

"No."

"When does all this (Ambrose wanted very much to say "all this nothingness") occur?"

At last, Mrs. Annesley spoke aloud. "The present time, generally."

Ambrose brightened. "So, there is mention of the Prince Regent!"

Silence descended once again. *"No."*

"Beau Brummell? Lord Byron?"

"No."

"The unpleasantness with the French Revolution? The rebellion in the Americas? England's twenty-five years of war with France, interrupted only by one year of peace?"

"No."

"Is there a romance?"

"Yes," she said.

"Finally!" a relieved Ambrose said to himself. With eager hopefulness, he said aloud, "Is it love at first sight?"

Again, she wordlessly shook her head, *"No,"* but then she mused aloud, "Actually, she does not much like him for most of the book."

"But, in the end, they fall into each other's arms and share a passion that causes cheeks to redden and handkerchiefs to flutter, do they not?" wished Ambrose, but doubted his own words as they were escaping his lips.

Mrs. Annesley looked at him as though he was suggesting that her characters would sprout wings and become Chinese dragons.

"No. They never actually…kiss. Not even after they have married."

Ambrose was silent. And then he said, "A novel, you say? Hundreds of pages, you say? About…?" He stopped. He, himself, could think of absolutely nothing to say.

So, Mrs. Annesley said, "It is an observation of ladies and gentlemen and their daily life in country shires. It started as an epistolary (a series of letters exchanged between various parties), but that format became somewhat awkward. Then, I obtained a copy of *Cecilia*, Fanny Burney's book, and I realized that I needed to write my novel in the same style as Miss Burney had written hers. It is mostly conversations, you know. In polite company, of course. And, conversations that include ladies because…I have no idea what gentlemen talk about amongst themselves without a lady present, or what servants discuss when their masters are not present, or what the inside of a pub even looks like. Obviously, I have never been privy to such things!" she laughed.

Ambrose laughed, too, but ventured, "I believe many authors rely on their imaginations for much of what they write."

Mrs. Annesley agreed, but, "I wish to write about what I know and rely on imagination only for advancing the general plot. The people, their conversations, their daily life (which is in actuality very little affected by what is happening in the world that exists outside their own neighborhood), I want those things to ring true."

It was then that Miss Darcy floated into her music room – and stopped cold. She began by staring at Ambrose, and then staring at Mrs. Annesley…who was NOT knitting. Clearly, Miss Darcy was a bit discomfited. "Mr. Terwilliger, I did not expect to see you."

"You asked me to come, Miss Darcy. For another music lesson. Have you forgotten?"

"Yes. No. Yes. I mean, since I did not hear you playing, I thought you had not yet arrived."

"Mrs. Annesley and I were locked in conversation about…"

But, just then Mrs. Annesley looked up at him, bit her lower lip, and implored him with such a wounded expression, that Ambrose knew he must change direction immediately.

"…knitting versus crocheting. She strongly prefers knitting. My mother is firmly in the camp of crocheting. Were you aware, Miss Darcy, of the controversy that exists concerning the merits of each?"

Miss Darcy stated that she had not taken a fixed position on either side of that wall. What she did not state was that she had taken note of the look that passed between her teacher and her Companion and would in future be certain that she was not merely on time, but comfortably early for all her coming music lessons with Mr. Terwilliger.

CHAPTER FIFTEEN

Fairy Fans

Summer days in France are within a range of warm temperatures. Humidity, wind, rain, all within a range. But summers in the north of England change from day to day, sometimes from hour to hour. Each day Etienne met Mademoiselle Anne (he was often told by others that he should address her as "Lady Anne," but he was waiting for her to mention it, and she never did), and they began their conversation by talking about the weather. This afforded enough time for the maid (that is, Anne's chaperone) to surreptitiously fall behind and rendezvous with the Second Footman, and that allowed Etienne and Anne to engage in private conversations.

Foucauld was trying to be casual about it, but on this particular day, he was rather fascinated by her profile. The sun was shouldering a cloud out of its way, and the suffused light caught flecks of gold in her eyes. Each tip of each hair on her head, too. Tiny glowing lights, surrounding her face and accenting the line of her jaw, her cheeks, her mouth. Odd. She seemed so ordinary when he first met her. Now he saw that she was really quite lovely. Her lips particularly. Very…moist.

A thought troubled him, and he asked, "What will you say if someone sees us together without a chaperone?"

"That I have outgrown chaperones."

Foucauld stopped. "Mademoiselle Anne, I would be devastated if I did anything that might compromise your reputation in this community."

"Wealth brings privileges, Monsieur. A title brings additional advantages. Is that not also true in France?"

"Yes. You put me in mind of someone who used those privileges extensively. He called himself a Marquis before he was elected to the National Congress. When he took his seat, at the beginning of the Reign of Terror, he became "Citizen de Sade.' Now, since Bonaparte, he is a Marquis again. His family is very wealthy."

"I do not understand. If he was a nobleman, how did he escape the guillotine?"

"Nobleman!" Foucauld laughed, a laugh that bit and spat. "There is nothing noble in that man! French Aristocracy is not the same as English Nobility, Mademoiselle. In England, all titles are conferred by the King, no? In France, if a family is old (like mine is) and rich (as mine once was), one takes the title one wants. My father was 'Count Foucauld,' my oldest brother a Marquis, and my younger brother was 'Vidame Foucauld'."

"You did not take a title, Monsieur?"

"No," he replied acidly. "As a second son, I was enticed by the ideals of liberty, brotherhood, and equal treatment. I was very public in my criticism of my family's self-aggrandizement." He frowned, "It was that, I think, that preserved my life."

She changed the subject.

He circled back to it. "But your family? Your wealth and title would not deflect *them*. What would they say?"

She chuckled. "Oh! They would be horrified! I would receive a very stern lecture from Mother. Then, a severe spinster twenty years my senior would be hired to follow me everywhere. And, the maid would be discharged."

"So, the cost of your folly would be paid by a servant?"

At this, Anne laughed out loud. Foucauld was shocked. While he deplored the Terror, he embraced the ideals of the Revolution. The fact that Lady Anne did not demand constant use of her title had convinced him that, even though she might not embrace those ideals as he did, at least she was willing to tolerate them. He was severely disappointed to learn that Anne de Bourgh would be so callous in her treatment of someone so vulnerable.

Once Anne had regained control of her voice, she explained. "Monsieur Foucauld. My family would hush the whole thing up! Only (and this is the important part, so pay attention!) ONLY the women I told would know that this maid could be relied upon to disappear upon request. There are many young ladies, and even more married women, that yearn for a chaperone like that! The girl would have another position in no time, and probably at a significantly higher wage."

Foucauld stared at her. When he was able to speak again, he said, "You have thought this through, beginning to end."

"Of course."

"But it is worthy of Machiavelli," said he.

"Merci," said she.

"No, Mademoiselle, I can see that I am outmatched, so it is I who must ask for mercy!" he smiled.

"Mercy I will give you, Monsieur. It is victory that I shall withhold."

Lady Anne's lips curved in a smile, but her eyes smiled not.

CHAPTER SIXTEEN

Blood Drops

Mrs. Annesley was quite displeased. The pattern had said "Knit two, Purl one" and she had Knit one and Purled two. Across twenty-three rows. So, she had to unravel an hour's work. This swaddling blanket would never get done!

Actually, what troubled Mrs. Annesley was the fear that Mr. Terwilliger might reveal to Miss Darcy that she had written a novel. A novel that disclosed a tale of seduction! How Mr. Terwilliger learned of it, she was not certain. Well, she had told him about it. And, somehow, he had acquired it! Well, she had given it to him. But he wasn't supposed to read it! Well, she did ask him for his opinion. She thought he would give it right back to her, half un-read. But he disappeared!

It was her only copy, and he did not return to Pemberley. Miss Darcy was clearly peevish about his absence, so Mrs. Annesley dared not raise the subject with her! On Mrs. Annesley's day off, she managed a casual encounter in town with a GanderGlen servant and learned that the Bingleys had gone to London for two weeks to visit Caroline Bingley (who had remained at their Mayfair house). Mr. Terwilliger, who had never seen London, had gone with them as companion to Peter.

They would be locking up the house for the season, and all five would return in another ten days.

Ten Days!

Anne de Bourgh entered the music room, smiled at Mrs. Annesley, and said nothing to Georgiana. Mrs. Annesley knew that the ladies wished to conspire, so she would not be needed until after dinner (if then!). She gathered her knitting and found a sunny corner in the observatory to finish unraveling and begin knitting *twice*, and purling *once*.

"When is he expected to return?" Anne asked, once she was certain they could not be overheard.

"Who?"

"Oh, Georgiana!"

"Well, if he cares not that my lessons fall two weeks behind, why should I care when he will return?"

"He has never seen London! How could you expect him to refuse it! Parliament! Kew Gardens! The Beefeaters! Are you so mean-spirited?"

"You forgot the pubs. The barmaids."

"Oh. You have heard those reports."

"Mrs. Annesley does not confine herself to the comings and goings of Etienne Foucauld, Anne." Georgiana shook off her mood and changed her tone. "He has made no promises to anyone. What right have I to expect him to refuse whatever opportunity is thrown in his path?"

"Still," said Anne, gently.

"Excellent idea, Anne. Let us be still on that subject. Instead, we will address a different subject. Monsieur Foucauld."

"I spoke to him yesterday, while you were visiting the dressmaker with Elizabeth." Anne paused and tilted her head to one side. "Strange man. His memory is so clear on some things, but he cannot retain the fact that three days each week you, and your brother, and your sister-in-law, take your noon meal in Lambton."

"Oh! And, what does he remember, Anne? Your favorite color? Your favorite poet? The name of your first kitten?"

"Stop it!" Anne laughed. "We both know he is trying to discover information that will help him secure custody of Peter. I have been flattered by fortune-hunters extraordinaire, Georgiana. This man is an amateur!"

"And, what have you learned?"

Anne pondered. There was something. Something awful.

Foucauld had told her of a…friend, a second son of an aristocrat. The guillotine took 40,000 lives during the Reign of Terror: Some had been men of the church, some were lawyers, some were doctors, but most were aristocrats, and some of those aristocrats were children. This friend of Foucauld's had been desperate to save his haughty and defiant teenaged sister. To deflect the attention she seemed determined to attract, he denounced his parents and his brothers. The denunciations were a mere formality – all of the aristocrats were known and were being herded into prisons as quickly as possible, anyway. But the betrayal of the family had some value as an endorsement of the rightness of the revolution's cause. So, the revolutionaries let this "friend" live. They let his sister live. The only thing they asked was that he operate the guillotine himself for one hour on one day, to demonstrate his devotion to the Glorious Revolution. He had known, the moment they said it, who would be in the tumbrels on that day, at that hour. So, his father spat on him. His brothers cursed him with their last breaths. The worst was his mother: She forgave him. The sister? She ran away with the first man who promised to take her out of France.

Even now, Anne heard Foucauld's own voice. *"While he stood on the platform, raising the chain and freeing the blade, he told himself* that he was doing it so his little sister could have a life, a husband, a home, children. He killed both his brothers, he killed his father, he killed his own mother. They all died at his hand. Now, the sister is gone. He lives. He convinced himself he was doing it for her. In the end, he did it...for himself. Only for himself."

"He is as cautious as I am, Georgiana. He has told me nothing." Anne could not look at her cousin. She could not say, *"We have him! He murdered his entire family! He is a monster! No English court will give him custody of Peter once it learns what he has done!"* Instead, Anne said, "Peter is his only family, now. He intends to seek custody."

"Darcy will not allow Foucauld to win in court," Georgiana said with absolute certainty.

"Not in an English court, I agree," replied Anne. "That being the case, the Frenchman's only recourse is abduction, removal to France, and a hearing before a French judge. We must prepare a countermeasure."

The next hour, they advanced and rejected several plans. Finally, they decided that any plan would require ready transport. "The Brougham," said Georgiana, "is rarely used. We must ensure that it is in good repair and that provisions are at hand, so that it can be taken in an instant if it is needed. At the same time, Foucauld has spies everywhere, so we must not alert him to our preparations. But how?"

"Picnics," said Anne. "You must invite your admirers on picnics, so the kitchen keeps on hand a supply of food that can be eaten cold. That way, if a swift departure is required, we will have provisions for the journey."

"Do you not think my brother will be suspicious of my sudden interest in encouraging acquaintances I have so diligently discouraged in the recent past?"

"If he were not so eager for them, he might. I think he will be so grateful for your interest that he will not look this horse in its mouth too closely," Anne said with confidence, for she saw the pieces falling into place. "Nor will anyone else. Your suitors and your marriage plans are a constant topic for all the gossip-mongers throughout Derbyshire." Anne chuckled at Georgiana's show of annoyance.

"But the Brougham cannot be used for picnics. It only seats two! What of my chaperone?" exclaimed Georgiana. "Unless you are suggesting that Mrs. Annesley take on the duty of handling a team of horses!"

"Hardly! You and I will use the Brougham to visit neighbors. Once we put that carriage in steady use, Tom will ensure that it is kept well-prepared for all of our demands at any hour."

Georgiana had seen nothing but a snarl of impediments. Now, however, she found herself marveling once more at her cousin's gift for seeing and accessing multiple seemingly unconnected elements so that they would all blend one with another until they intersected at the desired point.

They resolved that Georgiana would speak to the cook about picnic baskets and that Anne would speak to the butler about bringing up the Brougham in the morning. But before they could proceed, the servant approached and advised that the evening meal would be served in the garden, it being such a pleasant evening. They would have to wait until after dinner to initiate their separate tasks.

CHAPTER SEVENTEEN

Silver Rod

For the past month, preparations had been underway for this year's Summer Ball at Pemberley. Now that it would finally occur on the morrow, Mr. Darcy's primary responsibility on this day was to assure that as many of the male houseguests as possible were communally entertained, preferably at some distance from the house. Fortunately, Pemberley's woods contained a variety of wild game, and the stream was rich with trout. Darcy had settled on a morning of birding, followed by an afternoon devoted to angling.

The hunting party gathered at an early breakfast and included William Collins (the former Rector of Hunsford, and now the owner of Longbourne), Sir William Lucas (Mr. Collins' father-in-law), the Baron of Coxcroft, and Mr. Gardiner (Elizabeth's uncle). Darcy had also invited Charles Bingley, Bingley's brother-in-law Mr. Hurst, Sir James Culpepper, and one Monsieur Etienne Foucauld.

Although Darcy did not crave Foucauld's companionship, he certainly did not want "Uncle Etienne" visiting Peter any more than could be prevented and certainly not while Bingley was away from GanderGlen. Hence, Foucauld was frequently invited to Pemberley and warmly received.

Ambrose Terwilliger was also present. Ambrose had not exactly been invited by his host, but Miss Darcy presumed that he would be in attendance at the ball and had alerted him that his name was already filled in on her dance card. His cousin Charles also presumed that Ambrose had been invited, so he had purchased for him the proper attire for both the hunt and the ball, and had brought the tailor in to ensure that Ambrose would be comfortable wearing his new clothes. When Darcy saw Ambrose at the breakfast, Darcy stopped. Then, "Good of you to come, Terwilliger. Shot pheasant before, have you? No? Well, Bingley will set you right. Any angling in your past? No? Sir James, here is a student for you."

Sir James appeared to be quite ancient from a distance, but as he drew nearer his years escaped their captor and ran away. Clear blue eyes twinkling, Culpepper closed in nimbly, dropped his voice and said, "Saw you, my boy. Was there when you wagered you could drink a jigger out of an unopened bottle!" (There was one brand of whiskey that had such a deep indentation in its bottom, that the bottom of the bottle itself could hold a full shotglass of liquor. Hence, one could pour a jigger of whiskey into the indentation and drink the whole of it – from the upside-down, unopened bottle, which is what Ambrose had done to collect on his bets. But if Mr. Darcy learned of this, Terwilliger's hopes for a living were dashed.) "Between us, lad!" Culpepper winked. "If you get a placement, that is the church for me!" Ambrose could not suppress a laugh, and Sir James beamed with a young man's conspiratorial glee.

"Hello, Cousin!" called out Colonel Fitzwilliam, arriving late to the breakfast.

"Good to see you, Fitzwilliam," Darcy replied, as he kept an eye on Foucauld. The Colonel had arrived late last night, so Darcy had not had the opportunity to acquaint him with all of the details surrounding Etienne Foucauld's presence in

Lambton. The morning shoot was a particular concern: If Foucauld had discovered the identity of his sister's last lover, the father of her child, would he engineer an "accident" in the field? *"No. Surely not. Foucauld seeks to avenge his sister's honor. Murder will not suffice. He will insist on a public duel. I hope."* Darcy shuddered.

William Collins, as silly as ever, wanted a complete biography of all the participants in the day's hunt. He fawned over the Baron so insistently that Coxcroft could barely eat, for having to say "thank you" to so many frivolous compliments. Finally, the Baron changed his seat, which gave Colonel Fitzwilliam an opportunity to inquire after Mrs. Collins.

"Oh, Mrs. Collins is well enough! I have a son, you know!"

The Colonel acknowledged that he did know it and asked if Mrs. Collins was also visiting Pemberley. This struck Sir James as odd because he thought he had seen Mrs. Collins in conversation with the Colonel upon Culpepper's somewhat surreptitious arrival at Pemberley. (Sir James' long-time cook had decided to return to Scotland. So, the old gentleman was in need of a cook and was not above plundering a neighbor's kitchen to acquire a good one. Sadly, Pemberley's staff was too well-paid. Sir James would next negotiate an invitation to GanderGlen, in the hope that Charles Bingley was not nearly as generous as his friend, Darcy.)

"These ladies, they cannot miss a ball! She spent for a new yellow dress, though why she would not wear her good blue dress to another ball, I cannot fathom." Collins babbled on, not realizing that the only persons that listened to him did so solely for the purpose of criticizing him.

Darcy had long admired Charlotte Collins' forbearance, patience, and sense. *"That a good wife, new with child, should be criticized for the purchase of one dress! Why do I even let this man in my home?"*

But Darcy knew the answer to that question. Mr. Collins was inescapable. William Collins had begun as one of the genteel poor, in much the same position as Ambrose Terwilliger found himself: A gentleman by social standing and education, but with no income to support his living. Mr. Collins had the good fortune to attract the attention of a wealthy landowner with considerable patronage in the church – Mr. Darcy's aunt, Lady Catherine de Bourgh. Lady Catherine enjoyed Mr. Collins' toadying ways and rewarded him with the parsonage at Hunsford. While the Rector at Hunsford, Collins became acquainted with both Darcy and his cousin, Colonel Fitzwilliam. However, Darcy did not encourage a friendship, and he thought that his cousin was equally indifferent to the man.

But then, Collins married Sir William Lucas' daughter, Charlotte. Charlotte Collins was a close childhood friend of Miss Elizabeth Bennet, and because of their friendship, Darcy had been able to advance his acquaintance with Elizabeth and eventually convince her to become his wife. Now, whenever Darcy held a gathering at Pemberley, Mr. Collins heard of it through either his wife or Lady Catherine and hectored them both until the invitation arrived. Silly man! Of course, Charlotte Collins would be invited to every social gathering at Pemberley! And, she would be warmly welcomed at any time she wished to visit the Darcys, whether it be at the family mansion at Lambton, or the winter house in Mayfair. And because the Darcys could not exclude a woman's husband from a social invitation (although, Darcy did ask Elizabeth regularly if she was aware of any recent changes in the rules of etiquette), he could come, too.

As the ladies drifted into the dining room, the men drifted out, first to the courtyard where they gathered their guns and field gear, and then to the field.

The air was unseasonably crisp, the woods were full, the dogs were alert, and all in the party bagged a number of birds. All, that is, except Ambrose Terwilliger, whose shots strayed right or left, or high or low, no matter how skillfully Bingley sought to guide his young cousin's aim.

While the other men nudged each other with every missed shot, rolled their eyes, and turned away to hide their smiles, Darcy watched the way Ambrose handled the gun. Ambrose was careful with it, but he was not afraid of it. He did not absent-mindedly point it in anyone's direction, a common mistake by those unaccustomed to the use of firearms. He did not wince when his weapon recoiled from a shot. Terwilliger's family was poor; Darcy surmised that this boy had probably hunted for food since he was a child. But Ambrose Terwilliger was not hunting for food today. He was hunting for sport.

"This man," Darcy pondered, "*would rather be thought a hapless fool than kill a living thing unnecessarily. There is more here than I have credited.*"

Foucauld and Colonel Fitzwilliam bagged the most birds and chatted affably. "Your name is Fitzwilliam, Colonel? Is that not our host's first name?" asked the Frenchman. The Colonel confirmed their connection, Darcy having been given his mother's family name as his Christian name, and the Colonel being related to Darcy as a cousin, on his mother's side.

"Does it not become confusing, Colonel? Do you not have a first name all your own?"

"I have never used it, sir." Then the Colonel lowered his voice and confidentially added, "Being an unmarried soldier stationed far from family and friends of family, my first name is not the only Christian article that has fallen away from me over the years." Both men laughed with unshared memories of exploits and escapes and spent much of the rest of the morning in each other's company.

The servants brought the fishing gear and took away the guns and birds.

While they proceeded to the trout stream, a mist formed and a drizzle grazed the air. Darcy migrated toward Sir James to remind him that Terwilliger would be needing help with the hook. However, before they could pick their spots and free their lines, Ambrose somehow managed to slip down the muddy bank and fall into the stream. He was drenched from head to toe and began to sneeze miserably. Poor Ambrose! He had no choice! He had to return to Pemberley to dry himself and his clothes.

Terwilliger's absence and general ineptitude provided the chief topic of conversation for the bulk of the remaining day. Bingley would not let the criticism of Ambrose's manly attributes get too far, but he did little to conceal his own bemusement, particularly if the comments were not overly cruel.

Foucauld, however, did not participate at all in the castigation of Ambrose Terwilliger. Instead, he contented himself with counting the number of times that the Baron of Coxcroft uttered slurs on the boy's character, appearance, personality, and manliness. Etienne wondered why a Baron would even notice the existence of an Ambrose Terwilliger, let alone disparage him so aggressively.

As Etienne waded through the very cold spring-fed stream, and as he gloried in the slimy joys that the fishing process affords all its participants, he thought often of that bumbling naïf whom the other men presumed devoid of all common sense.

Finally, Foucauld could tolerate no more. "He misses every target...with a gun loaded with birdshot. What a feckless marksman. Then, we are to fish, in the damp and the cold, for hours on end. But, again, the hopelessly incompetent Monsieur Terwilliger! He falls into the stream at his first opportunity! He develops pneumonia in a matter of moments! Now, he is the only member of our party who is inside the walls of Pemberley, probably wrapped in a blanket, and undoubtedly partaking of a hot meal. Forced to suffer as the only male in a house filled with beautiful, lonely, sympathetic women! You are correct, Messieurs. The boy is witless." Foucauld hunched his shoulders and pulled his collar tighter around his neck. He cleared his nose of a slight sniffle. *"We are the clever ones."*

After the hunt, there was dinner, then the guests broke into smaller groups. Ambrose, Georgiana, and Anne slipped into the music room, Darcy and Bingley belittled each other mercilessly at the billiard table, Jane and Mrs. Hurst and Caroline Bingley strolled in the garden, but the bulk of the group played cards in the parlor. No one noticed that two of the guests had slipped away.

Magdeleigne Foucauld's grave was in a rarely-tended public cemetery, nowhere near a church or chapel – the place where the suicides and the criminals and the poor and the unbaptized are laid to rest. Few graves had markers, but those few were graced with rotting wooden ones. Her grave, however, did have a stone – "Magdeleigne Foucauld, Beloved Mother." *"That had to be Darcy's doing,"* Foucauld thought to himself.

Etienne was waiting for another visitor: One who visits "every day he is in Lambton," as Wickham had described him. So many guests were coming into Lambton for the Pemberley ball, the inns were all filled. Foucauld was certain that the last man that took his sister, and then threw her away, would be among these guests. But would he visit at dawn? Dusk? Not during daylight, surely. Not this poor excuse for a man, who would abandon a woman carrying his child and refuse to claim his own son. Foucauld now stood under the shadow of a chestnut tree, over a hundred yards away from his sister's grave. The night was clear and the moon was full. *"Please come tonight, Monsieur, for I want you to see me. I want you to know that she was not alone in life and is not forgotten in death. I want you to see that death waits for you because I am death and I have already waited too long."*

There was a sound. Finally, the visitor that Wickham promised had indeed come to stand at the foot of Magdeleigne Foucauld's grave. The man was cloaked, his face hidden, and Foucauld at first look thought him to be Mr. Darcy, for this man was like him in very many ways. Gradually, Foucauld saw that the visitor was taller and a little older than Mr. Darcy. It was not too long before he saw the man sink to his knees, put his head in his hands, and weep.

"You could have married her, English," cursed Foucauld, to himself. *"You could have legitimized her child. Your child! You could have provided the protection of your name, your family, your home! Instead, you left her to charity and gossip and ostracism. That is why you are alone in a graveyard. That is why you dare not claim your own son."*

The moon came out from behind a cloud, and Foucauld recognized the man's red soldier's coat. He knew this man! He was in the hunting party! This man had spoken with him as though they could become friends! Although resentment was hard upon him, Etienne Foucauld made no move to interrupt Colonel Fitzwilliam's grieving. Foucauld vowed to wait until tears and sobs were done with, and then he would confront this man and kill him.

But the Colonel's mourning did not abate, and finally Etienne could tolerate no more of it, and he quit the place.

CHAPTER EIGHTEEN

Yellow Carnation

The Summer Ball at Pemberley!

Every year, all of Lambton and the surrounding communities wait eagerly to learn the date. The announcement ripples through the servants at Pemberley, splashes into Lambton, gushes through the finest homes in Derbyshire, cascades into the Lucas household, and positively floods the Collinses at Longbourn. Milliners, bootmakers, tailors, dressmakers, inns that rent rooms, stables that rent carriages, greengrocers and fishmongers, butchers and candlemakers, bakers and blacksmiths, they all rejoice in the opportunity to provision the Darcy household and the Darcy guests. At the center of this raging maelstrom stand Fitzwilliam and Elizabeth Darcy, insulated from the buffeting winds and lashing rain by an experienced staff dedicated to its own invisibility and the Darcys' serenity. As they dressed for this final culmination of several weeks planning, Elizabeth and Fitzwilliam Darcy individually reflected on the joyful silence that would arrive on the morrow, when their guests would make their departures.

"Lizzie!" called Mrs. Bennet in a voice that had not mellowed with the years.

"Your mother is calling you," announced Mr. Darcy, tilting into the doorway that connected their separate bedchambers. "She probably wants you to explain, again, why this door is missing."

Elizabeth threw him a look that elicited a theatrical shiver. Darcy, she observed, was in a rare playful spirit. This night promised great rewards. She sent her maid to see to...whatever it was Mrs. Bennet wanted. Darcy in his own room with his valet, no doubt tying an elaborate, complicated knot in his newest necktie, Elizabeth Darcy was alone in her room. Her eye fell on the empty door jamb between their rooms, the frame with the missing door that so irked her mother.

"Lizzie," her mother had often impatiently explained, "wealthy husbands do not force their wives to share their bedchamber. Only poor people in small houses have to share the same sleeping room. Your husband should give you your due! Your privacy! You should insist on it!"

When first married, the Darcys did keep separate rooms. Of course, her husband was a frequent early-evening visitor, but each night he would withdraw to his own chamber. There seemed to be an unsatisfying reticence inside their marriage, for they were both naturally private in their thoughts and studied in their conversation.

Then, Elizabeth heard a rumor. She ignored it. The rumor grew a name, Madelyn Fox. She ignored it. The rumor grew a history of past association. She ignored it. The rumor asserted a continuing association. She ceased to ignore it but made no effort to pursue it. The rumor became a living child and a rumor no more. Elizabeth erupted in a hot fury, covered Darcy in burning lava, and slammed and locked the door between their rooms.

Each time Elizabeth saw two servants together, they ceased their conversation and busied themselves. Each time Elizabeth saw Georgiana, the girl would start to speak, then tears would begin to well in her eyes, and she would bite her lip, and she would turn away. Each time Elizabeth went into Lambton, there would be biddies pretending they were not watching her and were not accumulating details to augment their gossip.

Two weeks passed. Darcy and Elizabeth both went about their everyday acts speaking courteously and cheerfully to everyone, except each other.

Three weeks passed. Elizabeth relied absolutely on advice she remembered from years before: "Forgive a sinner, but never let them enter your home ever again." Then, in a sudden bolt, she remembered who had given that advice. It was the then-Rector of Hunsford, Mr. William Collins himself.

"Of all the people in the world to heed the advice of!" she exclaimed aloud when that realization became whole in her thoughts. She instantly called for a servant to "take down that door, break it into kindling, and use it to lay a fire in the library's fireplace. If Mr. Darcy asks, tell him that I am sick to death of seeing it, and that when he grows equally tired of seeing it, he may light a fire." Elizabeth now smiled at the memory of how, that very night, her husband ignited quite a fire.

That time, Darcy did not leave her in the nighttime. He stayed, and they talked of many subjects, gradually addressing the truth of Madelyn Fox. Darcy told Elizabeth everything, starting with Bingley's request that Darcy extricate him from a foolish entanglement, moving on to Madelyn Fox's attempts to seduce and blackmail Darcy himself, the name of the man who fathered the girl's child, and finally the reason why Darcy was still providing for her and the little Pierre.

Darcy then explained that, "I have become accustomed to autonomy, dear Elizabeth. But I know now that I have an ally, and I have learned that I will suffer if I waste the benefit of that alliance." He glanced at the empty doorjamb. "Suffer mightily," he said. He turned to her, kissed her cheek, and whispered in her ear, "I shall never fail you again."

Years had passed since that reconciliation. The firestorm had lasted long enough to excite every wagging tongue in Lambton, and the effect served what was now the Darcys' joint purpose: To convince everyone that Fitzwilliam Darcy was, in fact, the natural father of Madelyn Fox's son.

Darcy entered Elizabeth's room through the doorway that would never hold another door in their lifetime and went to her jewelry box. "The emeralds?" he asked.

She nodded, and he laid the heavy necklace carefully in place, taking a slow moment to stroke the back of her neck. Their eyes locked in their mirrored reflections, one the victor, the other the trophy. It was the fruit of a successful marriage that each held the belief that they were the fortunate champion and the other the envied prize.

There was a knock at the door that led to the hallway. A servant announced that the guests were beginning to arrive. Elizabeth took her husband's arm, and they proceeded to take their places downstairs.

CHAPTER NINETEEN

Ivy Geranium

It was not long before the ball was well underway. Miss Georgiana Darcy, of course, was at that age when romantically (and fiscally) ambitious young men appreciated the opportunity that existed only at a ball. Specifically, the opportunity to boldly speak to any young lady in the room, regardless of social rank, with the absolute social assurance that once asked, she must dance. Invitations had been issued to every fine family in the neighborhood, of course, plus relations near and far and friends and some politicians and business acquaintances (although mere merchants were not included). Several young men surrounded Georgiana, but it was the Baron's claim that she answered first.

Darcy was so delighted to see Georgiana at the side of the Baron so early in the evening that he did not notice that she danced only that one time with him. She danced twice with Mr. Terwilliger. Georgiana tried to engage each of her dance partners in conversation but they, all of them, approached her with a practiced script of what they would say, and she could not convince them to abandon their prepared speeches and simply talk with her. What was so easy with Ambrose

Terwilliger was not merely difficult with any other man, it was impossible.

Jane danced *"Earl Breadalbain's Reel"* with Monsieur Foucauld, as she determinedly searched for reasons to interpret his actions and motives as good. Everyone had heard of the scandalous confrontation of Wickham at a house in town, "but he did not harm Wickham," Jane emphasized. Still, she had a fear of the Frenchman because he insisted on calling Peter, "Pierre," and often spoke as though Peter would make an extended visit to France. Jane fretted constantly, but Bingley seemed perfectly at ease leaving the matter entirely in Darcy's hands.

One dance ended; another began. As Jane danced the *"Zephyrs and Flora"* with Elizabeth's husband, she studied his profile. He was handsome and educated and graceful. Oh, but so dull! Could he possibly be Peter's father? *"No."* Mr. Fitzwilliam Darcy of Pemberley would never pursue a French girl, never love her, never father a child out of wedlock. " 'Darcy the Pure,' Wickham calls him," Jane reminded herself. "Always noble. Always reliable. Always...punctual." How Elizabeth managed to tolerate the man's constant rectitude, let alone enjoy it, Jane did not know. Fitzwilliam Darcy and Charles Bingley had been friends from their school days, long before they had become acquainted with the Bennet family. It was evident even at Jane's first encounter with both of them (for in those days, they were constantly in each other's company) that Bingley was determined to embrace life, while Darcy was more than satisfied with a firm handshake.

Now, Bingley! He was capable of loving anyone at the drop of a hat. Jane sighed. Why must our greatest strengths carry the seeds of our greatest failings? Jane had already miscarried twice when Bingley asked her to consider an adoption. When Jane consented, he told her more – much more – than she wanted to know. Mainly, that the deceased mother had been of his acquaintance when he has young and foolish. No, it was not remotely possible that the boy could be his. Oh, but with each hour of each day, how Jane wished it were the case!

Peter was almost five years old when Darcy first brought him to meet her and her husband. The little boy presented a tiny fistful of buttercups he had impulsively pulled from a patch of grass growing on the side of the road because "Mr. Darcy said you-you-you were pretty, and they-they-they were pretty, so I-I-I thought you-you-you would like them." Then, he looked down at them, and his lip trembled a bit, and he pulled them back and whispered, "Not-not-not enough." Jane remembered how all her stiffness and formality and trepidations at this first meeting melted away, how she went down on her knee, gathered *her* child into her arms and kissed him and comforted him, and took him into the kitchen and found a vase that would properly display his gift. What was to be a first meeting became the only meeting, for she would not permit Peter to be taken away that night, or any night thereafter.

While her husband danced with Jane, Elizabeth saw the Baron circling into an approach, so she took Charlotte Collins' elbow and asked for her help at the punchbowl. As Elizabeth fussed with some spoons and asked Charlotte a number of busy questions about napkin folds, the Baron was threatened by the possible conviviality of Mr. Collins and was forced to retreat.

"What is all this about, Elizabeth? Surely your servants displayed the napkins correctly! And, the spoons! And, the…"

"Oh, of course, Charlotte. There was just a guest that I…well, I would rather talk to you than dance with him."

"How fortunate we are good friends," Charlotte laughed. "The truth can be so unflattering!"

"I know! I am sorry! But I needed a friend, and here you are!"

"I am happy for it. I fear the day may come when I shall need a friend." Charlotte gazed at her husband, who appeared to be basking in the condescension of a well-dressed guest.

"Have no fear. I am your friend. And a friend with no questions."

Charlotte smiled. "Then a rare and true friend, you are." Mrs. Collins inhaled deeply and adopted a merrier mood. "I, on the other hand, have a multitude of questions! Who is this Frenchman? Why is he here?"

Elizabeth answered as economically as she could and also provided brief biographies of the widower Sir James Culpepper (who accidentally places his hand too low on a lady's back while dancing), the unattached Mr. Ambrose Terwilliger (who does not drink, does not smoke, does not gamble, and does not flirt), and the compelling Baron of Coxcroft (who freely admits that he does all those things – and more).

"How strange," Charlotte mused, "that Mr. Terwilliger is so opposite of the Baron in habit. They are so close in appearance, are they not?"

"Close in appearance!?" Elizabeth almost shouted her response. "They are completely different! So completely different, one could never mistake one for the other!"

"No. There could be no mistaking them." Charlotte's eyes hopped back and forth between the two, comparing every outward particular. "But that is because one is older and ostentatious in his manner. The younger is quiet. But they are both of the same frame, their hair color is the same, and they have the same color eyes (whatever color that may be). Do they not claim an acquaintance?"

"None that I know of. Although…" Elizabeth stopped. "I am trying to remember. Mr. Terwilliger came to us from Cornwall. The Baron may have mentioned Cornwall…but I am not sure."

Darcy came to collect his wife for the *"Pins and Needles"*, and Etienne Foucauld gathered in Mrs. Collins.

"What of your family, Monsieur Foucauld? Your parents?"

"They are…as I left them, Madame Collins."

"Brothers?"

"They are as I left them, Madame."

"I have heard that you had one sister…"

"Just the one, Madame."

"Please accept…"

The Frenchman quickly nodded once, so she did not continue to express her sympathy.

She tried to find a more pleasant subject. "You have been in England for some time. I am certain your family must be eager for your return."

Foucauld smiled delicately and murmured something about a "joyous reunion, someday."

Mrs. Collins was silent for a few moments, then said, "All of them? Gone?"

"My family…aristocrats, Madame."

Mrs. Collins became silent. France was not a sheltering bower for aristocrats twenty years ago, before Napoleon. "Liberty, Fraternity, Equality" did not apply to the well-born. But, if the National Razor took Foucauld's parents and brothers, why did it not take him? Why did it not take his sister? This was not a question for a dancefloor, so Charlotte Collins cast about for some other topic.

"Can I impose upon you, Monsieur? Will you visit my son in the nursery, and carry him about the room a bit?"

"It would be my pleasure, Madame. But may I ask you why you wish me to do this?"

Charlotte smiled disarmingly, lowered her eyes just enough, and said, "Because when he is older, and becomes sullen and defiant as all young men do, I want to be able to tell him that he was once so tiny that he was cradled in the arms of a frog."

Foucauld stared at her. His mind had been in such a horrible place, trapped in a memory that could never be far enough away. And now, he was in a marsh, surrounded by weeds and reeds and flitting dragonflies and burping bullfrogs. He saw the swaddled baby. He saw the pacing frog. He felt his body rumble. His eyes watered. His shoulders shook. He was laughing! Not a snigger or a snort, but a true bottom-of-the-belly hoot! Wiping his eyes as his laugh ebbed into a chuckle, he promised her the visit she requested, but issued a firm instruction: "You may tell him of the Frog, only if you tell him of the Angel."

"What angel is that, Monsieur?" Charlotte searched her memory but found no reference to an angel in their conversation.

"You, Madame." Foucauld bowed low, kissed her hand, and cocked his eyebrow at Mr. Collins, who was oblivious to a bold flirtation happening right under his nose. "You are an angel."

The orchestra took its rest, and the guests called for entertainment. Mr. Darcy pushed his sister toward the piano. Looking to Mr. Terwilliger for assistance, she let him select a piece by Mozart. It was the perfect choice! She knew that vanity was not becoming in an unmarried woman, but she had never accomplished the precise fingering so fluidly as on this occasion. She tried to dampen her emotions, but the company's compliments emboldened her. She laughed aloud! They laughed with her! Darcy's chest puffed with brotherly pride. Her playful gaze lingered on Ambrose Terwilliger.

As for Ambrose, he had no illusions about his true worth to Miss Darcy. He was a distant poor relation of a family friend.

He would be an afterthought, except that he did not receive any thought at all. He was no one, nothing, soon to be gone forever. So, Miss Darcy found him easy to amuse, and easy to be amused by, until she selected a lover. Her lover! *"What a paragon he will be,"* smirked Terwilliger. *"He will hunt, he will fish, he will drink and smoke and smell of the field and smell of whores and cuff her across the cheek if she objects!"*

Terwilliger stopped smirking. Truth be told, he stopped smiling altogether. He cursed his many inadequacies, particularly his poverty, then shook off his resentment. *"Because I admire beauty, I admire Georgiana Darcy. But, not even the richest man in the world can possess every work of art. Some must be admired from a distance."*

Then, Foucauld saw Colonel Fitzwilliam enter the ballroom. Yesterday, the two men had conversed casually. They were both second sons, raised in wealth, well-educated, accustomed to being warmly welcomed at gatherings such as this. To marry a housemaid would have separated the Colonel from his family. To marry a common street whore (for that is what his sister had made of herself) would have barred him from even a merchant's house. Yesterday, the Colonel had not known that Etienne Foucauld was the brother of Madelyn Fox. Today – Colonel Fitzwilliam knew it now and stood ready to accept a formal challenge.

"There were so many men involved in Magdeleigne's ruin (including she herself), I cannot kill them all. Or, even find them all! I should kill the only one who still grieves for her?" Foucauld turned his back on the Colonel and walked away. His meaning was clear. There would be no duel. The issue was closed.

Foucauld had retreated to the sideboard and was now surveying the appetizers, so Ambrose drifted in that direction, hoping to practice his French. The Baron of Coxcroft was at

Foucauld's side, smelling of punch. Punch that had been visited heavily by a flask of scotch whiskey.

"When you were last in France, sir, did you hear of a philosopher, name of the Marquis de Sade?"

"Citizen de Sade, when I encountered him." Foucauld muttered.

"You met him? He actually exists?" The Baron tottered. Then he fell to the floor, and four husky housemen lifted him up and carried him to a chaise in the study, where he joined three other recumbent gentlemen who owned flasks.

"What was he talking about?" asked Ambrose.

"de Sade."

"Sod, Monsieur? Are you referring to a piece of dirt?"

Foucauld pondered the question. "Once again, I am astonished how English words and French words can be so far apart in their definitions, yet so close together in meaning. Yes, Monsieur, I *am* referring to a piece of dirt."

Foucauld went after the servants to see where they had taken the Baron, but he could not find them. He returned to the ballroom. It was nearly dawn. He wanted to find Mademoiselle Anne, for he felt a sudden concern for her safety.

He caught sight of her. She was dancing *La Boulanger* with a red-coat. "English," Foucauld growled with distaste. He saw her smile, he saw her lower her eyes, and he saw her incidentally stroke the sleeve of the man's uniform. Watching them dance, he grudgingly accepted the obvious: She had imagined this man as her husband from childhood.

Embracing every Frenchman's duty to don the quiver and bend the bow of Cupid when called upon, Etienne immediately began plotting the courtship, romance, and wedding of Mademoiselle de Bourgh and Colonel Fitzwilliam. *"They are too cold. Well, they are English, so they are dry and solemn, and their posture is too good. She will warm easily enough, I think, but the man needs a pricking. He needs to learn that she can be lost. Lost to someone he disapproves of. Someone who will take advantage of her, who will seek to seize and squander her fortune, who will cheat on her with the housemaids."* Foucauld sneered with malevolent delight. *"For that kind of villainy, any Frog will do."*

CHAPTER TWENTY

Plum

Ambrose Terwilliger proved himself a patient teacher, encouraging in correction, insightful in praise. His daily teachings had become Georgiana's central pleasure; she wished they would never end.

Now came the most rewarding minutes of each day's lesson, for this was the time that she surrendered her instrument to Mr. Terwilliger, and he played whatever melody came to him. Without fail, his selection always pleased Miss Darcy. This day, she sat by the open window, closed her eyes, and enjoyed a warm breeze as it caressed her cheeks and played with some loose strands of her hair. As a child, she had towered over boys her own age, and she was comfortable with that disparity. But as she aged, men passed her in height and at the same time began to presume a superiority in knowledge, discernment, and authority that edged her toward something like…resentment.

In the company of the shorter, younger, poorer Ambrose Terwilliger, however, she found a balance to her liking. He had once declared her bold, and in his presence she found herself determined to prove him correct. She had confessed her trepidations about Goya, debated the merits of Mozart, and even boasted (!) of the number and wide variety of books she had read. She had never before found it so easy to simply talk: It was as though she were merely thinking her own thoughts and providing her own candid responses, instead of engaging in conversation with another person. And, this was a young man! The introduction of Ambrose Terwilliger to her acquaintance had been a revelation.

He concluded his exercises, and Georgiana reluctantly bade him goodbye. Each day he stayed a little longer, but (since it was never long enough) Georgiana had not noticed the increasing length of his staying, only the absolute certainty of his leaving.

Today's lesson complete, Ambrose crept down the corridor that led from the music room to the main hall. He was a product of genteel poverty, which meant that people like the Darcys (who, technically, were his social equals) did not aspire to have such as a Terwilliger visit their home. It was Mr. Terwilliger's daily goal, therefore, to enter and leave the grounds of Pemberley without being seen by anyone, except the servant that would permit his entry, and, of course, Miss Georgiana Darcy, who each day would request another music lesson on the following day. He had his hand on the door latch when he heard a voice that froze him solid.

"Mr. Terwilliger, will you join me in my library, sir?"

Ambrose had never entered the Pemberley library. It was a fine, masculine room with the pleasant aroma of old leather. There were a few portraits, somber as their subjects, but mainly, there were books.

Darcy offered a glass of port. Ambrose fastidiously declined.

"You have been coming here daily for some time, Mr. Terwilliger. Are you aware that you enter and leave without one word to your host?"

Ambrose went white. Darcy was right! This was an unforgivable breach of etiquette! Ambrose stammered an apology and explained that his sole purpose was to accommodate Miss Darcy's requests for lessons on the piano. He had not felt that his visits were social in nature, so he had not wished to disturb the household.

"You feel then, that you are in the shoes of a teacher?"

"Well, yes, Mr. Darcy. I suppose that is how I see myself."

"Good. Teachers are paid for their labors." Darcy then proposed a daily fee.

Ambrose swallowed. More than anything else in the world, he wanted to secure an honorable placement and be able to express generosity to others, instead of having to be constantly grateful. Teaching was a gentleman's occupation – he *could* accept money for providing music lessons. He pulled at his shirt cuff to hide its frayed edge, which of course only served to draw Mr. Darcy's attention to it.

"I am very sorry, Mr. Darcy. There are no circumstances under which I would consent to accept one farthing for assisting Miss Darcy in her pursuit of the enjoyment of music."

Darcy smiled. This was the courteous reply that he had expected. Now, it was his turn to insist, courteously.

"Come, come, Terwilliger! My sister's playing has improved markedly! It is clear to me that you are the reason for that improvement. My sense of honor will not permit me to allow your generosity to continue, unless I am able to offer a small token of recognition for your efforts."

Darcy waited patiently for Ambrose to yield.

Ambrose pictured Miss Darcy. She had a natural gift, so she resisted the interference of instruction. Because his visits were at her request, she complied with his suggestions. But, once he became her employee, her servant, her lackey…No.

"In that case, Mr. Darcy, would you please make my apologies to Miss Darcy?"

Until this point, the conversation had been fairly routine. But this last remark was offensive. Terwilliger had virtually thrown Darcy's generosity back in his face. "Good day, Mr. Terwilliger," came the cold reply.

Ambrose left Pemberley as he had come, on foot. Five kilometers to GanderGlen. There and back, a ten kilometer walk every day. Darcy watched from the library window, as Terwilliger trudged across the meadow, then up the hill. Darcy left his sanctuary and went into the music room.

"Georgiana, are you expecting Mr. Terwilliger to assist your practicing, again tomorrow?"

As always, she tilted her head in her brother's direction but did not look at him. "I have asked him to come. He said that he would."

Darcy sighed. In twelve years, he had never seen his sister's eyes. She simply would not look him in the face. Whether it was the result of shame because of Wickham's seduction, or her desire to punish the dominating brother who had separated her from what she might still believe to be "her one true love," he did not know. Courtesy required that they never discuss the subject, so neither one knew the true feelings of the other. Darcy's one hope was that a marriage would erase every bad memory and that she would come to be at peace with the past. If, in the meantime, she was distracted by the visits of Ambrose Terwilliger, then Terwilliger must visit every day.

While plodding down the rutted road to the Bingley home, Ambrose realized that he now had no reason to stay at GanderGlen. Darcy would not offer a placement after that exchange! He resolved to announce his departure after dinner and leave in the early morning. He tried to concentrate on the particulars of his upcoming journey, especially where on earth he would go, but he kept returning to his memory of Georgiana Darcy's smile.

Ambrose wondered if it was all just thoughtless banter, or if it was possible she might truly care for him. A breeze played with the meadow grass and some forget-me-nots. He saw two spindle trees up ahead, one on the left side of the road, the other on the right. The way their branches spread above the road, it seemed like they were reaching for each other. *"Miss Darcy and me,"* he thought. *"We are like those trees. They grow where they have rooted, and neither one can move from its place. They will spend eternity each in full sight of the other, but never any closer or farther away than where they began. It makes no difference if she loves me or not."* He told himself that it was very good that he would never see her again.

He heard a horse coming up behind him. He turned and saw a rider approach from the direction of Pemberley, trailing a second saddled (but riderless) horse in his wake.

Darcy dismounted. "Mr. Terwilliger, if you will not permit me to offer you fair payment, will you at least allow me to lend you the use of a horse, to make your journey to my home less burdensome?"

Ambrose considered and, finally, agreed that the use of a horse would be an acceptable accommodation, except that he had never learned to ride, and except that horses terrified him.

Darcy was not really surprised. He almost said, *"Mr. Terwilliger, this is the horse I used to teach my son how to ride. My child is every bit of eight years old now and has moved on to a more spirited animal."* But Darcy did not say that. Instead, the most accomplished horseman in three counties held his tongue and spent a good hour in the middle of a public road, teaching a grown man how to mount, how to hold the reins, how to use his knees to nudge the animal forward, and how to shift his weight in the saddle to signal it to stop. When the lesson was concluded, Darcy returned to Pemberley, and Terwilliger went on to GanderGlen. Neither man thanked the other, there was no shaking of hands, and neither one ever mentioned the occasion again.

CHAPTER TWENTY-ONE

Dodder of Thyme

Each day when he returned to GanderGlen, Ambrose sought out the children. He loved music in all its forms and found the cacophony of innocence to be God's own artistry. Poverty had demanded that Ambrose leave behind his own innocence much sooner than he would have willingly surrendered it.

Nine years earlier, his mother's brother had offered him an apprenticeship. Ambrose was thrilled: Opportunities to learn a trade and earn actual money at the same time were rare in their little community. His father refused the offer, because it was *work*, and not a fitting occupation for a Gentleman. After his Uncle Benjamin took his leave, Ambrose loudly expressed his complete dissatisfaction with genteel poverty.

"You do not understand what it means to leave your class, boy. Doors that are open to you today will be closed to you tomorrow and forever."

"Those doors are not truly open, Father. They are barely ajar. I do not want to be a threadbare Gentleman of the leisure class; I want to *do* things. I want to *have* things."

So, that night, after all others had gone to sleep, Ambrose was yet awake, and he ran away to his uncle's house. His uncle took him to a raucous inn loud and damp, with music and gambling and real alcohol and women. And, his uncle left him there. Three days Ambrose stayed in that place, and then he was given his bill. Ambrose had never had money, and he had never imagined a debt like this one. The Publican slammed him against a wall and addled his brain. He threatened Ambrose with Debtor's Prison, public disgrace, and the assurance that everything his clergyman father possessed would be seized and sold to pay this debt.

Ah, but his uncle miraculously returned just in time. He was able to guarantee the debt, but – of course – Ambrose would have to earn the money to pay it. What could be more fair?

Cornwall is a beautiful shire. Shoulders to the sea, it has rocky shores and stretches of barren clifftops, punctuated by night-time beacon fires that provide warning and guidance to ships that approach its jagged coast. Treacherous shorelines during fair weather, terrifying monsters made of rock and wave during its storms. And Cornwall does get storms! Old timers still spoke of the time it was slammed by a tidal wave! Ambrose's uncle (known to his mates as "Jammin") was a dedicated worker in his chosen trade of shipwrecking; his crew would douse a reliable beacon, then build a fire of their own a few hundred yards up the coast. In the night, particularly during bad weather, there were no markers other than the beacons. If a ship navigated in accordance with a Jammin Hard signal-fire, it would find itself on the rocks. Hard's crew would then descend on the ship and seize its cargo for re-sale. It was a very lucrative trade. Very hard work.

Ambrose did not mind the work. Ambrose did not resent his indenture; after all, he created the debt and it was his responsibility to pay it. What Ambrose did find objectionable was the killing. English law stated that no ship's cargo could be salvaged if there was a single survivor of the shipwreck. So. No survivors. Ambrose volunteered for the rough and wet and dangerous labor and, by so doing, managed to be at a place other than where any murders might occur.

Ordinarily, boys brought into Hard's crew quickly craved the alcohol and the women, mostly to forget the work itself but also because they found they had a taste for alcohol and women. Their debts did not much increase, but never decreased either. So, once in Hard's grasp, they stayed in it. Ambrose gave every evidence of actually enjoying being a wrecker, enjoying the drink, enjoying the women, and enjoying the gambling. Jammin Hard was so pleased with the complete seduction and corruption of this fourteen-year-old boy, the pride of Jammin's own sister and that sickly simpering clergyman she married, that he did not notice that whenever Ambrose drank, it was as the guest of another, whenever Ambrose wenched, the woman would neglect to collect her fee, and whenever Ambrose gambled, Ambrose won. One day, while Jammin indulged his own tastes, Ambrose presented full payment (and a little more, to ensure a few short hours of silence) to the Publican. When Jammin Hard roused the next day, he learned that Ambrose Terwilliger had bought out of his debt and had left the Jamaica Inn for good.

When Ambrose reached his home, he learned his father was very near death. Soon, the parsonage would be given to another, and the Terwilligers would need to find some other place to live. Ambrose felt a desperate need of money. He resolved to abandon his class, and lower himself for any paying job that would provide for his mother and sisters. But, there was no honest work to be had for a man not fully grown. Finally, he went back to the cabin, but no one was there. He found no trace of Jammin Hard or his crew. Then, he heard of a reward offered by the Baron of Coxcroft for any news of Jammin Hard. He presented himself at Coxcroft Castle and came face to face with the new Baron of Coxcroft.

Ambrose's reward was a threat to his mother's life. Well, a threat to his life, too, but that did not matter so much. Ambrose was allowed to return to his home (perhaps because he mentioned how many people in his father's church knew of Ambrose's intention to visit Coxcroft Castle).

As it happened, Ambrose's father's parsonage was the result of the old Baron's patronage, and the old Baron (recently and somewhat suspiciously deceased) had remembered Ambrose's father's family in his will, leaving the widow an adequate living. There was enough for Ambrose to resume his education and for his three sisters to each have enough of a tiny fortune to offset their living costs (which made them each a viable marriage partner).

Ambrose completed his courses at the University, mostly music but also art and literature. He had prepared for his father's life – the life of a small community parson, perhaps a Vicar, and in time, a Rector. But there was no parsonage available to him in Cornwall. The new Baron of Coxcroft controlled the patronages there.

When his mother brought him the letter from his father's distant cousin (actually, it was the only reply to one of several letters his mother had written to a variety of relations), Ambrose saw an opportunity to put into practice the lessons of exploiting trusting fools that he had learned from Jammin Hard. He resolved to go to Derbyshire, to live for free in his wealthy cousin's house, and to convince this Mr. Darcy that Ambrose Terwilliger would be the clergyman of his dreams. It was a harsh and greedy Ambrose Terwilliger that first entered GanderGlen.

Now that he was here, he found it more difficult each day to carry it off. Ambrose was forced to face the truth; he was devious enough to exploit the innocent, but he simply could not maintain the amount of energy and determination that self-serving ruthlessness demands. It was just so much easier to be friendly, kind, and helpful. And there was that sad lonely memory of innocence that could not be persuaded to say goodbye. So, Ambrose wanted to help Mrs. Annesley become published, wanted to help Lydia Wickham become self-sufficient, wanted to help Miss Darcy…well, actually, to be honest…he wanted to help himself to Miss Darcy. He had to admit that in that one area, innocence had left him forever.

On this day, he found the children playing in the orchard, out of sight (and earshot) of the house. He saw Mrs. Wickham nearby, absorbed in her drawing. He knew that she would immediately close her sketchbook and if asked would insist that she only "scribbled" to have "something to do" while she shepherded the flock. She had never let him actually look at her sketches, although he had caught glimpses in the past and had become thoroughly intrigued. Today, he had a plan.

"Peter!" he called as he approached. Out of the corner of his eye, he saw the sketchbook close and fly under her skirt. "Will you go to the house and fetch my drawing pad? And, some pastels. I want to capture the cloud shapes. Quickly, now!"

Peter, however, was in the middle of the game, and the children pouted that they would have to wait for his return before they could resume play. So, Mrs. Wickham "found" a sketchpad, one that "just happened" to be at hand, and Peter returned to the game.

As Ambrose casually leafed through Mrs. Wickham's sketches, ostensibly searching for an empty page, he talked of an unpublished novel he had recently perused. "I have a friend from my schooldays. His father is in publishing. I left the manuscript with him when I was in London. He promised to read it and provide a critique. My friend explained that publication is unlikely, because its setting is in our own time. Few of today's writers attempt contemporary works. Even Sir

Walter Scott chooses to write of medieval days! But their caution is understandable. The Prince Regent is sensitive to criticism (what with his illegal – that is, *problematic* – marriage, his demented – that is, *discomfited* – parent, and his usurpation – that is, his *assumption of the duties* – of the monarchy)…well, both a writer and a publisher demonstrate great courage if they volunteer to speak accurately of our current English society. Speech alone can constitute treason, and the courts, of course, sympathize with the crown."

As Ambrose spoke, he studied her drawings of children at play and landscapes and flowers, and he recognized where her strongest talent lay. So, when he began to draw, he did not outline cloud shapes. Instead, he modeled the petals of a Chinese Chrysanthemum. When Mrs. Wickham saw it, she exclaimed on its perfection. "You make it look so real! It leaps from the page! How did you do that?"

He showed her the shadowing techniques that did exactly that, and she quickly mastered the lesson. Over the coming weeks, Ambrose taught Mrs. Wickham many of the tricks that artists employ to create mood and depth and movement. He knew his lessons had taken hold when she began to school her teacher! Just like the flowers she captured so perfectly, Lydia Wickham came into bloom.

CHAPTER TWENTY-TWO

Pussy Willow

Pemberley's Head Housekeeper, Mrs. Reynolds, fussed as Hannah Hill claimed illness almost every morning for over a month. The girl had begun as such a hard worker, but the trip to Rosings (which was a rare privilege!) had caused a change in her. She had become forgetful and morose. Was it because Pemberley was not as grand as Rosings? Did this sixteen-year-old girl think that she merited a better placement than Pemberley? Or was it because her friendship with a Lady's Companion had given her ambitions above her station? Then, Mrs. Reynolds drew in her breath when it became apparent that Hannah was gaining weight. Maids in fine houses do not gain weight – not for *that* reason.

The day Hannah Hill left Pemberley, it was raining. That morning, Mrs. Darcy saw the gathering clouds and called for the Brougham to take Hannah into town. It was unusual to place a carriage at the disposal of a servant, but Mrs. Darcy resolved that Hannah Hill would not leave Pemberley on foot; would not walk the distance to Lambton in the rain, and would not be dirtied by mud.

In Lambton, Hannah waited for the public coach in the shadow of a chestnut tree, imagining that every passerby knew of her disgrace. Of course, she was correct: Lambton keeps few secrets.

"Hello, Miss Hill."

Roused from her thoughts, Hannah was surprised – no, actually, she was shocked – that she was being addressed by Georgiana Darcy. Obviously, Miss Darcy had not been apprised of the pollution that Hannah Hill had brought to the shades of Pemberley. Hannah mumbled a reply and moved closer to the trunk of the sturdy tree.

Miss Darcy refused to be deflected by Hannah's reticence. Mr. Terwilliger had taught Georgiana Darcy the valuable strategy of talking, merely talking, until the other person could not keep away from a reply. Eventually, Hannah said that her future was "dependent on the generosity of my sister's family."

"With me, it is a brother's indulgence that is regularly called upon. That is what family is for."

Miss Darcy then raised her hand, and the livery owner came to her at once. "Miss Hill and I will be in the Fleur-de-Lis. Please notify us when the coach arrives."

He nodded, and he said, "Yes, Miss Darcy. Yes, Miss. Yes, Miss," as he backed away, still nodding, rotating his hat in his anxious hands.

Hannah did not know how to decline Miss Darcy's invitation and did not know how to accept it.

Georgiana took her by the arm and guided her toward the Fleur-de-Lis Tea Room. "You are as much at leisure as I am. You are my guest. I insist." And she did insist!

Delighted to be out of the damp air and equally delighted to be off her feet, Hannah sipped her hot tea and nibbled on her Squashed Fly Cake. Miss Darcy had ordered 'Eccles Cake,' which was the same thing, but sounded more elegant. Hannah looked about the tea room and saw that the other customers were peeking at her. Hannah Hill was no longer an object of derision, standing in the rain under a tree outside a stable, receiving pitying looks from passersby. Hannah Hill was now an object of envy, as she sat in the Fleur-de-Lis with the most elegant young lady in the entire county. Hannah resolved that, hereafter, she herself would order 'Eccles Cake,' even though she knew she would be ridiculed for talking above her station. It did not matter! She would order Eccles Cake, and she would remember Miss Darcy, and she would not forget how the most wretched hour of her life was transformed by one person and one act of kindness.

Hannah lost her thoughts in admiration of the crocheted tablecloths, and fine linen napkins, and bisque creamers. After a while, Hannah said, "My sister Mary has invited me to come to her home. Her husband…," she hung her head. "Mary says he has no objection, but her letter says that I should not speak to him, for he will not speak to me."

"The thing about family," Miss Darcy mused, "is that they know you. Sometimes, they know you too well. Sometimes, it is better to be among strangers, for strangers only know you by what you tell them." Georgiana delicately tasted her raisin cake and stirred milk into her tea and allowed her words to hang in the air for a moment. "Do you know your Bible, Miss Hill?"

Hannah nodded.

"Good. Then you know it says, 'Thou shalt be born again.' It means you have His approval to make a new life for yourself. A life of your own choosing."

Just then the livery's boy came and said the coach had arrived. It would be ready to leave in about one-quarter of an hour's time. Georgiana gave the happy young man a coin from her purse and drew out a knotted lace handkerchief at the same time. She gave the kerchief, which contained a hard, round object at its center, to Hannah Hill.

"It was my…my mother's. It is mine to do with as I wish, and it is my wish that you should have it." Then, Miss Darcy finished her tea, settled their bill, and stood up. "You know what you must do. You must live in a manner that best serves your child. That," *[she indicated the handkerchief's contents]*, "will be a great help to you, if you are wise. Goodbye, Miss Hill."

Hannah did not purchase passage to Meryton. She went instead to Manchester, a rapidly growing community in the north. It was growing so fast, Hannah hoped, that there would be many people that had no local connections and would be receptive to friendships with newly-arriving strangers. The coach was half-way to Manchester when the driver stopped at Whaley Bridge to change out the horses and take on new passengers. As she waited, Hannah recalled a signpost a few kilometers back. What was the name of that town they passed? Oh, yes. *"Buxton."*

It was then that Hannah Hill removed Miss Darcy's gift from the handkerchief, put the ring on her finger, and became the honorable Widow Buxton.

CHAPTER TWENTY-THREE

Adder's Eyes

The GanderGlen ball did not pretend to the elegance of the Pemberley ball. Pemberley hosted luminaries of the shire, in addition to family and friends. GanderGlen hosted only family and friends, so it was a little more…well, it was a little more fun.

This year, there would be a waltz. Even one such as Lord Byron pronounced the waltz to be scandalous! There had been no waltzes at the Pemberley ball. Georgiana and Anne had taken lessons, so they would know not only how to dance a waltz (well, all four different types of waltzes, actually), but so they would be prepared for the fact that their partners would…embrace them.

As usual, Georgiana was again besieged by partners. The first dance was not a minuet, as the Pemberley ball had begun, but the *"Crookie Den"*, a Scotch reel. Georgiana was certain that the horse lover had thoroughly exhausted the topic of "brown" at their other encounters, so she eagerly consented to his request for the first dance. *"He is good-looking. He is polite. In fact, he is quite dashing! What subject will he light upon? Art? Politics? Fashion?"* Georgiana was surprised to learn how many types of white markings can be categorized on a horse's face.

"There is a star (a white spot on its forehead)," he began, as she realized that this dance would last at least twenty minutes. "A stripe (narrow, middle of the forehead down to the muzzle of its nose)," he continued, as she remembered one reel that had lasted almost a full hour. "And a blaze (essentially a stripe, but wider and longer)," he concluded. And then, without taking a single breath, he proceeded to the subject of markings on horses' legs. "They are called stockings," he began again. She imagined herself in a corner, pounding her head against that wall right over there, and having a far less painful experience doing it than she was enduring at this moment. "On dark horses, the stockings are white, and on light horses the stockings are black," he said. Would this dance never never never end?

She could stand it no more. "White and black. Are stockings never brown?" she inquired, innocently.

He thought about it. "No. No. I do not recall ever seeing brown stockings."

"But," she ventured, giving every evidence of being captivated by his breadth of knowledge, "a brown horse could have brown stockings, could he not? I mean, just because you cannot readily detect something, that does not mean that it does not exist. We cannot see the Americas from this room, nor can we see the Continent, but we know they are out there."

Her dance partner had stopped talking. She did not know whether it was because he was trying to think about brown stockings on horses, or trying to remember the order of the dance steps, or wondering if her fortune was worth putting up with her. She did not care. She was just grateful that he had stopped talking.

"I did not know that you had an interest in geography, Miss Darcy. My leisure pursuit is mapmaking."

Until that moment, Georgiana Darcy thought that horse colors were the most boring topic in the entire world. She was wrong. The entire world was the most boring topic in the entire world.

When the music ended, he did not stop talking. She had to guide him to the edge of the dancefloor, as one would guide a blind man. He was still talking when the second name on her dance card appeared and claimed her for the *"Duchess of York's Slipper"*. "I did not know that you had an interest in geography, Miss Darcy. My diversion is navigation, the geography of the sea. Do you realize that the waters of the earth overwhelm the landmasses, as far as territorial area is concerned? Did you know that lodestones are used to guide ships where the horizon on all sides is one flat view of ocean and wave? That stars are signposts?" Georgiana wondered at her own capacity for ignorance. She had thought that geography was boring, but that was before she became acquainted with navigation and the endless (yes – endless) sea.

The third dance was the *"Sir Roger de Coverley"*, an energetic reel. She knew it would exhaust the Baron, which would allow her to escape a second dance, so she smiled at him invitingly and he eagerly fell into her trap. But, as with all her plans, Georgiana made a grievous mistake. She mentioned that the dance steps were inspired by the mad scramble of a fox to elude ravenous hounds, and that reminded the Baron of the fox hunt at Rosings.

"Been riding to the hounds for just over a year. Very first time I took the beast!" She tried to think of other things; fox hunting is a blood sport. Coxcroft boasted of how he held the exhausted terrified creature in one hand while he severed its tail with the other. The beautiful full tail, much the same color as his own hair (although he did not say so), was "a trophy, you know – I will give it to you if you like" (she declined, demurely), and then he told her how he tossed the breathing and bleeding carcass to the excited dogs. The Baron looked at his dance partner approvingly: She was so very like one of those dogs, thrilled and grateful to be favored by whatever he threw her way.

Georgiana smiled prettily at the Baron and silently mused that if women had invented fox hunting, country mansions would be overrun with plump lazy foxes reclining on feather pillows next to a warm hearth. And, Barons would be thrown to the dogs.

Darcy was so delighted to see Georgiana at the side of the Baron so early in the evening that he did not notice that she danced only that one time with him.

Ambrose pursed his lips as he witnessed Miss Darcy thoroughly enjoying the attentions of ever-more admirers. Suddenly, his left elbow was nearly jerked from its socket and a heavy right arm draped itself over his shoulders as Ambrose was being dragged from the room by a giggling Dennis Culpepper. Young Culpepper had been in The Hedgehog and Snake when Ambrose wagered that no man in the pub could lift a chair placed against a wall. A barmaid demonstrated how it had to be done (per Ambrose's precise instructions, of course), but no man could do it in the same way she had! When Ambrose was challenged to do it – *"That was not the wager, sir! I said, 'you could not do it,' and you cannot. In fact, it is a task that only women can perform!"* Now, Ambrose had to show it to the young men gathered in the hallway (for they had all heard of it from Dennis Culpepper) and they importuned a serving girl (actually it was the same girl from the pub – Darcy had to hire extra servers for the ball) to put down her tray and demonstrate how to pick up a chair. One young man would not stop trying to lift the chair because he was certain that no female could best a male in any endeavor. "I know in my heart that you are correct, sir," stage-whispered Ambrose as he returned to the ballroom. "In fact, I am so certain of your rightness that I promise to turn over all of my winnings to you…as soon as a rooster lays an egg."

The truly amazing thing was that the young man continued to try to lift the chair.

Terwilliger went to the groaning board. He found himself not alone. The Baron of Coxcroft had joined him.

"You have no friends, here." The Baron turned his attention to a lamb chop.

Ambrose loaded his plate, not even looking at the Baron. "I do not know how the old Baron died. But I do know that the constabulary of Cornwall is looking for Jammin Hard, and I know that you do not want him found." Now Ambrose deigned to look at the wealthy man beside him. "Feel free to ridicule and threaten me, Baron. Each slander confirms that you fear what I know."

The Baron hissed like an angered tomcat. "It occurs to me that I could save myself a great deal of annoyance if you were to disappear. I know several shipmasters who do not ask questions about first-time sailors who board their ships drunk or drugged."

"I am not a fool, Baron. I have written letters and left them in safe places. I will not tell you how many, so you will never know if you have them all. You dare not risk harm to me or mine!"

The Baron's language was not appropriate to a dance floor, but Ambrose was not listening to him. The Baron followed Terwilliger's line of sight and saw a tall, handsome young man dancing with Miss Darcy. When the Baron turned back to the object of his hatred, Ambrose had already taken his plate to a far corner.

So! Ambrose Terwilliger aspires to Georgiana Darcy! Well, why not? Thirty thousand pounds could intrigue any man. Even, a Baron.

For a while, Coxcroft observed the attentions bestowed on the younger Darcy woman. *"Pretty, yes, but so tame! Still, if one is to be burdened with a wife, there is much to be said for mute obedience."*

It occurred to the Baron that she might prove useful in a number of ways. She could provide an heir, for one. More importantly, marriage to her would provide constant access to the acquaintance of Elizabeth Darcy. Now there was a woman who would resist and defy and challenge until her last breath! It would be a great pleasure to conquer a woman of Mrs. Darcy's temperament. To have her beg...for respite? For favor? For death? What matter? So long as she begged! The Baron smiled a brilliant smile.

"Well, Ambrose," the Baron chuckled gleefully to himself, *"perhaps I shall condescend to invite you to my wedding, so that you may kiss the bride upon her cheek before she comes to my bedchamber. The opportunity to see that agony on your face!"* The Baron nodded pleasantly at Mr. Darcy, who was dancing with the piece of chattel named Georgiana. *"Now, that would be worth a wedding!"*

With so many happy thoughts tripping through his mind, the Baron left the ballroom and strolled through the covered path in the gardens behind GanderGlen. He plotted his courtship of Georgiana Darcy. He was certain he could rely on the ambitions of Mr. Darcy to support his suit. Mrs. Darcy, however, would be more of a challenge. At first, she had responded to his considerable physical magnetism, but lately *"she betrays a tasty repulsion."* He licked his upper lip, then his lower lip, and then he smacked his lips together.

It being a cool night, he had not expected to come upon any other person, so he was surprised when he heard muffled voices just ahead. He approached as silently as he could and was rewarded with a moonlit view of two lovers, framed by the outline of a gazebo. One was in uniform and unmistakably Darcy's cousin, Colonel Fitzwilliam. The other was more difficult to know. A woman, of course. Attractive figure, but not a young girl. The dress was a light color – beige, possibly white or a yellow – moonlight and shadow sometimes play odd tricks with the pastel shades. But this was no casual meeting. Indeed, it was furtive, almost desperate.

"We cannot continue this," she whispered.

Coxcroft furrowed his brow. *"If only she would enunciate her words clearly and aloud!"* he thought to himself. *"Then, I would know her voice, and I would know who she is."*

"Does your husband suspect?" asked Fitzwilliam.

"Delicious!" thought Coxcroft. *"Who is she?"*

"He has never accused me, but he regularly speaks of the importance of discretion."

The Baron licked his lips as Fitzwilliam gathered her into his arms and kissed her.

"My beloved," she whispered, "you cannot imagine my loneliness. Since the birth of our son, he has shown no interest in me. He cares only for the house and money and whether he can elevate himself in society. He talks of nothing but self-interest. I am just another possession. No! Not even that! I am just another expense."

"If only I had the means to make you mine! If we only had a single hope that we could one day be together, without scandal and poverty. But it is futile. There would be a divorce! My family would surely abandon us. And, your family…"

"We would be destitute." She clung to him. "Vilified by our families and all of our friends."

"Speak aloud! I cannot identify your voice if you continue to whisper! Unless…"

"I have given up all hope of happiness," her lover told her. "You are married. I must make a separate life."

"Say her name! Say her name!" The Baron exerted all his silent effort to will Fitzwilliam to speak.

"You must. You should have done it long ago," she whispered, on the edge of tears.

They kissed again, desperately, painfully, knowing that every word of separation had to be a lie. They had both thought that they could live without love, and they might have, had they never met. Now, having met, they neither one could breathe without thinking of the other.

The Baron was distracted by still other voices, distant but approaching. When he looked back toward Fitzwilliam, the Colonel was gone. So was the lady, gone.

Coxcroft cursed himself for being so slow. Who was the woman?

When the Baron returned to the ballroom, he saw Mr. Darcy dancing with Miss de Bourgh. And, he saw Mrs. Darcy, in a pale green dress, dancing with Colonel Fitzwilliam.

"Could it be?" he wondered. "Could it be that the jealous Darcy is jealous for a reason? They have a son, eight years old. Could he be the child she mentioned?"

The Baron spent the rest of his evening studying the relationship between Darcy's cousin and Darcy's wife. He saw looks pass between them; he saw two dances; he saw whispers and smiles. All innocent enough because it was open to all observation. *"They are clever,"* the Baron concluded, *"but there is a feeling there. She must have been the woman. Yes. It must be her."*

He smiled and rubbed the palm of one hand with the fingertips of the other and thought about a horse he coveted.

CHAPTER TWENTY-FOUR

Sweet Alyssum

Georgiana's latest dance partner indulged in hiking, hiking everywhere: mountains, seashores, heaths, rock outcroppings, dunes, caverns, meadows. Topography was his mania. "Have you ever heard of quicksand, Miss Darcy? Horrible stuff! You feel yourself sinking, sinking...every attempt to escape hastens the process of being pulled under. You are trapped, and it is inevitable that you will suffocate in its midst."

Georgiana gazed about the room, trying to breathe. Geography, navigation, and now topography. The music had changed, the dance partners had changed, but the burden of supporting courteous dialogues had not changed.

"I have never heard of quicksand, Mr. Wentworth, but your description of it has been so eloquent that I believe I know how it must feel to be in its power." Miss Darcy smiled at the preening young swain and silently concluded her thought: *"It feels like you are in a ballroom, with music and dancing and suitors whose company is crushingly tedious. It is not quicksand, Mr. Wentworth. It is slow torture."*

As soon as the *"Mad Robin"* ended, Georgiana resolved to find Ambrose Terwilliger and demand that he dance with her. Her search found Lydia Wickham in the conservatory, trying to capture the delicate unfolding petals of a night-blooming Nottingham Catchfly. Lydia went on and on about Mr. Terwilliger's patience as a teacher, his kindness as a friend. Georgiana was quite annoyed with Mrs. Wickham, until she glimpsed the drawing. It was still a mere sketch, but it was as delicate as the flower petals and as overwhelming as a cloud passing over the moon.

"And the children!" Mrs. Wickham prattled on. "How they adore him! Peter rarely stutters now, after those two weeks in London. Mr. Terwilliger has worked a miracle, there!"

The music for the leaping waltz was drifting out of the ballroom. Georgiana mentioned the ball and that Lydia was missing it.

"I am married, Miss Darcy. I could not possibly dance a waltz with anyone other than my husband! Well, I suppose it would be alright if he were present, but he was called away."

Called away! A ball in the house where she is living, and she cannot attend because her husband is…who knows where he is. Georgiana studied the spidery bloom of the white Catchfly, and recalled its meaning in the language of flowers: "I Fall a Victim." *"A woman's life is the product of the husband she chooses,"* thought Georgiana. *"How lonely you must be."*

Georgiana climbed the steps to the second floor and heard laughter and song coming from the playroom. As Georgiana approached, she heard an angry voice.

"I am not!" shouted Peter. Then he ran blindly from the room and found himself caught up into Georgiana Darcy's arms. "I am not a frog, am I, Aunt Joy-Jo?"

Georgiana looked into the room. Ambrose Terwilliger had her brother's pride and heir by the arm and was shaking a finger in his face. Ernestine and Evelyn Wickham were huddled together in eager conspiratorial guilt. It did not take tremendous insight to realize that they had dared Little Fits to call Peter a frog and that he had done so.

"Well, I do not know, Peter," Georgiana calmly replied, running one hand through his hair and lovingly searching his eyes. "Do you like to swim?"

Ambrose twisted around and looked at her. *"Can she really be this self-absorbed? Now, she is teasing him? Is it not bad enough that he knows he has no father? Must he endure ridicule as well as pity?"*

"Yes. I like to swim," Peter replied, bravely.

The children snickered. Peter was miserable. Ambrose wondered what would happen if he took Mr. Darcy's elegant sister across his knee and gave her the spanking she should have had when she was Fitzgeorge's age.

She put her hand on Peter's shoulder, looked him directly in the eye, and said, "Well, then, you could be a frog. Of course, I have it on good authority that princes also swim. Are you a prince?"

Before Peter could reply, Ernestine said, "Oh! Aunt Joy-Jo is going to tell us the story of the Frog Prince!"

"What story is that, Ernestine?" asked Miss Darcy.

"The Princess kissed the frog, and he became a Prince, and they lived happily ever after."

"What a foolish story! Do you not think so, Peter?" laughed Georgiana.

Peter allowed as how it was "a baby story." Lydia was right – Peter's stutter was gone!

Georgiana shook her head. "No, this is not the story of the Frog Prince. It is the story of the Frog Princess. There was a beautiful and artistically-inclined Princess in the land of…of…" she looked around the room, at all of Peter's stuffed toys and the beautiful lace curtains and the elaborate toybox that resembled a Rajah's elephant and the mechanical contraptions that were more like clockworks than like playthings, and she said, "…Mutchtumutch. This princess was being wooed by a dozen dukes and earls and…"

"And barons?" asked Ernestine.

"One extremely repulsive baron," Georgiana said, half to herself. She did not see Ambrose swell his chest and smile. "Her one refuge was her lily pond. Every day, she went to the lily pond and moaned about her fate. One day, a frog," she glanced at Ambrose, "a frog with freckles, told her that he was tired of hearing her complain. He said that she did not appreciate the wonders in her world. He asked if she would prefer a world that had talking birds and rocks that catch fire and beasts who obey spoken commands."

"Oh, Aunt Joy-Jo," exclaimed Evelyn, with tremendous authority, "that is so easy! Parrots talk, and coal burns, and dogs do what they are told!"

Georgiana put her hand to her breast in mock amazement. "Why, Evelyn, that is exactly what the Princess said! And, do you know what the frog replied?"

Evelyn did not know. Georgiana looked at Ernestine. Ernestine did not know.

"The frog said, 'How about a frog with a silver tongue? Am I not special?'"

All of the children laughed. Ambrose felt himself sinking oh-so-slowly through the floor.

Georgiana studied the rapidly reddening Ambrose Terwilliger dispassionately. He was not tall, not handsome, not commanding. She could not picture him declaiming forcefully in Darcy's library with a glass of port in one hand and a cigar in the other, nor could she see him haughtily ordering her about, nor throwing an injured animal into a pack of hungry dogs. She could see him at a piano offering suggestions, or under a tree bent over a sketchbook, or teaching children a new game. Thoughtful, gentle, patient, plain. He was every opposite of the husband she had always envisioned. No one in her acquaintance would ever select one such as Ambrose Terwilliger as a life companion for her.

"Well," Georgiana said, returning her thoughts to her story (which was necessary because she was making it up as she was telling it), "the Princess had to agree that she had become so accustomed to being a Princess, that nothing seemed very special anymore, not even a silver tongue over a meter in length. The Princess simply expected happiness to come to her every day, without any effort on her part. Not even the effort of appreciation. In short, she was bored."

"You mean spoiled," interjected Ambrose.

"Bored," repeated Georgiana. Then, under her breath to Ambrose, "Not spoiled! Bored!" Speaking again to the children, she said, "And, lonely. The lily pond was her only comfort."

"Lily ponds. Are they not damp? And cold?" mused Ambrose. "Would a Princess not starve on what a frog earns?"

"Princesses are notorious for their fortunes, Mr. Terwilliger," sniffed Georgiana, continuing her story. "The Princess told the frog that she envied him."

"How could she envy a frog?" cried Little Fits. "Aunt Joy-Jo, frogs eat flies!"

"People eat pigs, do they not?" the delicate and refined Miss Darcy retorted.

The children agreed in unison that people do eat pigs and that pigs were just as disgusting as flies.

"Anyway," Georgiana persisted (once the pig versus fly issue had been thoroughly debated and utterly resolved), "the silver-tongued frog told her that if she kissed him she could live in the lily pond forever."

"I do not remember this part," muttered Ambrose.

"So, she kissed him!" Georgiana proclaimed with a flourish. "But not," Georgiana now added, "*not* because he had a silver tongue. Oh, no!"

Ambrose raised a single eyebrow. Georgiana smiled and spoke directly to him. "It was because his heart was carved of the purest gold."

Ambrose felt more than his color start to rise, which always caused his otherwise imperceptible freckles to blossom, but he could not stop it, and he could not take his eyes away from hers.

"Is that when he became a Prince?" asked Ernestine.

"No, Ernestine!" Georgiana shouted in exaggerated surprise. "The last thing this world needs is another Prince! More music-making, silver-tongued, golden-hearted frogs! That is what is needed! So, that is why SHE became a frog!"

Peter was laughing so hard, he had to sit down on the floor, legs sprawled. All of the children wanted to finish the story their own way. Ernestine was insisting on a Prince. Little Fits wanted baby frogs.

"Tadpoles!" exclaimed the stubborn pedant that resided deep within Ambrose Terwilliger's heart. "Not baby frogs! Tadpoles!"

Ernestine wanted to know why the boy frog had freckles.

"Some frogs do, dear," Georgiana assured her with a tragic resignation.

The children returned to their games and made plans for the next day. Too soon, the servants came for the children, and Georgiana was alone with her frog.

"That had to be the worst fairy tale I have ever heard in my entire life," he said.

"They are all friends again, are they not?" whispered his Princess. "What good does it afford someone to win, or lead, or excel, if their reward must include the loss of companionship? I think it better for everyone to walk side-by-side. That is true success! Do you not agree, Mr. Terwilliger?"

Ambrose found himself lost in admiration. *"How is it I disparage her one moment and admire her the very next? And, for the exact same thing! The same words! The same acts! All that is required is that I open my eyes and my mind. What is wrong with me? Why do I insist on doubting her goodness?"* He was close enough to steal a kiss, so close, and she gave no sign of moving away.

Then, he snapped awake. *"Be realistic!"* he commanded himself. *"She may dally with a poor musician, but in the end, she will choose one of her own. He will be handsome, athletic, the best school, the best tailor, and…yes, he will be rich, but the other things first. If she knew how I think of her, the way I want her to think of me, she would be appalled."* He saw his distorted reflection in a polished silver bowl and believed it more accurate than any mirror could be. *"No. Not appalled. She would be dissolved by her own hysterical laughter."*

Ambrose turned his head and walked away from her. She wondered what she had said or done that would cause him to turn away so abruptly and leave her without so much as a single word.

Ambrose did not notice the hurt look on her face, or her bewilderment, or her discomfort at being left to return to the gathering unescorted. He had but a single thought: *"Even if I were the Baron of Coxcroft, she would not have me."*

CHAPTER TWENTY-FIVE

Maiden's Blush Rose

Foucauld had been studying the courting rituals as practiced by Colonel Fitzwilliam in his romantic pursuit of Lady Anne de Bourgh and wondered how the entire English race had not dissipated from lack of interest centuries before this date.

Etienne watched them together at every opportunity. His spies reported every meeting in town, every occasion they dined together, or rode together, or strolled together, or played cards in the evening. *"This is taking forever!"* fumed Foucauld. *"You, Colonel, soon you will muster out of the military. Your older brother is the heir...you are the spare. Had something happened to him in his youth, you were readied to inherit. But your brother reached his majority. He married and has a house full of children. There is no room for you, there! She has Rosings! That means that YOU will have Rosings, its lands, its income, everything. How many heiresses do you think you will find that can compare to her? So amiable, so intelligent, so sweet, and so rich? Do you think that you are her only choice?"*

Foucauld knew what had to be done, although he was loathe to do it because it would end the only friendship he had in this awful country. *"Well, I have sacrificed more than friendship. At least I will come away from my latest wickedry knowing that a rescuer will replace me."*

This was a Monday. He and Anne went for their usual walk. Foucauld stole an occasional backward glance until he saw Colonel Fitzwilliam rounding the bend at some distance. (Anne did not know it, but "she" had sent the Colonel a message, asking him to meet her and expressing some vague concern about the recent behavior of a certain acquaintance.)

Foucauld suddenly grasped Anne by her shoulders, spun her around and kissed her. He expected a violent reaction from the lady, and he received it. She kissed him back. He had thought it a placid day, but he was wrong. A wet, hot storm erupted, lightning, thunder, driving rain, howling winds...and then he was struck in the face by one Colonel Fitzwilliam, and the storm simply ceased to exist.

Laying on the ground, looking up at them, he saw the Colonel lead a trembling Anne de Bourgh back down the path to Pemberley. Before they reached the house, Anne accepted the Colonel's offer.

Although the Darcys (especially Georgiana) greeted the news of the engagement with unbridled delight, it seeped through Lambton drowsily. The marriage would undoubtedly occur at Rosings, near Hunsford, far to the south. There would be no appreciable boost to the Lambton economy.

Only one inhabitant of Lambton was thrilled to learn of Miss de Bourgh's upcoming nuptials. Etienne Foucauld rejoiced. She would marry her ideal lover! She would be a wife! Perhaps, she would even have children and grandchildren! He was filled with a sense of accomplishment. He found himself smiling for no reason he could think of and humming tunes from his childhood. In fact it was not until Wednesday morning, at eleven o'clock precisely, when he had no Mademoiselle de

Bourgh to walk with and no Mademoiselle de Bourgh to talk with, that he realized that he had made a terrible mistake.

CHAPTER TWENTY-SIX

Oats

Georgiana Darcy lowered her eyes and said, "Are you such a man, Mr. Terwilliger?"

Ambrose studied her profile, for she was not looking in his direction. In the course of these few weeks, he had become quite sensitive to the nuances of her moods, and her mood had suddenly changed. Her voice had dropped in volume and tone, and her manner had stiffened. They had been passing the afternoon most comfortably, with music flowing effortlessly, and with an amiable conversation about the symphony Ambrose had attended while in London. What could he have said that would alter her so?

"Would you feel cheated if you did not attend a premiere performance?" she pressed.

A lifetime of being a baby brother to three older sisters prepared him for this one moment. He knew that extreme caution was mandatory. She was not really talking about the symphony, he had discerned that much. But what subject was he being drawn into? And what response was she seeking? Of one thing, he was absolutely certain – this was not a moment for levity.

She swallowed. Why did he not answer?

Ambrose wetted his lips and spoke softly of the excitement of being an invited guest at a debut. She wilted. He stammered something about being witness to an initiation of beauty. He saw her shoulders jerk. He spoke of the privilege of being present at an opening. Her back stiffened. Miss Darcy was disappearing. He had said something that distressed her, and he had no idea what it was. Their acquaintance had taught him early on that she abhorred discord of every kind. If confronted, she withdrew. If she could not retreat from the room – a path often blocked by her oaf of a brother – she would disengage her thoughts and retreat to the deepest part of herself, letting others believe that she was still in the room with them, when in truth she had gone far away. That was what was happening now: She was leaving him.

He did not want her to treat him as she treated others. Those others did not realize when they were being dismissed, but he knew it and he rebelled. Did she not realize how much he had contributed to her progress as a musician? Did she not realize that with just the slightest guidance from him, her music had become bold, seductive, and playful? The others thought her shy. They thought her naïve. Their lack of understanding had stifled her. But he knew, *"No frightened child can play the music as she does. No, nor any untouched flower, either."*

And, in that moment, Ambrose realized that he had stumbled upon the true subject under discussion. He recalled his paeans to a first night and cursed his stupidity. He stole a glance at the ever-present Mrs. Annesley. She was fascinated by her knitting.

Ambrose knew that if he allowed her silence to persist, Georgiana Darcy would clothe herself in it and not emerge before he left that day. In fact, she might never return to him. So, the silence must not be permitted to remain in the room. He was not quite sure what to say, not sure if he would magnify his earlier gaffes, but he was certain words could always be explained, or elaborated upon, or denied – so long as a conversation continued, there would be opportunity to amend. Spoken words might create a temporary breach, but recrimination is limited to what was actually said. It is the unspoken words that fester, multiply, transform, and destroy. So, he gathered his courage and drove the silence out of the room.

"Of course," he plunged, "an opening night is not truly the first performance, you know."

"You refer to the rehearsal, sir?" she whispered, as she drifted toward oblivion.

"Oh, yes, there must be rehearsal. Several rehearsals! But, look here." Ambrose pulled a sheet of music out of his kit. It was a piece that he knew Georgiana had never seen nor heard, let alone played. He positioned it on the piano and stepped back.

"Play."

"But," she stared at it, her withdrawal interrupted, "I do not know this piece."

"Well, do not play all of it. Just play the first ten bars."

Georgiana began, stopped, looked at him – he waved her on – and finally finished the tenth bar. She had stumbled over it and hesitated and made mistakes, so she was most uncomfortable with her attempt.

Ambrose leaned close, whispered an encouragement, suggested a slight redirection, and waited while she played it again. After she had played it three more times, Ambrose came around to the front of the instrument, faced her, and smiled. "You see? The first time, it was just noise. Now, it is music. Only a man who values noise above music would demand to be present at the very first performance."

Georgiana felt the corners of her mouth edge upward. She studied her hands as they rested on the keyboard of the piano. She felt him watching her and sensed that he admired her. She felt proud and happy and womanly.

"Mr. Terwilliger. Do you not think..."

Ambrose saw her shoulders relax. The distance he had perceived in her manner had been replaced with a certain serenity. Her voice sounded like her music – bold, seductive, playful.

"...that a truly devoted music-lover would appreciate the unique pleasures of every performance, regardless of its iteration?"

Now, Ambrose smiled. She had completely returned to him. "Ah, yes, Miss Darcy. Every iteration of a performance does create the opportunity for a new delight. There are so many ways to achieve variation: A new introductory passage, or perhaps a different fingering technique, or pauses between refrains. But it would require a man who dedicates himself to regular practice."

"And," she looked into his eyes as the corners of her mouth capered with a smile, "are you such a man?"

"I am devoted to practice, Miss Darcy, but," he sighed theatrically, "I have not yet been gifted with the one perfect instrument with which I might play." He drew the fingertips of his right hand delicately across the polished surface of her piano as he admired the line of her neck and shoulder.

When he had drawn that line with his fingertips, she involuntarily inhaled, then averted her eyes. Now, she was not looking at him, but her voice held a twinkle of laughter. "But, if this instrument were to become yours, Mr. Terwilliger? Could you be relied upon to play with it every day?"

He grinned, basking in the effect of her artistry. "Without fail, Miss Darcy!"

"And how much practice would be required in a single day, would you think?"

Ambrose affected a scholarly pose and replied authoritatively, "That would depend upon the piece. If it were a lullaby, then I believe I could achieve the desired effect in not much more than an hour. But, if it were to be a nocturne, then I might require myself to devote as much as, oh, four or five hours to its consummation."

"Four or five hours!" Georgiana laughed with a kind of merriment she had never felt free to express before this moment. "You are an ambitious man, Mr. Terwilliger!"

"And you, Miss Darcy, have been delaying practice altogether!"

She lowered her eyes and composed herself.

He straightened the sheets of music and spoke of cycles of reverberation.

Her remark about his ambitions had been taken wrongly, she knew it. But how could she explain that she had not intended to accuse him of fortune-hunting? That, if anything, she wished to encourage it! *"What is the use of a fortune,"* she pouted, *"if it cannot secure for you the one thing you want most?"*

Ambrose could tell by her manner that he had offended her. What had he been thinking of, to allude to her unmarried state? Perhaps, she would even take it as a comment on her age! He could not conceal his complete mortification.

When the session concluded, Miss Darcy asked, as was her daily habit, if Mr. Terwilliger would be so kind as to return the next day for another lesson. Mr. Terwilliger promised that he would. During his ride back to GanderGlen, he explained to his horse that he absolutely must…"leave this house, this neighborhood, this shire. In fact, I need to get out of the entire country, before I make an absolute ass out of myself over a woman who is so far above me, that I must take it as a compliment when she deigns to address me by my own name." While he was speaking, the horse plodded along, nodding his head up and down in total agreement. But when Ambrose stopped talking, Butterball shook his head and mane vigorously, side to side, indicating complete disagreement.

"Make up your mind!" shouted Ambrose, which startled Butterball. Another horse might have bolted, or bucked, or reared. A startled Butterball, however, was merely a stopped Butterball. It took Ambrose ten minutes of nudging the horse with his knees and flapping the reins and pleading, to get the horse moving forward again. But then, Butterball merely moved far enough to reach some tender shoots at the side of the road. Realizing that he was defeated, Ambrose dismounted and walked the still-munching Butterball the three remaining kilometers to GanderGlen.

"You are as bad as Miss Darcy," Ambrose told him, as he pulled a fruit-laden tree branch low enough for the pixie known as Butterball to take his choice.

CHAPTER TWENTY-SEVEN

Carrot Flower

Foucauld had finally managed to corner his prey in Lambton, on that Wednesday afternoon. She had come into town with the Darcys. Mrs. Darcy was at the milliner's, Darcy was at his bootmaker's, and the elusive one had been on her way to the stationer's when Foucauld accosted her in the street, pulled her into an alley between two buildings, knelt down in a puddle and declared his undying passion. He begged her to be his wife. Anne de Bourgh said, "No," and attempted to leave.

Still on his knee, he implored.

She refused again and displayed her impatience. She did not want a report of this exchange to reach the ears of her intended.

He stood up and blocked her escape.

"Really, Monsieur. A gentleman would have abandoned this subject at the first refusal!"

"An Englishman seeks cover at the first shot, Mademoiselle. A Frenchman ignores his wounds and presses forward."

Anne de Bourgh stared at him for a moment, then said, "That explains how you lost the war."

He refused to be deflected. "I know you believe me to be the worst kind of – what was Darcy's word? – a dirty dog."

"I believe no such thing, Monsieur. I am as certain of your love for me, as I am certain of my love for you."

Foucauld literally felt his heart leap from his chest.

"But I love more than just you. I love Rosings, my home. I love England, my country. I love my friends, my family, my way of life. You ask me to turn my back on all of those and on a good man that I have promised to marry."

"A man you do not love!"

"A man I do love! Not as I love you, but I do love him. Etienne, try to understand: If I marry a French citizen, English law decrees that I am no longer a citizen of England, but a citizen of France. As a French citizen, I would not inherit Rosings."

"I see the truth, now, Mademoiselle. It is the money." Foucauld looked at her with a disgust he made no effort to conceal.

Lady Anne de Bourgh drew herself up to her full tiny height. "I have spent my life preparing to take on the responsibility of Hunsford. Hundreds of people, sir! The town's economy rests on the shoulders of the heir to Rosings. One irresponsible master and the entire shire suffers, perhaps irrecoverably. If it comforts you to believe me a servant of greed and not duty, then comfort yourself, Monsieur. I know where my responsibility lies, and I will not place my personal longings above it."

Etienne faded. The Revolution had repeatedly told him that women were the equals of men, but it had not been in his interest to listen. Instead, he had enjoyed easy rewards for exploiting the foolishness of flirtatious women. Mademoiselle de Bourgh, however, was not one to flirt. He had savored his successes with women susceptible to his outrageous flatteries. Mademoiselle de Bourgh had no patience with flattery. He had even occasionally been enslaved by women who pouted and required costly gifts. Anne de Bourgh possessed gifts that defied valuation by such women. There were flaws and horrors in the Reign of Terror, but there were truths, too. Etienne Foucauld thought he had embraced those truths, but he finally saw that there was one verity he had ignored. He had to come to this wretched English village to learn that the only woman he could truly love had to be just as proud, independent, and intelligent as he was.

She brushed against him as she left the alley. She almost collapsed into his arms, almost pulled him close, almost kissed him with the passion he had awakened in her. Almost called his name as she walked away. Almost turned around. Almost.

After she was gone, when she could no longer hear him, he said, "Je t'adore."

"What door?"

Foucauld looked about and saw two small children standing on the cobblestones, a boy about eight years old and a younger girl, probably his sister. Their presence reminded him of why he had come to Lambton and why he was still here. The little boy, holding his toy hoop and stick, cocked his head to one side, and said again, "What door? You said, 'Shut the door.' " The boy looked up and down the street, shrugged his little shoulders, and said, "What door?"

Foucauld smiled. Je t'adore. Shut the door. French and English, so easy to confuse. "The door to my heart. I must shut the door, as she has. The time has come for me to conclude my business and return to France." He went on his way, with a resolve in his thoughts that appeared in his stride. There was one thing he must do, and he would do it now.

CHAPTER TWENTY-EIGHT

Apple

Darcy had been watching for him, and now he saw Terwilliger dismount and give his horse over to the stableboy. He told his servant to show Mr. Terwilliger to the library, as soon as he entered. Ten minutes later, Darcy came out of his library and accosted the servant, annoyed that his instructions had been ignored. If Terwilliger had entered the music room, Georgiana would keep him in there for at least two hours (for she had become very devoted to the piano, of late).

The servant told his master that Mr. Terwilliger had not entered the house. As Darcy went toward the stable in search of the annoying Terwilliger, he glanced toward the pasture and stopped in mid-stride. There he saw the man who admitted he was terrified of horses. And there he saw Arabian Moonlight, eating an apple from that man's hand.

Elizabeth's grey had been a colt when the Darcys visited Lord Godolphin's estate in Cornwall. He was a distrustful, spooked young animal. He had become separated from his mother and cornered by a stallion. The stallion had kicked the younger horse and bitten him and almost killed him before the mare could reach her foal. "Ruined, damn shame," said the current Earl's second son. Elizabeth was four months pregnant and (stubborn woman!) had insisted on making the journey with her husband. As preparations were being made for their departure, she wandered over to the pasture fence. She had noticed that one side of a tree was rich in apples, but the branches hanging over the fence were stripped clean of them. So, she pulled a ripened fruit off a low-hanging branch, and offered it to the trembling grey yearling that stood alone and was almost invisible in the shade of the old tree.

"NO!" came a shout from the barn. But, by the time the stablemaster could reach Mrs. Darcy, the colt was nuzzling her belly and nickering gently and eating the apple out of her hand. The stablemaster gaped, eyes wide. All the grooms and stableboys and trainers stopped their work and went to the pasture fence, as though it was a wonder. The apple gone and the carriage ready, Elizabeth went to join her husband, clearly puzzled by the sudden gathering.

When the Earl heard the tale, he came out of his house and cursed aloud because he had missed the sight. But, in his next breath, he said, "You take him, Darcy, if you want him. I warn you, though, he's been worse than useless here. Whinnies and neighs at all hours, charges the other horses, kicks the fence rails, bites the stableboys. Would have gelded him, but no one could get close enough (well, no one was willing to *try* to get close enough)."

Elizabeth was at Darcy's side when the Earl spoke. She touched her husband's arm, for her husband did not look her way. Darcy did not need to look her way. He knew Elizabeth would not be peaceful if she did not help someone who asked for her help. Even if that someone had merely asked for an apple and that someone was a horse.

Darcy knew the value of a direct descendant of Godolphin's Barb, so..."I will take the colt, Lord Godolphin, but not his papers. I will not race him, and I will not offer him up for stud."

The Earl nodded, called a stableboy over, and instructed him to bring in the little grey from the pasture. The look of terror on the boy's face was heart-wrenching. "Take someone to help you," offered the Earl, but before his last word was spoken aloud, all of the awe-struck gawkers had fled.

Elizabeth took the halter and walked to the gate. She called to the horse (her horse) and it came to her, stood calmly while she slipped the halter over its nose and ears, and followed her docilely to the Darcy carriage. When Elizabeth handed the halter's lead to Darcy, the grey's head jerked up, his ears flattened, and he glared at him. But, when Elizabeth stroked the horse's neck with her left hand and laid her right hand on Darcy's shoulder, the grey acquiesced.

Not long after their return to Pemberley, Elizabeth received a letter from the Earl. It said in part, *"Please explain to Mr. Darcy that I did not gift you. The horse gifted you. His papers are his, so they must stay with him. You saved me from the sorrowful decision I had made: He would have gone to glue."*

She asked the boy to wait while she wrote a reply, but the boy said that his instructions were firm: There would be no reply. The Earl ordered that the matter was closed. In other words, Mr. Darcy could not courteously return the horse's extremely valuable pedigree. Moonlight's stud fee quadrupled the worth of Darcy's stable overnight.

A stallion now, the little grey still behaved like a fractious colt, except when Elizabeth was near. Moonlight was completely devoted to his chosen mistress. The grey would put any other rider on the ground in an instant, but Mrs. Darcy could ride him without a saddle, without a bridle, without a care. Elizabeth, who had never been much of a horsewoman, did not see anything remarkable in Moonlight's behavior. Darcy, on the other hand, had never known of a horse that distinguished one rider from another. Once broken to saddle, a horse can be ridden by anyone – unless that horse is Arabian Moonlight. Truthfully, it embarrassed Darcy to have a horse in his stable that would not let Fitzwilliam Darcy on its back. Over time, however, and at Elizabeth's insistence, Arabian Moonlight now condescended to let Darcy ride.

This is why, when Mr. Darcy saw that the grey thoroughly accepted Bingley's cousin, that he was truly impressed. Although Mr. Terwilliger was lacking in every attribute that Darcy required of a companion, Darcy had to acknowledge that this boy had a gift for inspiring the trust of others. Even though Darcy was aware that Terwilliger occasionally abused this gift (for although Darcy dismissed gossip, he welcomed information – and Ambrose's tavern wagers had become legend), Darcy was convinced that there was a great goodness there. This business with Elizabeth's horse thoroughly cemented Darcy's opinion.

When Ambrose noticed that Mr. Darcy was watching him, he feared that he had offended (for Ambrose was convinced that he had a natural gift for offending Mr. Darcy). Ambrose left the paddock fence immediately and joined Darcy in walking back towards the house. He began to apologize to his host, but the older man spoke first.

"Mr. Terwilliger. I was unhappy to learn, late last night, that an elderly parson long in the neighborhood has passed on to his eternal reward."

"Oh! That is very sad."

"Yes. Apart from the personal loss, I am now required to replace him, for his living was a result of my patronage. I have been very impressed with your gentle manner with children, and your patience as a teacher. I refer not only to the piano lessons you have given my sister, but also the art instruction you have provided to Mrs. Wickham and the assistance you have afforded Mrs. Annesley with her writing."

Ambrose was dumb-struck. How had Darcy learned of these things? Does not listen to gossip, indeed!

Darcy now came to the point. "I am convinced that the living at Kympton should be yours. Will you accept it, sir?"

Darcy braced himself for the joyous rush of gratitude that would soon crash over him and drown him in a multitude of excited utterances and handshakes.

Terwilliger, however, was not smiling. Kympton was the answer to his every prayer! But...Kympton was George Wickham's inheritance. Three children and a wife, all dependent on an indifferent provider, and Darcy offers their salvation to another? "No, sir. I will not accept it."

Darcy stared at him. To refuse a living? The easiest living possible?

Ambrose coughed, but said nothing more. It was obvious that there would be no expression of gratitude for the offer and no explanation of its refusal.

"I regret that I troubled you with my concerns, sir. Good day." Mr. Darcy increased the speed of his pace and left Mr. Terwilliger behind.

CHAPTER TWENTY-NINE

Calico Bush

Every afternoon, Anne would slip into the sanctuary of Georgiana's music room. The two would then giggle about local gossip, or share any new information about Madelyn Fox's brother, or tease each other about potential suitors (Sir James had visited Anne twice since the ball, but the caddish old rogue had surreptitiously winked at Georgiana each time!). If anyone other than Anne invaded Georgiana's music room, the penalty for that intrusion would be Miss Darcy's certain disappearance. This disappearance could not be characterized as a departure because one notices a departure. Miss Darcy's disappearances were never noticed as they occurred, only sometime afterward. So, if either Mr. or Mrs. Darcy wished particularly to speak with Miss Darcy during the day, they could be certain of finding her in the music room, but they could be assured of a conversation only if one or the other stood in the doorway while that conversation ensued.

On this day, Anne saw that both Mr. and Mrs. Darcy were standing in the door to the music room, so she went to the garden, instead. Later, she would regret that decision because Coxcroft was in the music room, making every effort to charm his way into her cousin's affections.

The Baron spoke of the beauty of Cornwall, its coasts and cliffs. Miss Darcy poked self-consciously at the black keys of her piano. He spoke of the immensity of the sea, towering waves, violent storms, monsters that lurked in the night and jerked the sails, tossing the unwitting onto the deck or into the depths. She smiled and eyed the blocked doorway. He drew closer to her and spoke of his desire for a family, a wife, a home. She coughed and asked to be excused.

"Delightful!" exclaimed Coxcroft after she had gone. "Modest!" he added. "Shy!" he confided. "Beguiling!" he marveled. And he went on: "Demure! Lovely! Soft-spoken! Sweet!" The list did not end. She was also, "Charming! Intelligent! Patient!" Darcy paid attention a little longer than Elizabeth did, but not much longer.

Finally, the Baron stopped ejaculating and merely stared rapturously at the territory of carpet where Miss Darcy had once stood.

Mrs. Darcy rolled her eyes heavenward. Mr. Darcy, benefitting from an apprenticeship of ten years in marriage, delicately extracted his wife from the room before she gave voice to her thoughts. He knew that if she uttered just one puncturing remark, they would not stop laughing for several minutes together. And, he knew, the Baron would not laugh with them.

Darcy was surprised, therefore, when he had her alone and she said nothing.

"What, Eliza? No biting axe? No telling thrust? Are you not feeling well, my dear?"

Elizabeth was not merry. "No, Darcy. There is something wrong here. He gives every impression of a man besotted with love, but I do not believe it is true. If he were one of these second sons, salivating for her fortune, then I would understand it. But he has wealth, so much wealth that he must be indifferent to hers. So...what purpose does this pretense serve?"

Darcy found her remarks, well...a little offensive. "Why are you so certain it is pretense? Georgiana is beautiful and accomplished and amiable. Why would any man not wish her to be his wife? Are you the one who is jealous, now?" jabbed her husband.

She colored and heard herself speak with more anger than she had any reason to express. "What do you mean? I am trying to tell you that he has some hidden purpose, and you accuse me of...of what?"

"He has turned his interest from an older, married woman to a younger, unmarried one. That is all." Darcy shrugged. "Elizabeth!" he then laughed, attempting to engage her in his own good spirits. "This is the only time I have ever seen you pettish about where an acquaintance's attentions are bestowed. Usually, you find these flirtations as amusing as I do!"

"Mr. Fitzwilliam Darcy, I demand that you answer! Do you accuse me?" Elizabeth exclaimed in a burning fury that even she did not understand.

The intensity of her response struck a chord in Darcy's possessive nature. His temper, too, flamed ahead of his thinking. But they were no longer newlyweds. Dedicated practice had taught them how to condense several hours of argument into a few choice remarks so that the pleasure of reconciliation would more rapidly overtake incidental wounding. Real argument was futile anyway, for in the end, they would agree, whatever the issue.

She conceded that she might be a little jealous, he confessed that he had been very jealous (and for quite some time), and they laughed at each other's foolishness.

Later that evening, while Lady Anne and Georgiana were busying themselves elsewhere, Elizabeth set down her crochet hook for a moment.

"Mrs. Annesley," Elizabeth began cautiously, "what subjects do Mr. Terwilliger and Miss Darcy discuss during their musical lessons?"

"Why, they discuss music, Mrs. Darcy!"

"Nothing else?"

"Fairy tales, occasionally. They are very fond of discussing the story of the Frog and the Princess."

"Fairy tales and music," Elizabeth repeated. She shook her head and looked at Darcy. He was pretending that he had not overheard the conversation, but she could tell by the rippling of his coat upon his shoulders that he was stifling violent laughter.

Once Mrs. Annesley had shut the door behind her, both the Darcys were overcome with glee.

"Ho, Elizabeth! What did you think? That Georgiana saves her deepest thoughts and tenderest confidences for impoverished piano players? That Ambrose Terwilliger is a clandestine seducer of beautiful women?"

"Say what you will, Husband. He is a young man, and not I, and not any of my sisters, would have wasted the attentions of a young man!"

"A man, you say? You are misinformed, dearest wife! He is no man, but the tallest leprechaun have ever I seen!"

Elizabeth laughed aloud at this new picture of Ambrose Terwilliger, dressed in woodland green, with pointed ears, sucking on a long-stemmed pipe. "So, Darcy, you think he sits on a hidden pot of gold, do you?"

"There would have to be a dozen pots of gold, my wife! And jewels and silver bars, as well! You cannot tweak me on this! There is not an evil demon on the face of the earth -- No! Or even below it – that would be so cruel as to tempt my sister to consider such a lackluster representative of masculinity. Fairy tales and music, indeed!"

"Sometimes, Cupid suffers from impaired vision," murmured Elizabeth Darcy, remembering her own initial failure to recognize the qualities in Fitzwilliam Darcy that made him so ultimately perfect in her eyes. She picked up her crochet hook and resumed her work on a wee bootie. "But, Darcy, Georgiana likes him! To what other man has she ever shown such solicitude? She sees him every day he comes, and he comes every day it does not rain severely. On the days he does not come, she pouts, and her music is positively morbid. What say you to that?"

"That on rainy days she is bored and depressed. Who is not? Oh, Elizabeth, really! Ambrose Terwilliger? When there is a Baron to be had?"

"A title is not everything, Mr. Darcy."

"No, it is not! There are lands and their incomes, plus various patronages, plus jewels, a vast estate in Cornwall, a large house in Mayfair, tin mines, copper mines, and stables, and foreign holdings – I agree with you, Eliza! The title is the least of it!"

CHAPTER THIRTY

Love-Lies-Bleeding

The next day, Ambrose entered the music room and found Miss Darcy not at the piano as was her custom, but standing by the windows looking out on the lawn. She seemed, to him, upset.

"Mr. Terwilliger," she cautiously began, "I have been informed that you have refused the parsonage my brother offered you. I know this must be a misunderstanding, for it cannot be true."

"It is true, Miss Darcy."

She studied him for a moment, choosing her words very carefully. "I had been under the impression that you aspired to the life of a clergyman."

"The truth is, I aspired to the money. I have not heard a calling."

She fingered the keys of her piano but did not actually create any sound. "I believe there are many clergymen who have not actually heard a call. They seem to find great comfort in silence." She paused, then rushed on. "To be honest, Mr. Terwilliger, I had a selfish interest in the matter. I had hoped that you would find occasion to continue your visits and that our acquaintance would continue as well."

"No, Miss Darcy. I am returning to Cornwall."

Georgiana was startled. She looked at him with a mixture of hurt and astonishment. His tone was cold, his jaw was set, and his manner almost offensive. Actually, his manner was intentionally offensive, but she was determined to excuse it. Her abhorrence of conflict was at war with her fear of loss. She pressed him further.

Terwilliger heard her speaking but gave her words no credit. As she went on, he felt himself softening at her apparent sincerity, but then he remembered what he had been telling himself for months. *"She is beautiful, so she is vain. She is clever, so she is manipulative. She is rich, so she is callous."* Finally, he could stay silent no more. "Then, since you will not abandon this subject, I will make myself plain. Your father intended Kympton for Wickham. If your brother wishes to punish his father's favorite because of some childish jealousy, and he has the power to withhold the inheritance, then your brother will have to act alone. I will not be a party to it."

Georgiana bristled. *"Wickham! Has this man not taken enough from me? Having devoured my past, must he also feast upon my future?"* Aloud and in a carefully controlled voice, she said, "This is old news, Mr. Terwilliger. I assure you that my brother acted honorably. If you have denied yourself on Wickham's account, you are a fool."

"Very well, Miss Darcy. Since you raise the issue, let us examine the quality of your brother's honor. Almost a dozen years ago, a young unmarried woman was with child. She was a maid at Pemberley. Your brother discontinued her employment and forced her into the streets. She died! Mr. Darcy then took her child and gave the boy to my cousin. Have you noticed, Miss Darcy, how much Peter Bingley resembles your brother?"

Georgiana turned away from him and walked to the other side of the room, as far away from him as she could be. She pulled herself up, lifted her chin, and faced him. "My brother is without blame in that matter. I give you my word on it."

"Your word!" Ambrose laughed in her face. "What do you know? Do you know that I take every opportunity to frequent taverns, to outwit drunkards in foolish wagers, and to seduce barmaids?"

"Yes, I know it!" She snapped out her reply with so much vitriol he stepped back. "Lambton is a small community, Mr. Terwilliger. There are precious few secrets here. I tell you again: My brother has never done anything that could possibly be characterized as wrong, unless it was done to protect his family or his friends. Even in that case, he would never renege on his responsibility to a helpless innocent, nor would he allow any member of his family to renege on it. If you think otherwise, then you are allowing vicious gossip to cause you to ignore your own best interest."

Terwilliger's mind was reeling. She knew of the things he had done? She knew and pretended regard? *Heartless lying minx! It was all a tease!* he seethed. He knew now that she had judged him unworthy from the start, that all her smiles and witticisms were designed not to enchant him, but merely to torture and humiliate him. Aloud, he raised his voice and almost shouted, "My best interest does not include becoming a lap dog to a spoiled, self-centered, self-righteous hypocrite!"

With the smallest of voices, one that was barely discernable as sound, Georgiana said, "Are you referring to me?"

"I am referring to the fine young lady of the Darcy household that sat in the Fleur-de-Lis Tea Room and ordered Hannah Hill to leave her home, leave her family, leave her friends, and go to a place where no one would know her name. The wealthy young lady who told an impoverished, pregnant, unmarried girl to disassociate herself from her past so that no one would connect her to the glorious virgin purity of Pemberley. The elegant young lady who finds the physical evidence of love to be a pollution of her Derbyshire air. Yes, Miss Darcy, I am referring to you!"

She turned her back on him! "You have said quite enough, Mr. Terwilliger. You may leave my brother's house."

Turned. Her. Back. On. Him.

"Oh, no! Not yet! Before I go, I will cleanse my mouth of all the things that I have left unsaid for these many months!" He gathered his breath and his resentment and his cruelty and plunged into her. "Because your family is rich and powerful, you have indulged yourself in the unkindest of ways. You wanted me to visit Pemberley because you enjoyed toying with me, knowing that my poverty and lack of connection made it impossible for me to even so much as speak to your brother, as I was told to step aside each time another man came to call on you. I excused your cruelty, and I returned every day to endure more of it, but your heartless dismissal of that young girl (little more than a child herself!), *that* I cannot excuse. You think yourself so different from her, and you are right. She has the proof of her kindness and selflessness and generosity, for it lives within her just beneath her heart, until it can have a life all its own." Miss Darcy winced, but did not face him. "You, on the other hand," he spat, "are a woman who has no feeling." He took a step closer to her, so close he could have whispered in her ear. But he did not whisper. He spoke clearly and aloud, jutting his chin closer and closer with each word. "You are cold and stale and lifeless." At this, Miss Darcy did not wince.

There was no denial. There was no explanation. She did not turn around. She did not even look at him. He watched as she disappeared into herself.

This time, he was glad to see her go.

He left the music room. He left the house. On his way out the door, he passed Anne de Bourgh.

Anne thought it quite odd that Mr. Terwilliger would pass right by her without the slightest acknowledgement. She watched as he set off for GanderGlen on foot. Why did he not go to the stable to collect Butterball? She went into the music room and found her cousin standing erect in a dark corner. Suddenly, Georgiana was in her arms, weeping as though the world had ended. Anne questioned her but received no replies, only sobs and tears. In the end, Anne learned only that, "Mr. Terwilliger will not return to Pemberley."

The next afternoon, when Bingley told Darcy that his cousin had suddenly become homesick and had left on the morning coach to return to Cornwall via Liverpool, Darcy was delighted. The boy had occupied too much of Georgiana's time. She had been using her piano lessons to avoid the pursuits of eligible bachelors. Now, Darcy was confident, she would finally select a man from her many callers and would become a beautiful bride. She would come to know happiness, at last.

CHAPTER THIRTY-ONE

Mourning Bride

"Mr. Darcy, may I have a moment of your time, sir?"

As the gentleman and the peer shared a fraternal glass of port in Darcy's library, the Baron nonchalantly described his passion for the delicate Miss Georgiana Darcy. He extolled her value as an ornamental accessory, while he examined the leather bindings of the books on the library's shelves. He poked the curved leg of a sofa with his foot, as he revealed his innermost longing for a home and serene marriage. In short, he condescended to plead for the merciful bequest of Georgiana Darcy's hand. It quite exhausted the Baron, for he could not conceal a yawn as Darcy enthusiastically accepted the offer.

After Coxcroft withdrew, Darcy struggled with an irritant. It was there, and it was irritating, but it hid from him and he knew not how to bring it to the surface so that he could see what it was. There was a knock at the door. Mrs. Darcy sought permission to enter, and Darcy half-heartedly waved her in.

"What, husband?" she laughed. "Have we been married too long?"

Darcy shook off his preoccupation and went to her.

Elizabeth twisted in his grasp to study his face. "What is wrong, Fitzwilliam? First, you greet me as though I am a stableboy, then you hold me as though you are afraid I will run away!"

"The Baron has asked for Georgiana's hand. I have given my permission, of course. But he was so casual in the request! He acted as though, as though..."

"As though she is nothing more than a pauper, and she should be grateful for his munificence?"

"Yes!" That was the irritant! Elizabeth had put her finger on it!

"I seem to remember another man..."

Revelation came too late to Mr. Fitzwilliam Darcy. "Stop it! Do not remind me!"

Elizabeth laughed merrily as her husband covered his ears. The former Miss Elizabeth Bennet had first refused the insolent offer of the vain Mr. Darcy, forcing him to spend many months in wretched suspense. His punishment (for his presumptuous certainty that she would leap at his offer) was her temporary flirtation with the despised Wickham and her deeply-felt friendship with Darcy's cousin, Colonel Fitzwilliam. Painful as it was, the experience had taught Darcy patience and brought him a small measure of humility.

"How will Georgiana manage to humble the Baron of Coxcroft?" Darcy asked, aloud.

Elizabeth smiled indulgently at his concern. "Your sister has arts we know nothing of, sweet husband, for I was with her all this day, and she made no mention of the Baron's offer."

"She retired early last night, did she not?" pondered Darcy, speaking as much to himself as to his wife.

"Yes. She claimed a headache. I think Mr. Terwilliger's decision to return to Cornwall is still troubling her."

Darcy flagged his hand impatiently. If there was one thing he did not want to hear, it was another verse in Elizabeth's annoying song about 'Ambrose Terwilliger, Cupid's chosen target for Georgiana Darcy.'

"The point is," Darcy pushed each word to the front, one at a time, "when did the Baron secure her promise?"

Darcy looked at Elizabeth piercingly. She sat down on the sofa, then cautiously replied, "I do not think that he did ask her." Genuinely alarmed, she came to attention and rushed on, "Darcy, I think you gave your consent, and she has not been consulted!"

Darcy stared at her, genuinely horrified. "Impossible! He would not dare!"

They stared at each other for one slow moment, and then both rushed to the music room. They heard no music, but went in anyway. Georgiana was there, at the window, her back to the piano. She did not acknowledge their entrance, perhaps because she did not notice it, or perhaps because she did not wish to notice them. When Darcy spoke her name, she responded lethargically. When asked if she was well, she said that she was "well enough."

"Georgiana," Elizabeth ventured, "is this unhappiness or is it love?"

Miss Darcy winced, but said nothing.

"The Baron has asked for your hand," Darcy said.

"Well, give it to him," replied Georgiana as she dumped herself into her grandfather's monstrous leather chair. The last time she sat in this chair, Mr. Terwilliger played one of his own compositions, one that caused her to envision a huge moon and misted stars and comets with long, feathery tails. She burrowed her shoulders into the soft leather, wrapping herself in a memory. She heard Mr. Terwilliger's voice, *"You are cold and stale and lifeless."*

"Georgiana," Elizabeth tried again. "You did accept the Baron, did you not?"

"He has never spoken to me of an offer. So...no." She picked at the arm of the chair. Mr. Terwilliger spoke to her again: *"You are a woman who has no feeling."*

Darcy fumed. "How dare the man! Baron or no, I shall withdraw my permission immediately!"

Georgiana was helpless. Mr. Terwilliger would not stop: *"I excused your cruelty, and I returned every day to endure more of it."* She had thought that he liked her. Enjoyed her company. She had convinced herself that he might love her. Once again, she was so stupidly wrong.

"Oh, what difference does it make? Is it not time that I married? Is the Baron not the man you have chosen for me? Is this not the life you want me to live?" Georgiana's voice sounded of resignation and defeat.

Elizabeth gasped, "Georgiana! If you do not love...Do not be cynical! Do not deny yourself!"

Darcy pleaded, "I thought this is what every woman wants! Wealth, jewels, servants, society..."

He stopped. She was staring out the window, not the least bit interested in the subject under discussion: The subject being – her life. She sighed, rose from the chair, and wandered across the room. She stopped at the doorway long enough to add (in a colorless voice), "Do not withdraw your permission, brother. I truly cannot bear another day of this procession of supplicants. Let me marry the Baron and be done with it." Then, she evaporated into the hallway and was gone.

"It is Terwilliger," said Elizabeth, sadly.

"It is Wickham," said her husband, more sadly still.

CHAPTER THIRTY-TWO

Flax

Ambrose Terwilliger had planned to take the public coach to Liverpool, and then try to stowaway on a ship that would port somewhere along Cornwall's coast. But the coach had stopped at Stockport, just on the outskirts of Manchester, and he had taken his meal at the station inn. His server was Hannah Hill, wearing very loose clothing...and a wedding ring.

"Mr. Terwilliger, sir!" she fairly shouted and led him to a table in the farthest corner of the room. "Please, sir, please," she pleaded in an urgent whisper.

"I am Ambrose Terwilliger," he said, loud enough to be heard, "but, from where did you learn my name, wench?"

"Hey, hey," said the innkeeper, a man with whiskers turning white, piercing eyes the same color as mud, and a disapproving frown. He was watching Terwilliger like a falcon studies a field mouse.

"I meant no disrespect, sir." Then Ambrose turned to her and winked with his left eye so the Publican would not see it.

Hannah relaxed. The wink told her that he understood enough to say nothing. "I am Hannah Buxton, sir, Hannah Hill before my marriage." She looked at him meaningfully. "Widow Buxton, now."

"Yes. I remember, Hannah. Sad, that was. Well, we will not talk about the sad things, will we? You look wonderful!" He glanced at the glowering Publican. "They treat you alright, here?"

She assured him that she was very happy. Then another table called for a refill of their tankards and she whisked away.

The Publican served Ambrose his food. The plate hit the table so hard it made Ambrose's tankard jump.

The coach Ambrose had taken to Stockport was not going to Liverpool, so Ambrose had to wait three hours for his connection. During that time, Hannah and he managed a few stray words, but they were always cut short by some task that the Publican needed her to perform.

Eventually, some workers came in singing and laughing. With the Publican busy at his bar and the coach customers all gone on their way to Leeds, Hannah and Ambrose finally had a real conversation.

"Miss Darcy, is she well?" Hannah asked with no small amount of concern.

"She was when I last left Pemberley," Ambrose replied, slightly baffled. *"Why would you care, Hannah? She was so cruel to you!"*

"She was so kind to me!"

Ambrose's mouth was open, but he could not form words. *"What? What did you say?"* He thought them, but he did not say them.

"When next you speak to her, will you tell her I am well? And that I followed her advice and am happier now than I have ever been?"

"Her advice?" Now, Ambrose was truly baffled. *"Was it not Miss Darcy's advice that you isolate yourself from everyone that cares about you? Did she not castigate you with scripture?"*

Hannah twisted her wedding ring around her finger. It was leaving a green halo on her skin. "Miss Darcy told me that I had a duty to choose the best life for my child." Hannah had tears in her eyes. "She told me that if I went where no one knew me, they would know only what I told them about my past. I would never have had the courage to come here and make a life for myself and my little one, if she had not given me her mother's wedding ring." Her tears were evidence of her deeply-felt gratitude, but from across the room, the Publican saw only tears.

"Mrs. Buxton! Have the boys completed their chores?"

"They were about them, when last I looked in, Mr. Morton."

"Best look in again," he commanded.

Once she was out of the room, the Publican explained (while he was quite decisively helping Ambrose to his feet and to the door) that Ambrose should wait for his coach outside.

Ambrose bought passage only as far as Manchester. Hannah had given him the name of a man who was starting a pleasure garden there and was in need of musicians. A few weeks' work, and he would not have to stowaway and risk impressment. He would be able to afford to book passage on a ship from Liverpool to Cornwall and arrive home safely.

He tried to focus on Manchester and music and what a pleasure garden might be (for he had never heard the term). But he could not drown out the laughter of the fiend that had controlled him since he learned about life from Jammin Hard – the fiend that insisted again and again that trust and honor and generosity were merely subterfuges for self-interest.

"*Mrs. Reynolds collected larger-size dresses for Hannah. Mrs. Annesley knitted baby things. Mrs. Darcy gave her money. I was all sympathy. But it was Miss Darcy that gave her a wedding ring. Only Miss Darcy realized what help was truly needed, and only Miss Darcy provided that help.*" He watched the scenery hop past his eyes as the coach bumped relentlessly forward to Manchester on the rutted road, and he gave himself one more reproof. "Now I know that when I hear of some wrong that Georgiana Darcy has done, I must begin my evaluation of it by saying, 'You, Ambrose Terwilliger, are an idiot.' If I start at that point, I will save myself a copious amount of time and a bushelful of reproach because I now know that is where I will end."

The only problem with his resolution was that he had left Pemberley on terms that absolutely ensured that Georgiana Darcy would never condescend to see or speak to him ever again.

CHAPTER THIRTY-THREE

Women's Bane

Coxcroft licked his lips. "This alliance will allow the two of us to grow closer, will it not…Elizabeth?"

Mrs. Darcy was finding it more and more difficult to keep the Baron at a comfortable distance. First, because the Baron's engagement to Georgiana allowed him to visit more frequently and with less formality and, second, because after each encounter with the Baron, Elizabeth wished to be further away from him. Initially, she had found the man attractive. That sensation had inspired in her a certain level of not unpleasant discomfort. Having gotten to know him better, however, she found herself ever more eager to escape his company – but she did not know why.

Was it his undisguised hatred of the French? She did not think so. Many Englishmen despised the French. Twenty-five years of war! But the Baron never mentioned the war. His animus seemed to focus entirely on Etienne Foucauld. Yes, the Frenchman was annoying, but he had done nothing hateful (except for all of the threats and the challenges and the sneering). And the Baron's eating habits! Yes, he had spent most of his life as a merchant sailor, but do all sailors talk and eat at the same time? Dripping food? Expelling foul odors and making odd noises? Hands covered with grease? Food bits nestled in their beards?

Elizabeth wondered how Georgiana, fastidious as she was in her own grooming, could tolerate the Baron's uncombed hair, greasy fingers, and – his aroma. These things did not seem to trouble Georgiana. Since the engagement was announced and the banns put up, it seemed as though she were not quite present and did not quite notice him – no – did not quite notice anyone, at all.

Elizabeth found the Baron at her side, his hand gripping her elbow, guiding her out the door into the garden. She did not want to accompany him, but short of creating a scene, could think of no way to decline his 'invitation' to join him for a companionable walk in the moonlight.

He licked his lips again. She was beginning to find this behavior as distasteful as his smell.

"Elizabeth, I am eager – and able – to assist you in concealing the proofs of this clandestine love affair of yours."

She stopped. Her lips parted. Her facial expression, which revealed her astonishment at his remark, he interpreted as confirmation of her realization that her secret was no longer safe.

"What a scoundrel!" the Baron continued, melodically. "Be assured that I know he has used your loving sweetness and your husband's unconscionable indifference to cause you to behave in a manner that is not compatible with your true nature. Your husband and his friends shall not learn of this matter. I promise it! But you must help me in my effort: My plan for your protection requires that you transfer ownership of your horse to me."

Elizabeth stood in rapt shock. Did the Baron think that she – Elizabeth – was involved…Wait! Darcy indifferent! Was the man mad? She needed time to think, so she quickly ran over what had been said and ventured, "I do not understand: How exactly is my reputation to be rescued by the sale of my horse?"

The Baron smiled angelically. "Mrs. Darcy. The less you know of these matters, the safer your personal reputation. Trust in me, my dear. We are family, are we not? I am a man who has lived in the world. I am not like your husband – unsophisticated, insulated, proud, craving the good opinion of others – such a man would be mortified if his wife's honor were exposed to wicked innuendo. Particularly, when there is proof."

"Proof?" repeated Elizabeth.

"You were overheard," he whispered, his breath stinking of rampion. "Your promise is sufficient, my dear, to ensure the eternal ignorance of your husband."

Elizabeth did not like the exaggerated courtesy of the Baron's manner, his opinion of her husband's character, his confidence that she would betray her husband (either by taking a lover or by paying a blackmailer), and most of all, she detested his foul, reeking stench.

There was a sound behind them. They both turned and saw it was Darcy. Coxcroft beamed lovingly in Darcy's direction and greeted his brother-to-be with a hearty affability that made Elizabeth recoil with disgust.

"Your wife has shown mercy, Darcy! She has promised me the Godolphin stallion! But you are to set the price."

Darcy took a moment, and then recalled that he had seen this expression on this man's face before. Ah, yes! During the hunt, one of the Baron's shots was not true. A bird was injured but not killed. It was in great pain. Darcy saw the expression on the Baron's face before Terwilliger put the poor thing out of its misery. The same expression. And the Baron was now looking at…Fitzwilliam Darcy.

Darcy grinned at the Baron with such a foolish admiration that Elizabeth wanted to run away. But she did not run. She lifted her chin and held her ground.

Darcy actually chuckled! "Well, dearest Elizabeth, how has this villain seduced you into abandoning a creature that loves you? My sweet wife, I am convinced that if you can turn your back on a dumb animal that serves you with unquestioning devotion, you can surely walk away from an even less intelligent husband."

Elizabeth realized that her husband was speaking to her, but his eyes had not left the Baron. She, on the other hand, did not wish to look at Coxcroft at all – actually, not ever again. "The Baron presumes that I will sacrifice Moonlight in order to conceal a piece of gossip from you."

"Then, the Baron has erred," Darcy addressed her evenly, his smile still aimed directly at the bridge of the Baron's nose. "My wife knows that I do not listen to gossip, Baron. In fact, on those occasions when it is foisted upon me, I neglect to retain it." Elizabeth knew again why she loved her husband as much as she did because, at that moment, her adoration surged through her body and out every pore. Darcy drew her arm around his own and laid his hand on it. She murmured a request that they return to the house, and Darcy gave his back to the titled peer.

The Baron, realizing that his pretense of courtesy would no longer gain him his desires, discarded all semblance of civil behavior. "See here, Darcy. The deal is made. Your wife has given her word."

"Has she? Well, her reputation means more to me than my own." Darcy squeezed his wife's hand to assure her of his unbending support. "Mrs. Darcy, did you make the promise that this man asks me to enforce?"

"No, Mr. Darcy, I did not."

Coxcroft exclaimed aloud, using a word that Mrs. Darcy had never heard before. "See here, woman. I caution you! You are making me out a liar!"

Although Elizabeth did not know that word, Darcy clearly did. "You are a *vulgar* liar, sir," calmly replied Fitzwilliam Darcy. "Do not trouble yourself that it is a woman that has called you out, for I would have taken even the horse's word above anything you might say. And, the next time you seek to achieve your end by extortion, I suggest you select a victim who does not command and deserve the respect, admiration, and devotion of every member of her family."

Coxcroft was shocked into silence. Unconditional loyalty was not a barrier that often confronted him.

Darcy called for a servant and told him that the Baron had been suddenly called away. "Bring up a wagon immediately. Provide it with an escort so that the Baron does not lose his way between this spot and Lambton. The Baron does not wish to tarry." Darcy waited for an acknowledgement, for all the servants knew that his demand of an acknowledgement required that his order be carried out exactly as given.

At the nod of the servant's head, Darcy then left the Baron without a single word of farewell, escorting Elizabeth into the dining room for their evening meal. The Baron watched the Darcys turn their backs on him, as though he were nothing more than an insect. He witnessed the elderly butler summon a younger, brawnier servant to stand with them and saw other servants receive instructions and scurry away. The Baron heard the servants talking among themselves as they ran to carry out their instructions. "He said 'wagon'! Not 'carriage'!"

Three men politely surrounded the Baron of Coxcroft and guided him to the front of the house, where an open wagon waited, but no driver. The Baron would have to take the reins himself. Also waiting were four stableboys on horseback who would accompany the wagon all the way into Lambton and bring it back. The Baron knew he had been turned out. And these servants knew it. Tomorrow, all of Lambton would know it! Where the Baron had once felt nothing more than mild disdain for this easy-to-impress country gentlemen, Coxcroft now felt a raging gluttony for revenge against a mere piece of backcountry arrogance and his haughty trollop of a wife.

As they walked with arms entwined, Elizabeth leaned a little closer to her husband and said, "I am sorry, Darcy. I have ruined your hopes for Georgiana."

"Elizabeth," Darcy grumbled, "I would not let the man have a horse. Do you think I would let him have my sister?" As Elizabeth sighed with relief, Darcy frowned. *"At least,"* he said to himself, *"the horse would fight back."*

The dinner meal proceeded with little conversation. No one at the table remarked on Coxcroft's absence. As the entrée was cleared, Darcy finally approached the subject. "Georgiana, I asked Coxcroft...that is, I *told* Coxcroft..."

"GOOD!" declared Georgiana with an immediate huzzah from Anne. The balance of the meal was shared with great conviviality, and everyone's appetite and digestion showed marked improvement over the coming days.

CHAPTER THIRTY-FOUR

White Heather

Mrs. Annesley had never had a day like this one.

She had a visitor in the morning. Her brother had business in Nottingham and was returning to his home in Rotherham. It was not too much out of his way to stop at Pemberley, so he did. His business was flourishing, he had taken a larger house, and his family was about to increase. Would Fanny consider becoming Governess to the two older boys, so that his wife could devote her full attention to the newborn? Mrs. Annesley welcomed this offer. Being a lady's companion was pleasant enough, but it lacked the stimulation that two mischievous and curious children could provide.

She was weighing various approaches that she might take to apprise the Darcys of her change in direction. She would have to tell Georgiana Darcy first, of course. But should she tell Mr. and Mrs. Darcy herself, or ask Miss Darcy to do it? And should the Darcys be told together, or separately? If separately, then Mrs. Darcy should be told first. What words should be used? Mrs. Annesley was totally lost in her own thoughts at the lunch hour, while the Darcys were in Lambton. It was just after lunch when she was asked to receive another visitor. Sir James Culpepper asked if she would walk with him in the garden.

Certainly! Sir James was always courtly; he held to the old ways and that appealed to Mrs. Annesley's stiff sensibilities about proper behavior. While they walked and talked, she remained preoccupied with thoughts of her brother's visit. Sir James prattled on about the different plants in the garden, the best soil for each, blooming seasons, and would she consent to be his wife, and she said, "Yes."

He promised to return that evening, after dinner, to secure Mr. Darcy's approval (since he was the man in the household). She thanked him, and they said "good-bye."

Then, he kissed her upon her mouth, and she woke up.

As she watched him ride away, she knew she had to talk to someone. Anyone. She went to the music room. Miss Darcy was not there. No, of course she was not. She would not return to Pemberley until after two o'clock. Anne de Bourgh would be in the library. So, Mrs. Annesley went to the library.

"Lady Anne?"

"Good afternoon, Mrs. Annesley. The light is good today…oh, you do not have your knitting with you. I presumed…" Anne let her voice trail off.

"Sir James…"

"Oh. Is he here? Does he want to see me? Or was he hoping to see Miss Darcy?" Anne thought about rabbits and how they dug holes everywhere and could hop into one at a moment's notice. How she longed to be a rabbit!

"He was here. He has left."

"Good!" (No need for rabbits.)

"He will return after dinner."

"Oh." (Where are those rabbits?)

"To speak to Mr. Darcy."

"Good!" (Never mind, rabbits, you may go.)

"He seeks…consent."

"Oh." (Thousands of rabbits. Digging madly.) "Really?" (Anne was scouring the library carpet for a rabbit-hole.) "Oh! He is ancient! No doubt any wife will be a widow within the year. And that oldest son! He will begrudge every mouth of food his father's new wife consumes, he is so jealous of his inheritance. And the younger one! He will spend each waking moment attempting to seduce her, for not even the serving girls in Lambton will have him and his rough ways. One must take care to avoid dark corners in that house! (Rabbits everywhere. On the furniture. Under the furniture. Bouncing off the windows in a frenzy to escape.) Tell me, Mrs. Annesley! Do not let me twist and turn! For whom will he come?"

"Me."

Anne's jaw dropped. But she recovered admirably and said, "I wish you every happiness."

Mrs. Annesley nodded and left the library. Her conversation with Lady Anne had put words to her own thoughts. Marriage to Sir James meant marriage to his entire family and his family...Lady Anne had not even mentioned the daughter and her six children. Those children! No governess stayed as much as a year!

She picked up her knitting and went again to the music room, hoping that her thoughts would clear. But she was accosted by the butler – two letters had come for her! One was from London. The book publisher that has her precious manuscript had written her a letter, no doubt to tell her that there had been a fire, or a flood, or a robbery, and sixteen years of her life no longer existed. That could wait. She opened the letter from Stockport. The envelope said that the sender was a "Widow Buxton", and the postage was pre-paid! But...Mrs. Annesley did not know a Widow Buxton.

"Dear Mrs. Annesley,

You were so kind to me when I was at Pemberley that I felt I must write you and tell you that I am well-settled and happy.

I am sure you know that Miss Darcy invited me to lunch on the day I left Lambton. We talked about many things, and I decided that I would not go to my sister in Meryton (as you and I had discussed), but would instead go to a new city and make a new life. I planned to go to Manchester and find work in a factory. But the coach lost a wheel outside Stockport, and I had to sit for over an hour in the public room at the inn. It was a rainy night, so the innkeeper had time, and we talked. He was widowed by the epidemic. She left him with three little boys, and he fretted about them being too young to be left on their own so much. He said, too, that it was hard to find workers because they all wanted the factory wages and the exciting life in the city. When the coach left, I stayed. I help him with his children, and I keep up the rooms in the inn. Sometimes, I help in the pub. It is better than factory work for me because he lets me rest whenever I need to.

I have my own room, and my meals and wages. He is a good Christian man, well known in the local church. He is also the postmaster, and he has offered to frank any letter I wish to send! His sister is a midwife, and she has been helping me prepare for my confinement. He will stop my wages when I cannot work, but he has promised to continue the room and meals and hold my job open until I can work again.

I do not know if you would want to write me, but if you do, please address the letter to Mrs. Joe Buxton, Widow. I will understand if you feel you cannot.

Thank you for comforting me at Rosings. If you will, please tell Mrs. Darcy and Miss Darcy that I am grateful for their kindness.

Hannah"

Mrs. Annesley decided that she would not delay in making a reply. *"A person can use any name they want,"* she huffed. *"Miss Burney used no name at all when she published her first book. Its cover said, 'Written by A Lady.' And that is how my book…"*

Oh. Yes. Her book. The letter from the publisher. Mrs. Annesley sighed so heavily that her shoulders went up, then down. *"Let me guess what this is about. Is it a tactfully-worded guffaw? Could it be a bill to pay for the postage required to send my manuscript back to me?"*

The letter said none of the things her imagination suggested. Instead, the letter was surprisingly complimentary, and it included two items: A contract wherein she gave up her copyright, and a bankdraft for one hundred ten pounds [Two Years' Allowance!]…made out in her name, alone.

No, there was never a day like this one.

She heard the Darcy carriage in the courtyard. The Darcys were there, but where was Georgiana?

Carolyn Bingley, she was told, joined them at the Fleur-de-Lis in town for lunch, and invited Miss Darcy to GanderGlen for dinner and an evening of cards.

"Oh, Mrs. Darcy!" cried out Mrs. Annesley, who then covered her face with her hands and ran into the house.

Elizabeth and her husband stared at each other, then Elizabeth quietly followed in Mrs. Annesley's wake.

By the time Elizabeth reached Mrs. Annesley's room, the traveling bag was open on the bed and already half-filled. "I must leave," said Mrs. Annesley, with more firmness than Elizabeth had ever heard from her before.

"Well, certainly, Mrs. Annesley. You may come and go as you wish. May I ask when you might return?"

"Never."

Elizabeth was at first baffled, but now she was concerned. "Are you alright?"

"I am fine. But I cannot stay here. Please do not ask me to explain. I will write when I am settled. But, right now…I must leave at once."

"But you cannot travel alone! Mr. Darcy and I…"

"NO! Mr. Darcy needs to stay here! He has to speak to Sir James when he comes."

"Sir James is coming?"

"After dinner. To plead for my hand. I do not want to be here!"

"Plead for your hand?"

"Please, Mrs. Darcy! It was a mistake. I was thinking of something else. I do not want his children."

"Children? At his age? At your age? Mrs. Annesley, I fear that you may have an unrealistic…"

"Please let me go!"

"Mrs. Annesley, you are not a prisoner here! But I cannot allow you to travel alone." Elizabeth gathered her thoughts. Then, she smiled. "You are the same as family to us. You know that. We will take the carriage to Rotherham, you and I together. We will stay at the inn in Rotherham tonight, and you can go from there to your brother's house in the morning. Mr. Darcy will ride to Rotherham tomorrow to provide me with an escort when the carriage brings me back to Pemberley. Perhaps I can persuade him to let me visit some shops before we return! Will that be alright, do you think?"

Mrs. Annesley nodded, hesitated, then hugged Elizabeth Darcy with grateful emotion. She had never hugged Miss Darcy!

Elizabeth let Mrs. Annesley finish her packing and braced herself for what would be a challenging conversation with her husband. He refused to let her go. He refused to allow her to stay overnight at an inn. He refused to tell Tom to bring out the coach and four. He refused to ride to Rotherham. Shopping was out of the question! And he absolutely and positively refused to explain Mrs. Annesley's sudden and permanent departure to Sir James. If she had accepted him, then propriety demanded that she withdraw her promise personally.

While the footman loaded the luggage into the coach, Elizabeth reminded her husband that Moonlight had not been ridden in three days (since none of the exercise boys dared even approach him), and it would please her if Darcy would ride her horse to Rotherham.

Darcy was not fooled. There was a certain mare in a certain Sheffield stable, not far from Rotherham. Elizabeth was hoping to mollify Darcy with the temptation of a generous stud fee.

Elizabeth turned back toward the house. "Fitzgeorge is at his nap now, Eliza," Darcy reminded her. "If you wake him, he will fuss and your departure will be delayed for at least an hour. You will be back at Pemberley by tomorrow at this time. You can wake him and spoil him then."

As he watched the coach in the distance, Darcy imagined his conversation with Sir James. He shuddered.

He must send word to the cook. Mrs. Darcy would not be dining with them tonight. Nor would Mrs. Annesley. Oh, and Georgiana was dining at Bingley's house.

Dining at Bingley's house!

"Tom! Ready the Brougham! And saddle Dark-of-the-Moon. Lady Anne and I will have our evening meal at GanderGlen tonight." Darcy felt fresh air in his lungs! He would not have to wait for an eager Sir James to come calling. Darcy could go to Culpepper Manor now and acquaint Sir James with the news that Mrs. Annesley had left her employment and gone to live with her brother's family as a Governess. Yes! This would forestall a request from Sir James, so there would be no embarrassment of a refusal. Darcy would then proceed to the Bingleys' in time for dinner. Lady Anne could proceed to

GanderGlen at her leisure from Pemberley in an hour or so. And, at the end of the evening, Darcy would provide escort to the ladies as they returned to Pemberley in the Brougham.

It was a confident and content Fitzwilliam Darcy that dined at GanderGlen that night, and he reveled in his mastery of the tangle his impulsive wife had created. It was good that he appreciated this gift, for it would be his last peaceful moment for quite some time.

CHAPTER THIRTY-FIVE

Nightshade

Darcy planned his departure for early in the morning, while the dew was still on the grass. The nurse had struggled with Little Fits *("Curse you, Georgiana, now you have me saying it!")*, who wanted his mother to read to him, wanted his mother to listen to his prayers at bedtime, wanted his mother…Period! *"Where does all this stubbornness come from?"* Darcy wondered. *"It must be from Elizabeth's side, for the Darcys have always been known for their patience and affability."*

As Darcy sauntered toward the barn, he saw two riders approach at full gallop. They appeared to be locked in a race for life itself. One was Bingley, of that Darcy was sure. The other -- red cape whipping behind, almost standing in the stirrups -- undoubtedly Foucauld.

"Darcy!" Charles Bingley pulled up his lathered white stallion with three spirited hops. Foucauld's rented gelding ran past both men and circled back. Foucauld dismounted as Bingley demanded, "Tell him who Peter's father is!"

Mr. Darcy silently turned back toward the house and signaled them to follow. This was not a topic he wished to discuss in an open courtyard, or within easy earshot of the servants. He led them into his study and closed the heavy door himself.

Bingley paced and cursed, flinging filthy looks in the placid Foucauld's direction.

"Damn it, Darcy. Speak, man! This French toad has filed with the court! He intends to take Peter out of the country!"

"Why not, Monsieur? I am the boy's only blood relation. At least, I am the only one who will claim him."

Bingley glared at Foucauld, then turned to his friend. "I am sorry, Darcy. I know it is embarrassing. But this toad will not go away!"

"I am a Frog, Monsieur," sniffed Foucauld, proudly. "Try to apply your insults correctly."

"You are a damn ugly toad!" Bingley roared, wounded and afraid. "This is personal, Foucauld! It has nothing to do with your nationality. Besides, my son is half-French…"

"Pierre is not your son, Monsieur."

"I have raised him! I have loved him! He is mine! And his name is Peter!"

"Your own courts will not support you, Monsieur. I am blood. They will not refuse my claim." Foucauld smiled at Bingley. "That is English law."

The man that had introduced himself as Etienne Foucauld months ago was almost comically French: Romantic, emotional, blindly devoted to an ancient family honor, even chivalrous. But this man, this French man now standing self-assured in Darcy's study, was a cunning antagonist who came to England fully prepared to negotiate the courts of a foreign land, as administered by unsympathetic judges and juries, and which adhered to a system of law completely alien to his own country's legal system. This was the man who had hired spies, had conducted interrogations, had established friendly relationships with Peter and with members of Darcy's own family. Darcy knew that this Fox had secured his victory before he entered this room and was now ready to snap the neck of any victim that foolishly presented itself. Darcy had not seen this man before.

Madelyn Fox had mentioned her brother only once to Fitzwilliam Darcy. "You and he are much alike. The only difference is that you will stop at murder, Monsieur Darcy. Murder is where my brother begins."

Darcy inhaled. Then Darcy exhaled. He had to get rid of Bingley.

"Darcy!" Bingley was pleading now. "Tell him! Tell him you are Peter's father."

Foucauld shrugged. "I asked the monsieur that question. He denied it." Foucauld fixed a disinterested gaze on the man who had not spoken since they had entered his study. "Do you wish to claim him now? As you once reminded me, Monsieur Darcy, there are sabers in your library."

"I make no claim."

Bingley's jaw dropped. "What?"

"Not mine, Charles. Peter is not my son."

"But...you told me he was!"

"I lied." Darcy stood straight and tall, his chin up, his gaze steady.

When Charles Bingley entered this room, he knew that he was stepping onto bedrock. Now, he found himself on shifting sand. "Have you forgotten how you begged me to take the boy? Your promise that my wife could invest her love safely? Have you forgotten your words of gratitude, when you learned that Peter could remain a part of your life?"

Bingley shook his head uncomprehendingly. Darcy crumbling? Had Gibraltar itself fallen? And then, he knew. "Georgiana. You are willing to deny your own son to avoid the scandal. Destroy my family. Throw aside every principle you have ever held dear, for what? So your sister can marry some sycophant second son? Or, is it that you hope Coxcroft will return? Does a title mean that much to you?"

Darcy said nothing. He felt every mortification imaginable. A lifetime of rectitude and honorable dealings was now the same as if he had crawled through every gutter in London.

"I thought more of you," mourned Bingley for a friend lost forever. "I know you better now."

Bingley drew in his breath and steeled his spine. He turned his back on his dearest, oldest and now most despised friend and gave his full attention to Etienne Foucauld. "I will fight you. Every step. Every day."

"I expected that, Monsieur. What I did not expect is that Monsieur Darcy would abandon you. That will make it easier for me. You will lose."

"I may lose, sir. But my son will know that he was taken, not surrendered. He will know that I fought for him."

Very seriously, Foucauld said, "Merci."

Bingley stared at the man who threatened to deprive him and his wife of their cherished child. "For what are you thanking me, sir?"

"For teaching my nephew what it is to be a man." Foucauld glanced at Darcy, then turned his back on Mr. Fitzwilliam Darcy and for the very first time, gave his complete attention to Charles Bingley. "Thank you, Monsieur Bingley."

The two stood across from each other with a shared respect deeper than the ravine that divided them. Then, without the slightest acknowledgement to his host, Bingley strode from Darcy's study.

Once Bingley left, only pall lived in that room.

Foucauld began to leave. Darcy cleared his throat. "Monsieur Foucauld. The Bingleys do not know this, and I ask you not to tell them – or anyone else: Peter Bingley is not your sister's son."

Foucauld leaned back on his heels, studying his enemy. "Clever," he finally said.

Darcy shook his head. "As I told Bingley: I lied." Darcy motioned to a comfortable chair. Foucauld glanced at it but remained standing. "It is a long story, Monsieur Foucauld, so I will be seated. You may stay on your feet as long as you wish."

"I know what you are attempting, Monsieur. But I have all of the facts. I am certain that you will not be surprised to learn that Monsieur Wickham confessed everything."

"Are you saying that Wickham is claiming Peter?" asked an alarmed Darcy.

"No, Monsieur! Hardly! That one would not claim his own if he could avoid the cost of it, let alone claim another man's child. Wickham told me of your cousin, the stalwart Colonel."

Darcy nodded. "I thought you knew that he had fathered your sister's child. I wondered how you learned it." Darcy sighed. "Wickham is…"

"A dirty dog. I agree."

"My cousin did make an offer to your sister. One offer. She refused him."

"Why, Monsieur? Why one offer? Why did he not press her, again and again?" For a moment, his thoughts ran to Anne de Bourgh. "I would have."

"I really do not know, Foucauld. I know there was a passion there, but…I can only guess that it was because he did not truly want her. He did want the child."

"Very well. But why would SHE refuse an offer that would have cleansed her name and legitimized her unborn baby?"

"Again, I am guessing, but I suspect it was because she nursed the hope that she could obtain a wealthier husband."

"And that would have been?"

"Me. She made several offers, all of which I refused. Nevertheless, she attempted to convince several persons that I was a seducer and an exploiter." Darcy shifted his position in his chair. He ruminated, and the tone of his voice changed. "Your sister, Monsieur, was a very manipulative woman, indifferent to truth, and sensitive to her own comforts."

"Yes, she was encouraged in that, by our parents. It is charming behavior in a child. Not so charming in an adult."

"She made it very easy for me to convince Bingley that I was the boy's rightful guardian. Her own child, which was ultimately interred with her, was Colonel Fitzwilliam's son. That is why my cousin is inconsolable, and that is why he continues to visit her grave."

"Not for Magdeleigne," said Foucauld. "Then, I am the only one. The only one that loved her. The only one who remembers her."

"Have you already forgotten Peter?" Darcy asked. "He loved her. He remembers."

Foucauld lowered his head and looked away.

Darcy poured two glasses of port. "Magdeleigne Foucauld's son was born sickly. He died not two weeks after his birth. Mademoiselle Foucauld did not come through the birth well and was quite ill for several months. Naturally, she did not have very much contact with her child during its short life, so," Darcy sighed very deeply, "she did not notice that a second child was substituted for her own. Before you accuse me of the basest of cruelties, Monsieur Foucauld, let me say that your sister, in the last months of her confinement, had changed. Dramatically changed. She focused on the child. She lived for it. She bathed, she forswore hard drink, her mood brightened. Truly, sir, when her baby died, her nurse and I both feared how she would react to the news. There was another child, another boy, born at almost the same time. It occurred to me that the child was in need of a mother, and the mother was in need of a child. At the time, it seemed fortuitous, even blessed."

Darcy leaned forward in his chair, his legs apart, rolling his glass of port between the palms of his two hands. "Your sister was a wonderful mother, Monsieur. Loving, patient, gentle, kind. Had she been that woman before…but she was not."

"As I said before you began this fairy tale, Monsieur Darcy, you are very clever."

"You think it a fairy tale, Monsieur Foucauld?"

"Did you not begin this day by admitting that you are a liar?"

"As you wish, Monsieur. I will continue the lie. If you bring the matter to a courtroom, I will claim Peter Bingley as my own. His resemblance to me is strong enough to sustain my claim. My wife has agreed to testify that I admitted it to her several years ago. Bingley will testify, truthfully, that I confessed my paternity of Peter to him. The courts will support my claim, Monsieur. Your claim will fail."

"Perhaps you will risk the scandal, Monsieur Darcy. Perhaps not. You will not succeed with a bluff, Monsieur."

Darcy pulled himself to his feet. "Foucauld! Have mercy! This boy is not your sister's. You will spatter mud across this child's entire life!"

"And yours too, Monsieur Darcy! Will it cost your sister a wealthy husband? Might it cost her every husband, do you think?"

"I had not thought you vicious, Foucauld. Angry, vengeful, relentless, yes. But I did not think you would do harm merely for the pleasure of it."

"You are a monster, Etienne. Who told you to kill my parents? Who told you that my life is worth four lives? How dare you make me live with this horror? How dare you live? I shall never forgive you. I shall never see you again."

Those were the last words Magdeleigne Foucauld had spoken to her brother. That was the last time he saw her. He finally did sit down in the chair Darcy had offered earlier. He reflected on the tragedy of his sister's life. Pampered as much as any princess, thrust into poverty by the Revolution, orphaned by a brother's devotion, discarded by her seducer, offered marriage by a man who wanted her child but not her. Her one friend was Darcy, and in the end, it was Darcy that hid from her the death of her own child and used her to foster another woman's baby. And now, she is grieved only by the monster she never forgave. Oh, yes. And a child that was not hers.

Foucauld jumped to his feet. "I do not believe this story! I do not believe that one child was substituted for another!"

"Then go to the nurse! You have hounded about Lambton for months, asking your questions and raking through the past. Ask her!"

"I have asked her several times, Monsieur. She remembers nothing. She says nothing. You have invested wisely in that one!"

"She is close-mouthed, yes, but she is also a Christian woman. Tell her that you know your nephew is dead, and you wish to visit his grave. That request, she cannot refuse. Then, you will know the truth."

Darcy sank into his chair again. What more could he say?

Foucauld studied his adversary for some time. "So, Pierre is not your child, nor is he the son of your cousin. Just who is this man, that you would betray your dearest friends and closest relations, and even ask your wife to do the same, to protect him from a scandal that he brought upon himself?"

Darcy bolted from the chair and took two steps toward Foucauld, their faces now inches apart. "Do you think I would debase myself for him? I damn him straight into hell!" Darcy stopped and breathed. "It is the mother."

"Until I know her name, I cannot judge whether you speak the truth." Foucauld folded his arms across his chest and waited.

Darcy looked out the window and shook his head, *"No."* He stole a sidelong glance at Foucauld. "I will tell you this much. She was convinced to elope and was married in Scotland, but the man was a base profiteer. He was bought off, and the marriage was annulled. It was not until months later that I learned of her condition. She was sent out of the country and bore the child in Europe. When I realized the opportunity of a substitution, the opportunity to keep the child close, I arranged the matter. Sir, she is in a position to marry and to know true happiness. I ask that you do not interfere, for to do so would damage many lives for the sake of one that is no longer salvageable."

For a significant period of time, Foucauld paced the room. Finally, he spoke. "Does Colonel Fitzwilliam know Pierre's true lineage?"

"No. He knows that his own son perished and that Peter is the child of another."

Foucauld pressed, asking his question one word at a time. "But he does not know the identity of Peter's mother?"

"No." Darcy heard it. Foucauld had called the boy "Peter." It was over.

After Foucauld had left, Darcy still wondered what the Frenchman had been thinking. Foucauld, on the other hand, found himself dwelling on a remark that Anne de Bourgh had made at their first acquaintance, about how much she enjoyed her visit to France – in Europe.

Eleven years ago.

CHAPTER THIRTY-SIX

Hydrangea

When Arabian Moonlight saw Darcy in his riding clothes, the little stallion came to the fence. As he saw his Friend's Favorite walk to the stableyard, Moonlight pranced prettily on his side of the rails, keeping pace and tossing his mane. Tom brought out a saddled and bridled Dark-of-the-Moon, for Darcy had determined he would not indulge Elizabeth's every whim, and he wanted her to know it. When Moonlight saw the Dark, Moonlight went wild, racing up and down, pounding the ground with his front hooves. But, when Darcy looked his way, Moonlight quieted. He came to the fence, stretched his neck, and nickered gently.

"He saw Mrs. Darcy leave, sir," said Tom. "Now he sees you're leaving. He thinks you're to join her, so he wants to go, too."

"Tom!" Darcy was aghast. "Do you really think that this horse is capable of reasoning? That he can make connections between me in my riding clothes today and Mrs. Darcy in a carriage yesterday? Do you really think that a horse can even remember yesterday?"

"Well, he remembers mistreatment, don't he? And that was years ago."

Darcy fumed. First, he was manipulated into this entire situation by his wife (*"Next time, dear wife, you can be the one to tell a long-time friend that he has been discarded."*), and now he was being dictated to by her horse! No! No! No!

"It is all of thirty kilometers, sir. And thirty kilometers back. The Dark will be completely spent, so you won't be able to ride him for the Ingersoll's fox hunt on Sunday. But that grey…sixty kilometers is nothing for him. And you wouldn't be riding him in the hunt, anyway."

Darcy was a realist. But he was still fuming. As he swung into the saddle, he told the little horse exactly what he thought of him. Silently, of course, because he would not want Tom to think that the master of Pemberley would actually talk to a horse, or expect a horse to understand what was being said to it. *"And I will teach you the lesson of your life, my lad. I will take you to Sheffield, and I will give you over to that mare, and you will discover what being at the mercy of a female with a mind of her own is all about!"*

As Moonlight trotted happily on his way to Sheffield, he passed two men lounging under a tree, just on the outskirts of Lambton. One nudged the other and said, "That's him. That's Darcy. Looks like he'll be gone a while. Now's the time!"

Fitzwilliam Darcy's true intention was to merely converse with Atherton Vinson, evaluate the mare, and perhaps come to an agreement on the fee and the dates that Vinson would bring his mare to Pemberley. A minimum of three days was the standard for a stud service. However, Vinson had a mare already in heat, and the stallion he planned for her had broken a leg.

Darcy led Moonlight into the paddock. Then, the mare was loosed. Her condition captured Moonlight's full attention, and he began to herd her around the pen. Darcy withdrew from the paddock and went into the stable, selected a mount, and left through the back entry of the barn. He would return in three days, with Moonlight none the wiser.

It was mid-afternoon before Darcy reached Rotherham. There were several inns in Rotherham, and it was the fourth innkeeper who confirmed the overnight stay of a Mrs. Darcy and a Mrs. Annesley. They had already gone on to Roderick Annesley's home, and the innkeeper provided directions. But the innkeeper had not known that Mr. Annesley had recently changed houses. It was nearly dinnertime before Darcy presented himself and asked for his wife.

Mrs. Annesley came back with the servant. "Mr. Darcy! Did you not receive Mrs. Darcy's message? Her sister Lydia needed transport to Manchester. Something about selling some of her drawings to pay down her husband's debts. Mrs. Darcy left this morning. Surely, she is half-way to Manchester by now!"

"What? Why…"

"I do not know all the details, but I had the impression that Mr. Wickham was in some kind of desperate circumstance, and his wife was quite distraught."

At this point, they were joined by Roderick Annesley, who said, "Your wife knows you were to meet her in Rotherham. No doubt she will send a message to you here or return here by nightfall. We are about to sit down for our meal, Mr. Darcy. Please join us."

"*Wickham.*" The meal could have been sawdust for all that Darcy tasted of it. Finally, the houseman brought in a letter.

"*Darcy,*

I am well. Lydia and I are traveling and visiting shops. I will return tomorrow evening.

Lizzie"

He stared at the letter. "Darcy," not "Fitzwilliam." "Lizzie," not "Elizabeth." No mention of Fitzgeorge! But it was Elizabeth's hand that wrote the letter, no doubt of that. *"Visiting shops? Is she joking?"*

"Is the boy still here?" Darcy asked the houseman. "Where did the letter post from?"

"The boy would not stay, sir. I do not know which direction he came from and did not see which direction he went. It was dark, and I was helping my wife in the kitchen."

Annesley would not hear of Darcy staying in town. Any message would come to the Annesley house, not an inn in Rotherham, and Darcy should have it at once. The next time a letter came, the houseman would be sure to hold the boy so that Darcy could question him. "But, hopefully," said Roderick Annesley, "our next visitor will be Mrs. Darcy, and we can all be at ease again."

CHAPTER THIRTY-SEVEN

Mock Orange

Georgiana Darcy stared at this second letter. The first letter had come less than an hour earlier. This letter had just now come. They both identified "Rotherham" in the sender's address. They were both in Elizabeth's hand. They were both addressed to Fitzwilliam, but Fitzwilliam was on his way to meet Elizabeth in Rotherham, so why would she send a letter to him at Pemberley? Stranger still, why *two* letters?

Georgiana wished Anne were here, so they could debate the meaning of two letters. But she and Anne had quarreled: Monsieur Foucauld had come to the house with Bingley, and voices were raised. Bingley had left in a black fury. Georgiana wanted Anne to catch Foucauld and find out what was happening, but Anne refused to even try to talk to the Frenchman. Now Fitzwilliam was gone to Rotherham, and Anne was gone to Lambton, and Georgiana was going mad with curiosity about two letters that were not addressed to her.

The butler approached.

"Miss Darcy? Tom wishes a word."

"With me? Are you certain?" Georgiana Darcy rarely went near the stables. What could the stablemaster possibly want with her?

Georgiana went to the front entry and saw a sheepish Tom, with his hat in his hands, and his head half-bowed, acting for all the world like he thought she would sic the hounds on him. So she smiled, addressed him by his name, and asked after his health. He answered, hunched his shoulders, and took a piece of paper from his hat.

"I don't understand what it means."

Georgiana read the paper and stopped smiling. "Why, Tom, this is a Bill of Sale. It says that…my brother has sold Arabian Moonlight!"

"Yes, Miss, I know it says that, but Mr. Darcy never said anything about selling Mrs. Darcy's horse. Mrs. Darcy never said anything about it. And these men say they are here to take him."

"Well, they cannot have him!" declared Georgiana.

"No, Miss, they can't. 'Cause he isn't here! It was Moonlight that Mr. Darcy rode to Rotherham today."

Georgiana tapped the piece of paper in her hands. 'Arabian' was spelled 'Arabyan.' It certainly was her brother's handwriting, but how could Fitzwilliam Darcy make such an error?

"What have you told these men? Do they know Darcy is not here? Do they know that Moonlight is not here?"

"I think they know both Mr. and Mrs. Darcy are not here, but I did not tell them anything about Moonlight. Well, they're demanding that I give him over, so…they must think he's here!"

Georgiana Darcy did not have a mind for puzzles. She never took up chess. She did not enjoy deciphering charades (or rather, she did not enjoy being exposed as a person unable to decipher charades). No – Georgiana's favored challenge was a brick wall. Years of living with one such as Fitzwilliam Darcy had allowed his much younger sister to develop a certain confidence when confronted by an unmoveable barrier: She had learned how to burrow beneath it, or scale it, or pull a few bricks loose and squeeze her way through it. But, no snarls, please – no myriad paths to some unknown destination. Just let her get to the other side of the wall, and be done.

So Georgiana considered for a moment, then addressed the butler. "I want the First Footman in this entryway and I want the Second Footman just outside this door. Tom, tell those men that Moonlight has been released to open pasture, and it may take days to find him and bring him in. Tell them you will send a boy into Lambton when you have the horse in hand."

"If they wish to help?"

"Thank them. And tell them 'No.' " Georgiana turned away, then turned back again. She waited.

It took a fair moment, but Tom realized she was waiting for an acknowledgement. He had received an order. From MISS Darcy! He bobbed his head.

Miss Darcy then gave her attention to the butler. He bowed his head, never once taking his eyes off of hers.

"Tom," she caught him just as he was on his way out the door, "when they are both well gone, bring up the Brougham, with two outriders. Also see that four men go into Lambton and trail Lady Anne's Barouche Box. Do not alarm her. But do ensure her safe passage home."

"Yes, Miss Darcy! Exactly as you say, Miss Darcy!"

Georgiana had it clear in her mind exactly what she must do. She went to the study to read both letters. The first letter was very short.

"*Joy-Jo,*

I am fine. My dear sister Lydia and I are enjoying all the sights of Manchester. We may visit Blackpool and visit Lady Catherine, your aunt. I have never enjoyed riding. I have asked Darcy to sell my horse.

Please visit the Wickham children. I am sure they miss their mother.

Lizzie"

Georgiana gasped. Had she read this letter, she would have let those men have Arabian Moonlight – had he been here. But why was her letter's envelope addressed to Darcy and not her? And, it mentioned the Wickham children, but not Peter. Nor Fitzgeorge! *"Really! Write a letter to one person and send it to another. This is so backwards, how could Elizabeth make such a mistake?"*

The second letter was also short.

"Dearest Fitzwilliam,
By now, I am certain you have been told about Lydia's upset. Someone has purchased all of Wickham's notes, and he is being threatened with Debtor's Prison. I have told her that you will not stand good for him this time. You have done enough, dear husband. Naturally, she is frantic and begs me to ride with her to Manchester. She has no one else. So, to Manchester I go. I am sending this letter to you at Pemberley, in the hope that I can prevent a fruitless journey to Rotherham.

Please read to Fitzgeorge and listen to his prayers and tell him I love him and will return as quickly as I can.

Always and All Ways,
Elizabeth"

Within less than an hour, Georgiana entered GanderGlen and asked for Bingley.

"Is Darcy with you?" Bingley asked, so coldly it would have sent a shiver through Georgiana had she noticed its tone.

"No. He is on his way to Rotherham. I need your help."

Bingley paused. Then his mind cleared, and he took her hands in his. "You may always call on me for help, Miss Darcy. Always."

"Today, two letters came to my brother from his wife. I opened them and read them both. I am deeply troubled."

"You opened letters…addressed to another?" Bingley was certain that he had not heard her correctly.

"They are both in her hand, but so different! The one was in an envelope addressed to my brother, but when I read it…the letter was for me! That is…she sent it to 'Joy-Jo' (only the children call me Aunt Joy-Jo), and it was signed 'Lizzie' (I have never addressed her as 'Lizzie,' my brother would have a fit!). One letter speaks as though Elizabeth and Lydia are on a lark, and the other reads as though there is deep cause for concern about Wickham's future. Here, read them yourself."

Bingley pushed the letters away. "I most certainly will not read a letter written by a wife to her husband!"

"Then at least read the letter that was meant for me!"

"If it was in an envelope addressed to her husband, then it was not meant for you!" Bingley sighed. "Miss Darcy, husbands and wives…little sisters are not told everything. This letter you think was intended for you – it is just some code that lovers share."

Georgiana stared at the letters that Bingley would not even look at.

Bingley could see her concern. "Listen to me. I know Lydia much better than you. She has decided that her sister needs a lark. So she has her on a goose-chase. Seriously, Miss Darcy! Why would you think that anything is wrong?"

"Two men came for Elizabeth's horse. Do you think Fitzwilliam would ever sell Moonlight?"

"To be honest, Miss Darcy," Bingley bristled, "there are many things that I thought I would never see from Fitzwilliam Darcy. The sale of a horse is nothing."

Georgiana stared again at the letters in her hands.

Bingley smiled at her paternalistically. "You are familiar with Mrs. Darcy's handwriting. Are both letters in the same hand? In her handwriting?"

"Yes."

"Well, there it is, is it not?" When he saw that she was still troubled, he postulated that, "if Mrs. Darcy was in a hurry, and she asked Lydia to mail her letter for her – well, then! Lydia sent it to the wrong person! I think we agree, that is something Lydia would do."

"Yes," Georgiana slowly agreed. "That is something Lydia would do. What remains as a mystery, though, is that both envelopes were addressed to Darcy, and both were written by Elizabeth. If Elizabeth were writing to me, would she not have addressed one of the envelopes to me? If Lydia addressed the envelope for her, would that envelope not be in Lydia's hand, instead of Elizabeth's?"

Bingley shrugged.

Georgiana returned to Pemberley with one hope remaining: Anne. Anne had a talent for devising and discerning plots. Anne would know instinctively what these letters were about! Georgiana did not care how unladylike it was, she bounded up the stairs and rushed into Anne's room without knocking. But Anne had returned to Pemberley in a foul mood and had called for a bath. When Georgiana asked to enter, entry was refused.

It was a defeated Georgiana Darcy who read and re-read the letters ten more times, and then went to her music room, where she sat in her Grandfather's chair and listened to music that used to be there, but would never return.

CHAPTER THIRTY-EIGHT

Fleur-de-Lis

Early this morning, Lady Anne de Bourgh had quarreled with Miss Georgiana Darcy about Etienne Foucauld, so Lady Anne was alone in Lambton, going through shops by herself. Lady Anne had decided to address her trousseau, so she was in the best milliner's shop in Lambton. Nothing would do. Not the hats, not the scarves, not the muffs, not the gloves, not the groom. Grooming brushes! She was thinking of clothing brooms! The wrong Broom! Not the wrong Groom!

She picked up a pair of yellow kid gloves. She inspected the color: There were no variations. She inspected the leather: Supple and blemish-free. She tried them on: The fit was perfect. She tossed them back onto the table with unconcealed disgust. The shopclerk hurried to her side, horrified that she may have found a flaw in his merchandise. She was trying to think of some way to explain her show of temperament when they both heard the shouts of "Fire!" The clerk looked from the door to Lady Anne, then back to the door, then back to Lady Anne...clearly, he needed direction from his most distinguished customer.

"Well, go on man! They need your help!" she commanded.

He nodded eagerly and tossed his coat onto a table of neatly folded scarves and lace handkerchiefs as he ran out the door. Anne de Bourgh swept after him.

Smoke was pouring out of the Fleur-de-Lis Tea Room. The customers were all out of the building – someone spoke of a candle that flared and set fire to someone's sleeve, which came into contact with a curtain, then raced across a trail of smeared butter on a countertop...Anne stopped listening. The building was ablaze. Its second floor was living quarters, and above the shouts in the crowd, Anne heard the screams of terrified children.

The crowd was one single body, and it did not move. Men had formed a line and were passing buckets of water, but no one, Anne included, moved to enter the burning building. But then, one man did. Anne's heart stopped when she recognized the flash of red. Then she started to push her way through the crowd. She had to turn and pry her way past each rooted pair of legs in her path. She was almost at the front when she saw him emerge, a child under each arm. Only then did an old woman and an old man rush forward to take the boys. Even at the distance from the fire where Anne stood, she could feel the intense heat. She was glad the children were safe, but her profound relief was the product of knowing *he* was safe. Once loose of the children, though, he turned back toward the tea room.

"NO!" Anne pushed and twisted, but the crowd had closed around her. He took off his red garment, shoved it into a bucket of water, and then threw it over his head as he ran back into the eager flames.

Just then a man shoved her out of his way and sent several of the unmoveables sprawling. He ran to the building and started to enter, but he was stopped and his arms were pinned by the man exiting. There was the sound of a woman's scream, and then the only sound was of the hiss when water turns to steam and the flames themselves give up their fight.

His arms no longer pinned, the rough stranger roared with fury and pummeled the man who stopped him from rescuing his wife. The man in red did not strike back but merely blocked the blows as the men and women in the crowd gathered around and urged their neighbor to look to his children.

Anne dipped her favorite Irish lace handkerchief into one of the buckets as she passed and knelt down next to a thoroughly exhausted Etienne Foucauld. She wiped the soot from his face, careful not to disturb the ever-alert twisted ends of his finely waxed mustache. As she did so, her mind filled with the sensation of how those pointed tips pricked her upper lip the last time…the only time…he kissed her. She willed herself to think of something else.

"You thought you did it for your sister, then you thought you did it only for yourself. Now, you know the truth." She lowered her head and nodded toward the grieving husband and his two boys. "You did it for them."

"I do not even know them, Mademoiselle."

"Listen to me, Etienne. There were only two men that were willing to enter that building. The children's father…and you. He came too late. If you had not been here…if you had not lived so that you *could* be here…the children would have died, and their father would have died trying to save them."

"Three lives, Mademoiselle." Foucauld refused to be consoled. "I took four."

"Your calculation is flawed, Monsieur. You are not counting their children and their children's children. You have no way of knowing how many you saved. Today they indulge their grief, but tomorrow they will thank you."

Foucauld stood up and helped Anne to her feet. "Let us hope their gratitude comes early in the day, Mademoiselle, for I take the noon coach to Kingston-upon-Hull. I return to France." As he spoke, he searched her face for a resemblance to Peter Bingley. He thought he saw it, just a bit, around the mouth. She would not go with him to France, no matter what persuasion he used. She would never leave her child.

Anne hesitated. Then… "Good-bye, Monsieur."

"No, Mademoiselle. My brain understands English, but my heart speaks only French. You must say 'Au Revoir' as the French do, or my heart will not understand that it will never see you again. It will always think of you. It will always hope."

They parted politely, with him pretending that he had not slipped her handkerchief into his pocket, and her pretending that she had not noticed it missing.

That evening, Georgiana tried several times to interest her dearest friend in a variety of subjects: Art, music, dance, fashion, gossip, cards. Anne's preoccupations would deaden the entire evening if she were not roused from them. Colonel Fitzwilliam, too, tried to encourage interest, but he also failed to wrest her attention from the fireplace and the licking flames that burned within.

So, there was an unnatural silence at dinner. That is until Charles Bingley arrived. A rare jewel of the perfect cut, he caught what light there was and shimmered in their gloom. His smile lifted the Colonel's spirit, his wink comforted Anne, and his voice had the same effect as music to Miss Darcy's ear.

"I have come to share some news with you all! Some of it is good news, excellent news! But some of it is very sad. Where is Darcy?" he asked.

The Colonel replied that Darcy had gone to Rotherham to collect his wife and bring her back to Pemberley. "Did he not stop at GanderGlen?" the Colonel asked.

"Yes, he stopped. But we did not…speak." They did not speak because Bingley had refused to see him. Darcy had left a note.

"Charles,

Peter is safe. I had to separate you from Foucauld. The man is determined to stab somebody with that foolish blade. He blames himself for his sister's death and much more. He wants to die. I did not want you to be the one who kills him.

I am your friend, as you are mine.

Fitzwilliam"

Charles Bingley wanted to settle with Darcy and tell him off. Darcy's absence was an annoyance because, frankly, Bingley never could maintain animus toward anyone, and it was even now dripping away from him. By the time Darcy returned, Bingley admitted to himself, *"I will be the one apologizing!"* Oh well. He was not angry with any of the gathering before him, so, "Well, which news first? Sad or merry?"

"I have had enough of sad news, Bingley," answered the Colonel. "Let us be merry!"

"You are very wise, Fitzwilliam! I have a letter from my Cousin Ambrose."

Bingley had captured Georgiana's full attention.

"You know he planned to return to Cornwall via Liverpool. But he never reached Liverpool! He encountered an acquaintance when he neared Manchester, and she…" *[Georgiana caught her breath, then hoped no one had noticed]* "…knew of a place that required a pianist, so he is still in Manchester! Well, he had some of Lydia Wickham's drawings in his own sketchbook, and a pamphleteer in Manchester purchased them! Can you imagine? Is that not the most wonderful news?"

"Yes, it is," remarked Anne, "unless her husband's creditors hear of it."

Georgiana nudged Anne's elbow. "That is excellent news, Mr. Bingley," said Georgiana. "Pray, does he write more?"

"Oh, he prattles endlessly," laughed Bingley. "But he cross-writes to save paper and postage, as though I would begrudge a shilling for an understandable letter." He gave the precious missive to Georgiana, so she could make it out at her own pace.

She immediately retired to the periphery, to give her full attention to Mr. Terwilliger's words and, particularly, to find if there was a clue to who this "she" might be.

Because the recipient of a letter was required to pay its postage rate, and because the rate depended on the number of pages sent, it was common practice for a sender to write on only one side of a sheet of paper, fold it with the writing inside, and use the blank side of the paper for the address. In order to put as much information as possible onto a single side of a single page, Ambrose had cross-wrote, that is, he wrote in very small and tightly packed script in black ink, filling the entire page. Then, he turned the page on its side and wrote perpendicularly in blue ink, across the already-written words. Thus, two pages of writing on one side of one page. Very clever, but Oh! So difficult to read!

Georgiana struggled with what was written. Mr. Terwilliger's handwriting was elegant, almost artistic, which was very pleasing but at the same time complicated the process of interpretation. The first part spoke of the urgent need for additional of Mrs. Wickham's sketches. The next part described his current occupation as a musician. The part after that mentioned that he had encountered a Widow Buxton, formerly of Lambton and familiar with Pemberley, who had found work as a housekeeper and governess at a local inn. Georgiana smiled with relief: Hannah Hill was the "she" and her condition made a romantic attachment most unlikely.

The letter closed with a single sentence:

"Please convey my thanks to Mrs. Bingley, and please tell Peter, Ernestine, Evelyn, and Emma, and Little Fitz, that I **Miss Darbyshire very much and think of them often."**

"It is not 'Darbyshire' (although that is how it is pronounced), it is 'Derbyshire,' " thought Georgiana as tears welled in her eyes. "And 'Fits' with an 'S,' not a 'Z.' He never really understood anything." His letter did not even mention her, did not ask about her, offered not one sentence meant for her. She gave the letter back to Bingley, shielding her eyes, and trying to hide her disappointment. But Bingley saw her tears and put his arms around her and tucked her close, and his kindness broke her down. She buried her face in his shoulder and sobbed.

Bingley was contrite. "Miss Darcy, I did not realize that you would be so moved by the Collins' loss. I should have been more careful in how I conveyed the sad news. Will you forgive me?"

"I will take her, Mr. Bingley," said Anne, who herself seemed quite shaken.

Colonel Fitzwilliam said nothing, but he swallowed several times.

Bingley stole more than one glance at Anne, trying to gauge her temperament. He scolded himself for not insisting that Jane join him in his visit, particularly since both of the ladies seemed so upset.

Finally, Anne spoke. "If you are going to write to Sir William Lucas, will you please enclose my heartfelt condolences on his loss? I will write directly to Mrs. Collins."

Georgiana now realized that there was something she had not heard and looked questioningly at her cousin. Anne, who was the only person in the room who knew that Georgiana was weeping over a love letter that never came, was tasked with re-conveying the news without arousing the suspicions of the others.

So, Anne chattered on like a demented squirrel (or like the dotty old maid she was on her way to becoming). "Such a shock, for Charlotte Collins to lose her husband in the very prime of his life. He was tending his honeycombs, you say? And stung to death? How sad." Anne did not look at her fiancé, who was now alternating deep breaths with his swallowing.

Georgiana looked at her dearest friend. Mr. Collins, dead? Mrs. Collins, free? She started to turn toward Colonel Fitzwilliam because she wanted assurance that his promise was firm, and Anne's happiness was not in jeopardy. But Anne's fingernails dug into the palm of Georgiana's hand and kept her attention on Anne alone. It was bad enough that Bingley kept looking at him – having the entire party stare at the Colonel, as he digested the impact of Mrs. Collins' widowhood, was not what Anne wanted. Now, it was Georgiana's duty to protect Anne's private thoughts and public dignity.

Georgiana asked Mr. Bingley if he intended to send Mrs. Wickham's art to Manchester. He replied that he would take her portfolio himself, leaving on the morrow.

Finally, Anne was certain she could rely on her voice to remain steady. "Colonel Fitzwilliam? Mr. Bingley? Georgiana is very tired."

"Yes, very tired," echoed Georgiana on cue.

"We will retire. Will you excuse our poor company this evening?"

The proper assurances were made, and the ladies went to their rooms. Actually, they went to Georgiana's suite, where they spent upwards of an hour discussing Mr. Collins and Mrs. Collins and Colonel Fitzwilliam and Anne's engagement.

"Must you allow him to withdraw his offer, Anne?"

"Silly child! If he wishes to withdraw it, he will do so whether I give him leave or not!"

Georgiana pouted. Anne's happiness was the one island of respite in the ocean of misery that had become Georgiana's life. That one last toehold was dissolving beneath her feet, and there was nothing left but tears. She was surrounded by tears and was sure to drown.

Anne had been lost in thoughts of her own, but when she caught the expression on Georgiana's face, Anne laughed. Not a merry laugh, but a laugh that betrayed an odd mix of both resignation and bewilderment. "When we are beset with the workings of a devil, we take solace in the knowledge that we can pray to the angels for assistance. But, Georgiana!" Anne's mood suddenly lightened, and now her laugh betrayed her exasperation with fate's frustration of her long-cherished plans. "To whom do we pray to when the angels themselves are engaging in the deviltry? When you are given no choice but your fondest wish, what then?"

Anne went to the door, turned, and said, "Colonel Fitzwilliam will not withdraw his offer, Georgiana. It would disappoint his family. He has never learned that family forgives." And with that, she was gone.

Downstairs, Fitzwilliam ignored the decanters of port and sherry and, instead, offered to share his flask of whiskey with Charles Bingley.

"What will you do?" asked a warmer and more awake Bingley.

"What I have always done," sulked Fitzwilliam, drawing again and once again until his flask was empty. "The easy, expected, stupid thing. When have you ever known me to do anything else?"

CHAPTER THIRTY-NINE

Iris

Now alone in Darcy's library, Colonel Fitzwilliam told the butler to bring him whiskey. The butler brought in a single glass, not quite full.

"Bring the bottle. Two bottles. And close the door."

The drapes were pulled, so he did not realize that dawn had come until he heard the cocks crowing in the distance. He climbed the stairs, found his room, and fell across his neatly made bed, fully clothed and still wearing his boots. When he awoke, he shrugged off the effects of alcohol, stood up, and splashed water on his face. By habit, he surveyed his surroundings. "*Oh, yes, this is Pemberley. Yesterday I returned from Hunsford, where I put up the banns announcing that Anne de Bourgh will marry me. In three weeks, I will be her husband.*" And then, Colonel Fitzwilliam did put his head in his hands and did curse the sun, the moon, and everything else. There was absolutely no possible way that he could escape marriage to Lady Anne.

He must have stared at the envelope that had been pushed under his door for several minutes, at least, before he realized what it was. His name was on the envelope, written on his fiancée's stationery in his fiancée's own hand. How long had it been there? Was it there before he even came upstairs? There was no way of knowing. He did not want to touch it. He knew it had to be some kind of love letter.

In fact, it was.

"Dearest Fitzwilliam,

Please forgive me for any hurt this letter may cause you. I have decided against a marriage that would unite us in a lifetime of tepid routine. Because I know that we have a sympathy for each other, which may be akin to love, I will confide in you the whole of the truth. I am passionately in love with Etienne Foucauld. He goes to France, and I shall follow him. He has asked me to be his wife, and perhaps that event will occur. Perhaps, it will not. I do not care.

This night, for several hours, I sat watching the fire in the fireplace. It was a careful, contained flame. I compared it to the conflagration in Lambton yesterday. One thing tame, the other wild.

I find that I prefer the wild.

I imagine, Fitzwilliam, that every time I see a candle flicker, I shall think of you and the marriage we might have had. Try to understand that because I know that there is not enough warmth in a candle to keep me content, I cannot believe that there would have been enough for you. I would rather you curse me today for my inconstancy, than curse me forever for my fidelity.

I am certain that it will not be long before you are grateful for this letter. That is, if you are not already grateful for it.

I leave you now with the same amount of love that I have always had for you.

Anne de Bourgh"

Colonel Fitzwilliam read the letter twice. Then, he read it a third time. He folded it and put it in his pocket. He resolved to go to the seaside and acquaint Lady Catherine with the situation, and then follow her instructions. Of course, he already knew what her instructions would be: To locate Anne, annul the marriage (if one had occurred), run off the fortune-hunter, and return Anne to Rosings. But, the more time Anne spent with this lubricious Frenchman, the less eager she would be to leave him. Fitzwilliam knew that he must act quickly or lose her forever.

As Colonel Fitzwilliam sat down to a leisurely dinner (for he had slept through most of the daylight hours), he contemplated the wonder of Anne de Bourgh. She was wealthy and titled and landed, but he had known all of that for years. Only today had he learned of her capacity for passion, a side of her that was willing – no, eager! – to embrace carnal pleasures. "How I would have wasted her!" he chastised himself. For a few minutes, all he thought of was Anne (not Lady Anne, not Cousin Anne, and not Anne de Bourgh, just — Anne), and how much he desired her.

He was halfway through his meal before he thought to ask where Miss Darcy might be. The servant replied that Miss Darcy had gone into Lambton for the day. With the discretion born of years of domestic service, the long-time retainer did not say that Lady Anne had roused the Second Footman in the middle of the night (to fetch the Brougham and a driver so that she might go into Lambton without companion or chaperone), nor did he mention that Lady Anne had not yet returned to Pemberley. Although the servant's first impression was that Lady Anne's behavior was capricious at its best and disgraceful at its worst, the servant could not help but note that while Colonel Fitzwilliam *did* ask about Miss Darcy, he made no inquiry whatsoever concerning the whereabouts of his fiancée.

The Colonel buttered his bread, attacked his venison joint, and devoured the potatoes and rocket. He steeled himself for the clucking sympathy that would be coming his way. His thoughts wandered again to the garden at Bingley's house and a stolen kiss and the mistress of Longbourne – a wealthy, well-born, proper English widow. His thoughts had found their true home and would not wander again. "A year. She must wear black crepe for six months, then black and white for six months more. Perhaps less, if her family specifies a shorter mourning period. I could secure a post in Hertfordshire, near Longbourne. Mrs. Darcy might be prevailed upon to visit Mrs. Collins, and then I could visit Mrs. Darcy while she was visiting Longbourne and renew my acquaintance with Widow Collins in the most decorous and innocent..."

He heard a high-pitched, furious, uncompromising voice coming from the hall entryway and knew that there would be no need for him to go to Blackpool.

"What do you mean, she is not in the house?"

Mumble, mumble, mumble, replied the terrified housemaid.

"Where is she?"

Whimper, whimper, whimper, begged the poor young thing.

"Where is my nephew?"

"Mr. Darcy has gone to Rotherham, Lady Catherine," interjected the butler, shooing the cringing housemaid away. "Colonel Fitzwilliam..."

"Has just finished his breakfast, Aunt."

Lady Catherine could not keep herself from glancing at the lowering sun, but nothing in her expression disclosed her pious disapproval of her nephew's schedule.

"I am glad you have come, for I have much to tell you," he cautiously began.

"I know! I received Anne's letter yesterday, and I have ridden all the day. Remind me to obtain more comfortable cushions for my coach. Fitzwilliam, my son! I have waited much too long to call you that! I am overjoyed. But where is Anne?"

"Aunt..."

"Mother!"

"Yyyessssss...Perhaps we should go into the library. Yes, that would be best. I have so much to share. And you have so much to learn."

Lady Catherine studied his face. She stiffened her back. She led him into the library, and she shut the door.

He tried to explain it, but she did not want explanations, she wanted facts. When he had imparted the details (all of them, including Lydia's artwork, the turning-out of Coxcroft, and the loss of Mr. Collins) and handed over Anne's letter and answered all her pointed questions, Lady Catherine was neither happy nor sad. She was business-like. "Anne has always loved all things French. Why, I cannot imagine. They eat snails, for heaven's sake." She spoke in an appealing voice to her nephew. "When you think of a table piled with succulent food, you imagine a roasted goose, do you not? Potatoes? A pig with an apple in its mouth, yes? Who envisions a heaping plate of dead frogs?"

The Colonel opened his mouth, but no words came out.

"The French do! And octopus! They eat that, too!"

The Colonel dutifully shuddered.

"And their gardens! Straight lines everywhere. How can chaperoned young lovers round a curve and steal a kiss in such a place?"

The Colonel dutifully shrugged.

"Well." Aunt Catherine threw back her shoulders, raised her chin, and finally asked the only question that mattered to her. "Is he good enough for her?"

"No," replied the Colonel. "But he is better than I."

Lady Catherine de Bourgh sighed. There had been so many second sons from distinguished families. A few were eldest sons of titled, but impoverished, lines. She had hoped the Baron would take an interest, but no. Rosings was getting a Frog.

"If I leave today for Gretna Green..." ventured Colonel Fitzwilliam, carefully.

"Why would you go there?"

"Why? Why, to investigate the marriage, to provide guidance to Anne, to assure that her interests are protected."

"Do not be stupid, Fitzwilliam. Why would he take a grown woman, above thirty years in age, to Scotland? She is old enough to marry, with or without parental approval. He plans to return to France, does he not? What port has ships bound for France?"

"Surely he will not take her out of England unmarried!" Fitzwilliam paused. *"No. He would put himself on his own sword before he did that. Not after the way his sister was treated."* Aloud, he said, "I am certain, Aunt, positively certain that he will marry Anne before they sail. Since the banns must be posted for three Sundays together..."

"Did you not understand her letter? She will not wait three days, let alone three weeks! If they are not already married, it is because Anne decided that consummation should take precedence over ceremony. Let us hope so because that would afford us more time to intercept them."

The Colonel swallowed air. What had his aunt said? Did she really suggest that Anne would...sacrifice her virtue?

Lady Catherine heard his gasp and stared at him. "Did you not even read her letter? What did you think she meant when she said, 'Perhaps marry, perhaps not. I do not care.'?"

"But, then they must go to Gretna Green, where the banns are not required, so they can be married immediately!"

"Fitzwilliam, you have known my daughter all of her life. When has she ever proceeded without a plan? The banns are not required when one obtains a Special License!"

"A Special License must be purchased from the Bishop of Canterbury, outside London. Three full days in a hot, dusty, uncomfortable coach. Do you think Anne would do that?" asked Fitzwilliam, already knowing the answer.

"No. But, at last, you are thinking!" Lady Catherine sorted through the possibilities. "She could get a Common License."

"Then, they must go to the church she regularly attends. They must go to Hunsford."

"Has she not been attending church while at Pemberley? Is there not a church in Lambton?"

"Yes, but I...I have not...," the Colonel coughed, self-consciously.

"Georgiana knows where it is and, undoubtedly, knows the Rector by sight and by name," Lady Catherine huffed, peering at her nephew disapprovingly. "Where is the girl? Why has she not come to greet me?" She went to the door, opened it, and accosted a servant who just happened to be dusting a table in the hallway very nearby. She closed the door and returned, now speaking at a volume akin to a mere whisper. "Georgiana rode one of the horses into town just before the noon-hour and took a second horse with her. She returned to Pemberley in the Brougham – the same carriage my daughter took into Lambton after dark last night – but stopped only long enough to tell the servant that she intended to visit a friend and will not return until the morrow."

"How odd," said Fitzwilliam. "Miss Darcy finds so little pleasure in riding horseback."

"Idiot!" shouted his aunt, no longer concerned about being overheard. "She helped them obtain the license! She witnessed the marriage! She brought them two fast horses from Darcy's stable! They have already fled! On horseback! They can travel much faster than we can because they can leave the road and cut across open land. We will be in my carriage, so we must stay on the road. How will we overtake them? How can we find them? We do not even know which port is their destination."

"But, surely Miss Darcy knows where they have gone!"

"Yes, and surely Miss Darcy will not tell us where that is!" Lady Catherine de Bourgh took several deep breaths. "I have no doubt that Anne coerced a promise of secrecy from Georgiana. My niece took one look at my carriage, knew I was here, and she herself fled! We are better served by using our own knowledge of Anne's thought processes, than by trying to locate and elicit information from Georgiana Darcy, the little traitor. Might they have gone to Liverpool on the west coast? No, that would be the long way around to France. Dover, to the south? Calais is just across the channel from Dover."

"Dover is further south than either London or Canterbury. We have already agreed that Anne would not go to London by a public carriage, so by that reasoning we must also surmise that her destination cannot be Dover."

Inspiration came. "Hull," said the mother.

As Lady Catherine refreshed herself and dined, the Colonel ordered her carriage's four horses changed out, depleted the kitchen's remaining supply of picnic viands, and prevailed upon two of Darcy's stableboys to be drivers. The horses could be turned at any stable along the way, tired for fresh, but the drivers would have to stay with the carriage and spell each other throughout, so the two-day journey from Pemberley to the coast facing Holland could be reduced to an uninterrupted trek of a single day.

Fitzwilliam had been mulling things over, and when Lady Catherine appeared and was ready to commence the trip, he said, "Aunt, she knows you to be in Blackpool, just a few kilometers north of Liverpool. She does not know that you have come to Pemberley. Do you not think it likely that she will go to Blackpool to secure your blessing, with the intention of ultimately departing from Liverpool?"

"That is what you would do, is it not, Nephew?"

"Yes!"

"And if your family voiced its concerns, you would delay your plans until you had secured full approval, would you not?"

"Well, yes, of course!"

"Anne is not so foolish. There is always some flaw in a potential match: Too old, too short, too loud, poor grammar, bad penmanship – always, something! She will give me no opening to impede her marriage or force an annulment. I have indulged my dislike of the French too freely. If she leaves England believing I am against her marriage to a Gallic husband, I may never see her again. She must see my face. She must hear my voice as I give her my blessing. A letter will not do. My only opportunity to keep my child in my life will come before she sails." Lady Catherine saw that Fitzwilliam was looking a bit abashed. "Now, Nephew, you are not going to be peevish about this marriage, are you?"

Colonel Fitzwilliam fought mightily to conceal his delight. He soberly averred that he had accepted his Cousin's decision.

"No doubt, Mrs. Collins will be equally heartbroken," observed Lady Catherine, as she permitted the First Footman to assist her into the coach.

Fitzwilliam searched the skies for the name of one person in his acquaintance who might not know every snippet of his business.

"Stop that!" ordered his Aunt. "Get in the carriage! You will have the luxury of months to resolve any complications that may present themselves in your relationship, Fitzwilliam. I have mere hours!"

CHAPTER FORTY

Pennyroyal

Georgiana Darcy had told the driver to stop at the side of the road and to alert her if he saw anyone approach. She had Anne's letter in her hand, but she had not yet removed it from its envelope. The letter would explain everything, Anne had said. But Georgiana was not sure she wanted to know the reason for all of this. Georgiana had no gift for intrigue. She lost patience with deception much too easily. She imagined being questioned by her imperious Aunt, or cajoled by a concerned Elizabeth, or commanded by her virtuous brother, and she saw herself throw her hands in the air and tell them the entire truth. And that would not do.

Georgiana's day had begun when she was awakened by a maid. Lady Anne had left in the middle of the night, Georgiana learned, and had given the maid instructions to deliver a sealed written message to Georgiana no later than mid-morning.

"*My Dearest Cousin,*

I have made a decision of which you will not approve. In fact, you may find this decision so distasteful that you will withdraw your friendship and refuse to acknowledge that I am your kinswoman. If you can imagine that such a thing could happen, that we could be parted as less than intimate friends, then I call upon our past loyalties and bid you to destroy this letter now and not read another word."

Often, Georgiana had voiced gratitude for Anne's unwavering loyalty, her discretion, her sympathy, her guidance and, most of all, her refusal to tolerate self-pity. Now, Georgiana knew, mere words of gratitude carried no value. Acts of gratitude were to be this day's requirement.

She inhaled deeply, and read on.

"*Thank you, my dear one. I have released Colonel Fitzwilliam. I have gone to Etienne Foucauld. Mother will be in a mad fury when she learns of this – she despises the French. You know better than I how your brother and his wife will react.*

I ask you to bring two saddled and provisioned horses to the livery stable at Lambton. Have them there just before the noon-hour. Also, bring me all of the money you can spare. The horses will not return to Pemberley. I do not know when the money will be repaid. Come alone. Tell no one.

If, after reading this, you cannot give me your help, I ask only that you destroy this letter and say nothing of it to anyone.

Forgive me if I have asked too much.

Anne"

Georgiana took a very deep breath, put the letter in the fireplace, and burned it.

She then sent the maid to the cook for "two picnic baskets of food, but securely wrapped in packages, not in baskets." She dressed, collected the packaged food, and went directly to the stable. Her "request" for two saddled horses was fulfilled, of course, but not without several polite requests for clarification and confirmation.

When Georgiana arrived in Lambton, she saw Anne waiting. With Foucauld. Georgiana embraced her cousin and whispered, "Are you sure?"

Anne's reply was, "Certain."

The Rector was clearly relieved to see Miss Darcy (for her presence signaled the whole-hearted approval of his patron, Mr. Darcy, which made the Rector's cooperation not merely acceptable, but mandatory).

The vows were spoken and the wedding recorded in less than five minutes, from the time of entry to the church to the leaving of it. Ah, yes…the leaving of it. That was when things became…odd.

The moment that Foucauld's boots left the church steps and touched the cobblestones, he turned on Anne and sneered, "Little fool! Who would want one such as you? I married you for your fortune, and now it is mine! I go now to the bed of another and will celebrate this marriage with her. And what can you do about it? Nothing! In France, a woman can divorce a man. But not in England! In England, only a man can sue for divorce. You may keep your virtue, Lady Anne de Bourgh. I shall take everything else." And then he strode away.

Georgiana's jaw dropped. Anne collapsed into the arms of the mortified Rector.

"Boo hoo hoo," she cried, dabbing at her eyes with a dry handkerchief. Then, over the Rector's shoulder, she made a face at a bewildered Georgiana Darcy, who understood that she was supposed to…um, something.

"Uh…the cad?" Georgiana stared at Anne and almost imperceptibly shrugged her shoulders, hoping for a clue.

Anne sniffed and gave her cousin a look that told Georgiana that she had better get more involved, and quickly.

"Anne!" Georgiana took her cousin into her arms. "Do not cry! He is not worthy of your tears!" Then, she lowered her voice to a whisper and said into Anne's ear, "Give me a hint."

"What...what...what did he say?" Anne sniveled, in a way that might have been truly convincing had it not been accompanied by so much throat-catching.

"He said..." Georgiana began, her mind racing, as she tried to remember. *"What did he say?"*

Ah, but those devilish angels must have been listening in, for the Rector was moved to speak! "He said that he married only to seize control of your money! Then he spoke of, of, of...adultery! It is a blasphemy on The Lord's House!"

"Yes!" Georgiana agreed. "And he left before...before..."

"Yes!" shouted the Rector. "He is a fool! He is a fraud! And he is a FROG! He does not know that in England he must consummate the marriage for it to be valid!"

"Oh!" said Anne. "What does that mean, Georgiana?" Anne eyed her cousin meaningfully and saw the light finally dawn.

"It means, dear Cousin, that you do not need a divorce to upset his evil plan!" Georgiana piped buoyantly. "You have grounds for an annulment!"

The Rector raised his arms in triumph, almost jumping in the air. "Yes! Yes! I am your witness! I will write to the Bishop!"

Anne looked alarmed. "No! No! Not the Bishop!" Then Anne leaned toward her cousin and repeated through clenched teeth, "NotTheBishop!"

"No," said Georgiana. "That would...take too long. I think. Not the Bishop?"

"Yes," nodded Anne. "Too long. Is there not another way? Someone we could...SOLICIT...for advice?"

"We could see a solicitor," Georgiana parroted. Turning to the Rector, she added, "For advice!"

And that is what they did. The Rector accompanied the distraught ladies to the office of Harold Humphrey Kirkpatrick, Esquire, and he somberly prepared the paperwork needed to propel the petition of annulment through the court (not the Church). Anne's desire to leave Derbyshire forever and return immediately to the safe haven of her own home in the shire of Kent would not delay the decree. The kindly Kirkpatrick would deliver the Certificate of Annulment to Miss Darcy himself, and Miss Darcy could convey the document to Lady Anne discreetly. The Rector and the solicitor volunteered oaths of absolute secrecy. They vowed that no one in Hunsford would ever learn of the marriage, the despicable behavior of the Frog, or the swift annulment.

Once they were alone in the privacy of the Brougham, Georgiana turned to her cousin eagerly and began to ask one of the dozens of questions that were tumbling through her brain. But, Anne shook her head and pointed at the carriage roof: She did not want to be overheard by the driver. When Anne instructed the driver to go north towards Rotherham, instead of west towards Pemberley, Georgiana made no comment. When Anne told the driver to stop at the edge of town, Georgiana said nothing. And when Anne dismounted from the Brougham and ran to the arms of the laughing Etienne Foucauld, Georgiana was not surprised. When the Frenchman lifted her cousin off her feet and spun her around, Georgiana looked away. Oh. Of course. There were the two horses, tethered to a larch tree. When Georgiana looked back, Anne was in Foucauld's arms, kissing him with a passion that made Georgiana blush. And tingle.

"Anne! Try to remember that you are frail and weak," called Georgiana with a stage-whisper that could have been heard in the farthest row of the highest balcony in London.

Anne and Etienne both approached the Brougham, arms entwined. It was quite clear that they were as far from estrangement as Georgiana was from comprehension. Anne withdrew an envelope from her purse and handed it to Georgiana through the window.

"Oh, good. Another letter." Georgiana rolled her eyes.

Anne laughed. "It explains everything. You will want to read it before you speak to Colonel Fitzwilliam or your brother or…Mother."

"You mean Aunt Catherine? Oh, she will not return until…"

"I would be very surprised if she is not at Pemberley before the day is out. And not surprised at all if she is waiting for you there, right now. I am certain she ended her stay at Blackpool the moment she learned of my engagement to Colonel Fitzwilliam."

Then, they said, "Goodbye," and they were gone.

So, now, Georgiana was in the Brougham, stopped on the road to Pemberley, contemplating a sealed letter.

Finally, she was hungry enough (for she had not eaten breakfast and had not eaten lunch) to open it, read it, and eat it. Although, she hoped that last would not be necessary.

"Dear Dear Dear Georgiana,

Thank you.

By the time you read this, all will have been accomplished, and you are aware of what happened, but undoubtedly puzzled by why it all transpired as it did.

I love you as a sister, Georgiana, so I hide nothing and will confide the entire truth.

As you know, English law will confer control of all that I possess (my fortune) and all I might inherit (Rosings) on any man that I marry – but, only if that man is an Englishman. Etienne is a Frenchman. By marrying him, I would (by law) be divested of my own

British citizenship and my title and become a French commoner. As a Frenchwoman, I could not inherit Rosings. The stewardship of Hunsford has been the responsibility of my family for dozens of generations, and one day that duty will rest on me – but only if I am a British citizen. Knowing this, I accepted Colonel Fitzwilliam's offer, in spite of the fact that I was deeply in love with Etienne, even then. I convinced myself that I was nobly sacrificing my own happiness in service to my ancestors.

The night Mr. Bingley brought news of Mr. Collins' untimely death, I realized the full measure of my own errors by observing our Cousin Fitzwilliam's reaction to the news that the love of his life was free and able to marry him. Never have I seen such a complete ass! He would have married *me*!

I went to Etienne. He accepted my love with an enthusiasm that I would find embarrassing to relate in detail. But then. Apparently, Etienne had convinced himself that I had given birth to a child, so he assumed that he would not be my first lover. Well, of course, he was! Upon realizing that fact, he compared his own behavior to that of the villain that debased his sister. I reminded him that it was I who knocked on his door, and it was I who insisted there be no delay, and finally, I reminded him that I was not a child but an adult. Still, he felt that he had compromised my reputation, and he was ashamed.

And so, Georgiana, we come to the heart of it. There had to be a marriage, to satisfy Etienne's honor. And there had to be no marriage, to satisfy mine.

It came to me that if we married, then divorced, I might re-secure my British citizenship. But there were so many pitfalls! Marry in England and divorce in England? I knew without asking that Etienne would never sully my reputation with an accusation of adultery. Marry in England and divorce in France? Would an English court recognize a foreign divorce of an English marriage? Marry in France and divorce in France? Would the marriage and divorce of two French citizens arouse any sympathy at all in a British judge?

I thought of you, and the answer came to me: Annulment.

An annulment would void the marriage from the moment it occurred, which would mean that I never married a French citizen and I never lost my British citizenship. Fortunately, in Etienne's estimation, a wedding ceremony in a church, performed by a man of God in the sight of God, far outweighs any post-wedding declaration that might be made by some obscure British magistrate.

Hence, the wedding – for him. Hence, the annulment – for me.

Speak freely of the wedding itself, Cousin, for I will live openly with Etienne, and I will heretofore be known as Madame Foucauld (not "Lady Anne"). However, because I will live as a married woman, I do ask that you refrain from making any mention of the annulment.

We go to France, via Hull. I will write when I am settled.

As I write this letter, I do not know if you will come to Lambton today. The fact that it is now in your hands means everything to me. Please ensure that no one else ever reads it. It contains admissions that could be used against me. You have trusted me. I trust you.

Forever,
Anne Foucauld
P.S. I know that Mother will forgive me – if we all live long enough. Until then, please love her for me."

Georgiana called to the driver, who had been allowing the carriage horse to graze, and bid him to gather sticks and build a small fire. Once a flame took hold, she sent him with the carriage a hundred meters up the road. She read the letter one more time, so that she might remember every word of it, and put each page separately into the tiny blaze, until it was completely consumed.

CHAPTER FORTY-ONE

White Catchfly

In his letter to Bingley, Ambrose had intended to include a heartfelt apology to Miss Darcy. He had gotten as far as, *"Please tell Miss Darcy…"* and then his courage failed. He was certain that their parting had been so distasteful to her that she would most likely refuse to acknowledge that she had ever been acquainted with anyone named Ambrose Terwilliger. *"Well, why should she? I showed less courtesy to her than she affords an insect that she intends to crush beneath her shoe."* Instead of the apology, he squeezed a goodbye to the children into the space between the end of one line (*'tell'*) and the beginning of the next line (*'Miss Darcy,'* which he managed to transform into *'Miss Darbyshire'*).

Now, Ambrose Terwilliger sat in a tavern on the southern edge of Manchester, waiting for the arrival of his Cousin Charles, pretending that he was not hoping for a message that his cousin might be conveying from the perceptive and forgiving Miss Georgiana Darcy. Bingley arrived and ordered their noon meal, all good spirits and alive with curiosity about Ambrose's employment at the…"pleasure garden (?)".

"It is simply a garden! There is a pavilion for dancing, and that is where I play their magnificent pipe organ. It is huge,

Cousin! Hundreds of pipes, each emitting a slightly different sound, all controlled and combined by the keyboards (there are five of them!) and foot pedals. You cannot imagine the challenge and delight of playing such an instrument. And there are garden paths for lovers to stroll, a park with structures that lure and thrill children, and tables for those who bring picnic baskets. Also, too, there are strolling musicians, so I can augment my earnings with a turn on the flute or the mandolin. Even my father would approve, for 'Musician' is an occupation that befits a gentleman. I am a fortunate man!"

As they dined and conversed, Ambrose learned that Bingley had seen Miss Darcy twice yesterday, once in the afternoon and again in the evening. Oh, yes, she had seen Ambrose's letter. Yes, she knew Charles Bingley was traveling that day to see his Cousin Ambrose. What was so urgent that she had to see Bingley before he left for Manchester? (Some message, perhaps?) "The sale of a horse!" Bingley laughed.

Ambrose ordered another pint of ale.

Once the pleasantries were concluded and the meal consumed, Ambrose unwrapped the watercolors that Bingley had brought from GanderGlen. He expressed relief at the sight of a precisely-drawn white Catchfly, for the owner of the pleasure garden had specifically requested a rendition of a Catchfly to decorate his office, and, "Mrs. Wickham said that she could not find it in the portfolio she has with her."

"Excuse me, Cousin, are you saying that you have spoken with Mrs. Wickham recently?"

"This morning," Ambrose replied.

"Excellent! This is wonderful news!" Bingley exclaimed. He had told Georgiana Darcy that there was nothing to worry about and there it was! "And how is Mrs. Darcy?"

"Is Mrs. Darcy in Manchester, too?" asked Ambrose.

"You did not see her when you visited Mrs. Wickham?"

Ambrose shook his head, *"no,"* then said that Mrs. Wickham had given him to believe that she was alone in Manchester.

"Alone?" Bingley repeated, a frown crossing his lips. Then his back straightened as he noticed something unexpected in Lydia's drawing of the Catchfly. His eye had fallen on the delicate lettering that identified each segment of its biotica. "What is this? Did my wife contribute to Mrs. Wickham's artwork?" he asked. "This cursive is Jane's!"

Ambrose grinned. "It is almost exact! Did you not know that Mrs. Wickham can duplicate every curve of her sisters' handwriting?"

Bingley did not grin. He slowly began to comprehend a truth that was quite chilling. "Can she duplicate Elizabeth Darcy's hand as well?"

Ambrose nodded cheerfully. "She is a brilliant artist!

"A brilliant artist," Bingley repeated, nodding broodily. "She is a brilliant FORGER!" Bingley pulled Ambrose erect and demanded to be taken to his wife's sister, at once.

At first, Lydia denied all knowledge of Elizabeth Darcy's whereabouts. Then, she said that their mother had sent word to Lydia that one of the Wickham children was ill, so Elizabeth decided to continue the trip to Blackpool alone.

"Let me understand this," said Ambrose carefully. "Mrs. Darcy and you were going to Blackpool together because it was *your* wish to visit Blackpool. Then, you heard that one of your children was ill, so you broke off your trip. Is that correct?"

"Yes."

"And Mrs. Darcy, who had no wish to visit Blackpool, continued to Blackpool...why?"

Lydia stared at him.

"And you did not return to GanderGlen to care for your sick child because...why?"

Lydia looked at the floor. While making a thoughtful inventory of every dust mote at her feet, she ventured, "Mother did not exactly say that Ernestine was very ill, it was more in the nature of a passing discomfort. Oh! Elizabeth was homesick! She broke off the trip to Blackpool and went to Derby, instead. To visit the shops!"

Ambrose persisted. "She was so homesick she broke off your trip to the seaside so that she could go shopping? And to do this shopping, she left Manchester to go to a town half its size and fifteen kilometers beyond the turn-off for her home? The home she is aching to return to? *That* home? And you stayed in Manchester, which means that she undertook that journey alone? Is that what you are saying?"

"Elizabeth was not alone. She had taken sick. So, she did not want to expose me to her illness."

Bingley had exhausted all his patience. He gathered her up by her arms and shook her. "Enough, Lydia, enough! Stop lying! You forged Darcy's name on a Bill of Sale! You forged her letters! Admit it! Where is she?"

Lydia began to cry. "I did not want to write that last letter! But, we needed the money to clear Wickham's debts. Debtor's Prison! Elizabeth refused to help! I knew Darcy could buy back the horse. It was free to him anyway. A gift! What is wrong with him having to buy it once?" Bingley's lack of sympathy was plainly obvious, so she importuned Ambrose. "I know it was wrong, but...prison!"

"That part is done and over, Mrs. Wickham." Ambrose patted her on the shoulder. "You mentioned a 'last letter.' Why did you not wish to write that 'last letter'?"

Between her sobs, she blathered that, "it was only a joke" and that Elizabeth was safely in the care of "my dear Wickham, who is as much her brother as I am her sister."

"There is a truth if ever I heard one!" shouted Bingley, who had let go of her arms, but was now pacing the room like a wild man and declaiming imprecations in her direction.

On and on did Bingley rant, so loudly that the tenant in the room beneath Lydia's used a broomstick to pound on his ceiling. All the while, Ambrose softened his own voice and spoke slowly with much kindness and gentle concern. "Mrs. Wickham," he edged forward, "when and where exactly did you last see your sister?"

"I tell you she was ill, and Wickham did not want her to travel alone, so he was taking her home to Pemberley on the public coach."

"Wickham going to Pemberley?" Bingley roared. "Knowing Darcy would shoot him on sight?"

Ambrose took a deep breath. Lydia was always difficult to connect with reason. Bingley's scattershot fury was creating additional layers of complexity. Now, Lydia was bawling. Ambrose took her hands into his own and tilted his head down and up, in the hope of forming an illusion of intimacy and calm in the midst of Bingley's frenzy. His voice was so soft that Lydia had to stop crying and give Ambrose her full attention so that she could hear what he was saying. Bingley continued his rant, but Lydia and Ambrose were able to converse underneath him, at a different volume and a different speed.

"Mrs. Wickham, tell me why your plans changed. Why did you break off your trip? Was it because Mrs. Darcy became ill?"

"No. That happened later. I think it was something she ate while we were in Stockport."

"Then, why did you change your plans?"

"Because Mr. Wickham asked me to. He had some money…"

"And who did he cheat to get that?" bellowed Bingley.

"Go on, Mrs. Wickham, go on. I want to know everything. I am worried about your sister's safety," Ambrose urged.

"But she is with Wickham! She is safe!"

"What was in the last letter you sent that carried Mrs. Darcy's signature?"

"Oh, that was just a tweak for her husband. So that he would not be so sure of himself."

"But what did it say?" pressed Ambrose.

"Only that…oh, it said that she was on a tryst in Goole! It was just a lark, to get Darcy's wind up and put him on a goose-chase."

"Was this joke…was it her idea?"

"No." Lydia blushed. "It was Wickham's." Then, she leapt to her husband's defense. "Well, why should Wickham not sport with him a bit? They are brothers!"

It is possible that Mr. Bingley's reaction to this last comment may have been considered unsuitable by some listeners because there soon came a pounding on the door. Apparently, the innkeeper needed to clean the room because he was insisting that the inhabitants depart at once. Bingley flung the door open, pressed several large heavy coins into the man's hand, and shut the door in his face. So, at least, the pounding on the door stopped. The pounding from the room below, however, continued unabated.

"Where did Wickham get this idea? Does he often indulge in whimsies such as this?" asked Ambrose, with not a hint of accusation or suspicion in his tone.

"And where, Lydia, did he get the money? Who gave him that?" demanded Bingley. "Because he could not have had it long – money is not water in his hands, it is steam!"

"Maybe the man at the bar," mused Lydia, clearly employing all her powers to recall the incident in every detail. Then her eyes widened, and she said, "Jammin!"

Now, Ambrose's eyes widened. "What? What did you say?"

"It was Jammin Hard! I did not recognize him because he has a beard now. NO! George!" she wailed. "What have you done? What have you made me do?" Lydia sank into her tears. "Wickham is afraid of him! He told me never to be alone with him. Elizabeth! Elizabeth!"

Bingley stared down at Lydia for a moment then turned to Ambrose. He pushed money into his cousin's hand. "I go to Goole. If you learn anything additional, send word to me there."

"Where, in Goole?" asked Ambrose.

"The Golden Cock," gasped Lydia. "My letter said that Darcy should come to the Golden Cock. It is a trap, is it not?"

The two men exchanged looks of rising panic, their imaginations running in every direction.

Lydia sobbed and brought them both back to this room and this time. She was a person who was all of the moment. Because she could not plan so much as a dinner meal without active guidance, she was incapable of recognizing the machinations of others. The perfect dupe.

Then, Ambrose noticed that his cousin was gone. No! Terwilliger ran to the window and saw Bingley mount. There was no way to catch him, so Ambrose leaned out the window and shouted as Bingley charged off to the east. "Jammin is short for Benjamin! Hard is shortened from Hardaway! You will know him on sight...he is the Baron of Coxcroft!"

CHAPTER FORTY-TWO

Peach Blossom

Elizabeth was unawake. She was not in possession of her own brain. It would not think. It was as though…it was avoiding her. There were words, and there were images, but nothing came together. Wickham was smiling, and she heard, *"Stumble and Seek,"* but that was not right. Where was she? She was someplace. *"Tremble and Sneak."* No, that was not right, either. She had been…in a carriage. But she was not in a carriage now. She had been in…someplace public. A store, maybe. Wickham was there. Yes! Lydia saw Wickham! He came over to where they were, and he said, *"Trouble and Shriek."* Why would he say that?

She had to stop. She was getting a headache, and she was getting dizzy. Someone else was there. Not Lydia. It was a man. *"Tumble and Tweet."* No, that was wrong. *"Rubble and Reek."* NO!

"Sign it, George. Sign it, 'Mr. and Mrs. George Wickham.' I will take it back to the desk, so Darcy will find it. The clerk got a good look at her. Darcy will be up the stairs in a heartbeat, once he arrives!"

She knew that voice! From somewhere. *"Fumble and Peek?" "Bumble and Bleat?"* So close. She was sure she was so close!

George Wickham saw Elizabeth Darcy staring at him, and he knew that she did not see him at all. "What have you done to her?"

"Nothing, George! A mild opiate in her Bubble and Squeak, that is all! She will be full alert by the time Darcy gets here."

YES! Bubble and Squeak! That is what it was! She was at a pub, and they brought cabbage and potatoes! She was coming back now! Wickham is here. And…someone else. She looked at her sister's husband, and this time he knew that she was seeing him for what he was.

She had a vision of the cabbage and the potatoes in a pot, bubbling and squeaking over the fire, and she realized that she was in that boiling water with them.

"Take her to the bed, George, and remove her clothes."

"Do you have any idea how Darcy will react to this?" asked Wickham, who felt as though he were on a forced march to his own doom.

"Yes! He will throw her out! Most importantly, the things that she holds dear will be disposed of. Especially, her horse."

"Her horse? But my wife forged the Bill of Sale for you. You have the horse."

Elizabeth tried to rouse herself, wanted to escape, but her body was too heavy, too tired. She hoped that her strength would find its way back to her, if she could only be patient.

The second man shook his lion's mane of a head. "The horse was not there. That Bill of Sale might have fooled his stablemaster, but it will not fool Darcy himself! No. Change of plan."

Wickham was aghast. "You bought up all my promissory notes and threatened me with Debtor's Prison. You forced me to cajole my wife into forgery. And now you expect me to ravish my own wife's sister…for a horse?"

"It is a very fine horse."

"Jammin, this is insane! You will have us all in prison! Just go to Darcy, tell him some blackguard has his wife and demands a ransom of every horse in his stable. He will not hesitate a moment! He will give them to you, every one!"

"You are so clever, George! Why did I not think of that? Could it be because I cannot race the horse, or breed the horse, or even be seen in the presence of the horse, without admitting that I myself am the blackguard?" He shook his head wearily. Clearly, he was in the company of a fool. "Just sign the Golden Cock's register, George. And take her to bed."

This second man stood between her and Wickham. She could see his back. She knew this second man's voice, but could not bring forth a name or picture a face. She knew she did not have the strength to flee or to fight.

"I want to thank you, Jammin, for you have found for me," Wickham savored the concept, "something I thought I would never find."

"What is that?" asked the Baron, warily.

"A level to which I will not sink."

Through half-closed eyes, Elizabeth saw the expression on Wickham's face. He was absolutely resolute. Was it possible that Wickham...Wickham!...would sacrifice himself to preserve her honor?

"BOLLOCKS!"

That word! He said that word! Then she saw his sledge of a fist arc into Wickham's belly, and she knew who this second man was. Wickham went to his knees in agony, desperate for breath. Elizabeth knew that a better man than Wickham would not refuse the Baron a second time.

Elizabeth tried to put it together. The Baron wanted...what? Power! Not over Wickham – he had Wickham. And not over Elizabeth – she was already at his mercy. This was all about Darcy! She did not have the strength to fight for her own honor, let alone help Wickham or warn her husband. The only thing she could do was…surrender.

Elizabeth gathered all her strength and cried out, "George, dearest! Is it Darcy? Has he discovered us?" That took all of her strength. She swooned.

Benjamin Hardaway, Jammin Hard, Baron of Coxcroft, peer of the realm, stared open-mouthed at the unconscious woman. *"Ho, now. What is this?"* he wondered. *"Have I underwritten costs and risked social censure and possibly criminal prosecution, all for naught? The proud Mr. Darcy, already a cuckold? The cherished Mrs. Darcy, an eager adulteress?"*

He lifted Wickham's head by its hair. "She is lying, is she not, George? You are too much of a coward to risk the wrath of her husband, and if he were to discover…"

Wickham could barely breathe, but he was a natural talent in the area of self-interest, so he knew what to say. "He knows. She has begged him for a divorce. He will not give her up."

Jammin's plan, so perfect in its formulation, was falling totally apart in its execution. The plan had originally called for a minion with a forged Bill of Sale to secure and remove Arabian Moonlight while both Mr. and Mrs. Darcy were off the premises. But the horse was nowhere to be found! Most inconvenient.

So, a new plan had to be formulated, and this new plan called for Darcy to find his pristine wife in the bed of the hated Wickham so that the enraged husband would cast her out in righteous disgust. Or, he might kill one or both in a fury. That would be good. Anyway, once Mrs. Darcy was disposed of, through either death or divorce, the horse would be available for purchase. Coxcroft had actually liked this version much better than the original and was looking forward to its consummation because it would put Elizabeth Darcy (if she lived) at his nonexistent mercy. But, *"If Darcy already knows of this liaison, a discovery would be meaningless – for Darcy himself would conceal the scandal! No death, no divorce, and no horse."*

Frustrated and angry, the Baron kicked Wickham in the side and was quite delighted to hear the sound of cracking bone. His lust satisfied, Jammin relaxed, and took a moment to think things through. "George, I have grave doubts about your sincerity. If you are already her lover, why did you choose to accept a beating? Why did you not simply take her into your bed?"

Wickham did not reply.

"George?" The Baron kicked him again, but not as hard as before because he did want a response.

"Are you dead?"

Wickham did not move.

The Baron was forced to accept the fact that Wickham was no longer conscious and, therefore, could not provide any further assistance. So, the Baron would need another new plan. First, Darcy was on his way and would no doubt arrive within the hour. Lydia Wickham's letter most certainly assured that fact. Second, Lydia Wickham did not know that the Baron was Jammin Hard, so even if she had recognized Jammin in that pub, there was no danger that she would tie the Baron of Coxcroft to this affair. Likewise, Mr. Darcy had no knowledge of the Baron's involvement. Wickham knew, but he might be dead. But, *"Even if he is alive, I can simply put him in Debtor's Prison. Then, any accusation he makes will sound like it is born of personal animus. He is a known liar, so all I have to do is vouchsafe a denial."* Mrs. Darcy, though…he had had such hopes for Mrs. Darcy. Leave her here? No. She had heard his voice, perhaps even seen his face. In time, she might remember…and *she* would be believed.

Ideally, Jammin Hard would have taken both George Wickham and Elizabeth Darcy with him, but neither one could walk without help. Mrs. Darcy would be easier to carry. Time was becoming thin; Darcy was on his way. Wickham could be left behind. If he is yet alive, it would be an hour or more before he roused and more time still for him to become coherent. *"He might even be dead – let Darcy deal with all of that, it should delay him."*

But Mrs. Darcy – she had to come with him. He could slit her throat and discard her body on any deserted roadside. He bundled the semi-conscious woman down the stairs and told the concerned innkeeper, "My friend has taken ill and cannot continue with us on our journey. Please do not disturb his slumber. His wife has exhausted herself caring for him and has fainted again. But we must reach Leeds by sundown or lose the inheritance." He settled the bill, generously, and so assuaged any suspicion on the part of the inn's proprietor.

In the carriage, on the way to Liverpool via Manchester, the much-revered Baron of Coxcroft reviewed his situation. Mrs. Darcy had gone from asset to liability in one stroke. This was particularly annoying because he had invested a great deal of money in this endeavor, and he hated that he would get none of it back and, on top of that – probably never acquire the horse. *"Forget the horse!"* he admonished himself. *"I must get rid of Elizabeth Darcy!"* And then, he remembered: *"There is one way to do it that will remove all trace of her and give me some return on my investment."* He nodded in agreement with his newest plan, then told his driver to change direction and proceed to Kingston-upon-Hull.

Elizabeth drifted in and out of lucidity, for the effects of the drug were still upon her. In her lucid moments, she feigned sleep. She knew that she would have no opportunity for escape while the carriage was moving.

Her captor studied her. The coach trip to Kingston-upon-Hull would take about one hour more. This allowed enough time for some diversion, but he found himself somewhat disenchanted by what he had learned about the genteel Mrs. Darcy. He had imagined her as a modest, loyal, sheltered wife, unacquainted with the variety of pleasures he could introduce to her. Instead, she had at least one lover (if Wickham could be believed) and possibly two (for if she was not the woman in the gazebo, who was?). If this were true, then seducing the esteemed Mrs. Darcy into abandoning her virtue would be no greater an achievement than overcoming the objections of a London streetwalker.

Still and all, defiance was a quality that Benjamin Hardaway much admired, and Elizabeth Darcy was a woman who would brace the Devil himself. Hardaway prodded her with the toe of his boot and licked his lips. She stirred, but could not seem to waken. When he saw that his efforts would yield no struggle, no invective, no despair, and no sensibility to pain, he reluctantly abandoned his debauch. His eye fell on a circlet of gold, which to him signified profit. He slipped it from her finger and pushed it deep into his vest pocket, knowing that a wedding ring would be of no further use to her.

For the rest of the journey, he napped as peacefully as an innocent child.

CHAPTER FORTY-THREE

Watcher-by-the-Wayside

Vinson had sent two messages requesting Darcy retrieve Moonlight earlier than originally agreed. The first said, *"at your convenience."* The second, *"NOW! PLEASE! NOW!"*

The stableboy stood as far away as he could, holding out the saddleblanket at arms-length, thanking Darcy over and over again for saddling Moonlight himself, instead of requiring the boy to do it.

Darcy barely heard him. Elizabeth's letter was torturing him. He could see every word, still before his eyes.

"Darcy,

I am gone to Scotland with a friend. I am sure that he will be a more pleasurable companion than you ever were. Come and join us, if you would like to learn how a man behaves toward a woman he loves. We will stop tonight at the Golden Cock, outside Goole.

Lizzie"

The letter was in her handwriting, but what could ever have induced her to write it? It suggests that she is traveling in the company of a man! Impossible! And she signed it "Lizzie." He never once called her "Lizzie"!

Another man might surmise that his wife was frivolous and unfaithful and, in truth that thought had presented itself to Mr. Darcy's thinking. But the answer came back with a brutish refusal to believe it. There was no doubt in his mind that he would never betray her (and since he thought better of her character than his own), he was certain she would never betray him. This fact (for he accepted it as fact) troubled him far more than any betrayal would have. If the letter had been forced from her, what circumstances was she in? With whom? And most importantly, how could he help her?

And then, there was the second letter. The one from Hannah Hill to Mrs. Annesley that arrived just before his letter was delivered. There was a line in Hannah's letter – *"I hope when you receive this that Mrs. Darcy has recovered from her illness and her brother was able to bring her swiftly home."* What could that have meant? Hannah Hill knows that Elizabeth has no brothers!

Was she on her way to Pemberley or on her way to Goole? As he tightened the girth strap on the saddle, he decided. At Pemberley, she would be safe. He would go to Goole.

Hours passed. Darcy rounded a woody bend, and there it was: The Golden Cock. The innkeeper acknowledged that a party of three had requested rooms earlier in the day, and then unexpectedly departed.

"There was a woman with them, but she was very ill. I did not see her clearly. She could be the woman you seek, just as easily as she could be anyone else."

"Did they register?" asked Darcy.

"Ah, well…" the innkeeper dissembled, then came to the point. "My Register has gone missing. It was here!" He waved his hand across the top of his desk. "Now, gone!"

"Did you see their direction?"

"What? Oh, he said, 'Leeds.'"

Darcy began to leave, then asked, "Do you know which Leeds? There is a Leeds College in London. Could he have meant that? Or did he mean the town to the north?"

"I presumed he meant the town, but…perhaps his friend, Mr. Wickham, would know."

Darcy took the steps three at a time. The innkeeper caught up to him as he banged on the door. "Wickham! What have you done?"

"Please, sir!" the innkeeper begged. "He is ill! I was told not to disturb him."

"If you have a key, open it! If you do not have a key, stand aside while I break it down!"

The key was produced, the door flung open, and the unconscious Wickham was seen sprawled flat on the floor in an unwholesome pool of his own making.

"Oh!" wailed the innkeeper. "Do not let him be dead! No one will take a room if someone has died in it!"

"George!" shouted Darcy, then to the innkeeper, "Get a physician!"

"It might be best if we moved him to…" the innkeeper struggled to finish his sentence, without giving voice to his actual thought, which was *"someone else's inn."*

"A physician! Now!"

Darcy saw a pitcher of water on the dresser and poured all that was left of it over Wickham's head. "George!"

Wickham did revive a little. When he recognized Darcy, he struggled to speak. "Port," he croaked.

The innkeeper and the doctor arrived in time to overhear Wickham's remark. The relieved innkeeper ran for a bottle (praying that Wickham would live long enough to crawl into the hallway before he expired), splashed the wine into a glass, and forced it into the hand of the doctor. The doctor drank it.

"Elizabeth," exhaled Wickham as he began to fade.

"There is better air in the hallway," offered the innkeeper. "Perhaps we should move him."

Darcy was atop Wickham in an instant. The doctor did not interfere, as he was preoccupied with pouring a precise dosage of medicinal wine, undoubtedly intended for his suffering patient.

"What do you know of my wife?" Darcy demanded.

Wickham was in the process of reclaiming his senses and croaked again, "Port."

"Coming!" sang the doctor.

"You know, the floorboards in the hallway are much more comfortable than the floorboards in the rooms. Perhaps we should..." interjected the innkeeper.

Wickham clutched Darcy's arm and carefully enunciated every word. He looked at Darcy full in the face, and his look was desperate. "The. Nearest. Port."

Darcy furrowed his brow. "They go to Leeds."

Wickham's body wrenched about like he had been violently kicked. His head flung from one side to the other. He grabbed the lapels of Darcy's coat, pulled himself up, and growled out his words close to Darcy's face. "He will make her gone forever with the next tide." This took all his strength, for then he fainted and the doctor could not revive him.

Darcy had stopped to feed and water Moonlight at Gilberdyke, and it was good that he did because Moonlight had a loose shoe. While he wolfed down his meal in the pub and waited for the farrier to finish, Darcy was inattentive to the arrival and departure of the coach and four that stopped only long enough to change out its horses. Since the coach was well-stocked with picnic food, neither Colonel Fitzwilliam nor Lady Catherine left the carriage, not even to stretch their legs. But, had they done so, it was unlikely that Darcy would have seen them. He was thoroughly immersed in his own thoughts. Was Wickham so perverse that he would misdirect Darcy at this critical time? *"Yes. He hates me enough to do that."* But, Darcy had one other thought, the memory of a rebuke he had once voiced, and which now held all of his hopes: *"I suggest you select a victim that does not command and deserve the respect, admiration, and devotion of every member of her family."*

While Darcy fidgeted in Gilberdyke, Bingley reached Goole. He spoke with the innkeeper, spoke with the doctor, and sent word to his Cousin Ambrose that Lydia must be brought to Goole at once. Then Bingley left his mount at the Goole stable and put his saddle on a rented horse. He was determined to catch up with Darcy and assist him in any way he could.

Bingley was just a quarter-hour from Gilberdyke when the farrier's work was done. "I'm sorry, sir, but that horse's hoof is smaller than what we have around here, but larger than a pony's. Couldn't shape anything I had on hand. Had to make the shoe to get a proper fit. Then, had to let it cool," he said, as Darcy swung into the saddle.

The farrier shook his head in real sorrow as he watched the little grey horse disappear in the distance. "You poor thing. Gave you as much of a rest as I dared."

CHAPTER FORTY-FOUR

Horse Hoof

Etienne and Anne Foucauld were on the foredeck of the *Marit Buck,* a two-masted ship that took cargo primarily, but also had a few berths for passengers. Although their thoughts were occupied with recently-made memories, their conversation focused on the activities on the dock. Barrels and crates were being loaded on all the ships, and instructions in various Nordic languages were being shouted back and forth between the sailors. It was all very colorful and romantic in a frost-tinged way. It was cold enough to see their breath, but there was surprisingly little wind at this time. No doubt it would pick up soon, fill the sails, and require Anne to nestle gleefully inside Etienne's cape, hugging his body, enclosed by his arms. The thought of it made her smile, then grin. She was confident, comfortable, and very, very happy.

Suddenly, Anne twisted violently in Etienne's grasp, nearly falling over the ship's railing. Etienne clutched at her waist and gathered her in. "You must not do such things!" he reprimanded her.

"But I saw Elizabeth! Mrs. Darcy, Etienne! She has come to see us off!"

Etienne was skeptical. Madame Darcy? In Kingston-upon-Hull? "You are mistaken, Anne. You are homesick, already. You are imagining..."

"There!" Anne thrust out her arm and pointed into the crowd.

Etienne glanced in the direction indicated, but he did not see Madame Darcy. He did see the Baron of Coxcroft. "Are you certain, Anne, that you saw Madame Darcy?"

"Yes, Etienne!"

"Stay here."

Etienne Foucauld's cape billowed out behind him as he descended the plank and returned to the dock. As he advanced on the Baron, he saw two ruffians removing a woman from a carriage. *"It is Madame Darcy!"* he confirmed. *"Is she ill?"*

Coxcroft had abandoned his old associates once he came into title and money, but he still had a smuggler's eye for a ship's captain who was amenable to profit.

"She's a trollop I have grown tired of," Coxcroft told the master of the *Sea Urchin*, not that the man had bothered to inquire. "I want her out of England. You can get much more than I am asking if you take her to a Gobi port. White women sell at a premium in the desert country." The Baron had momentarily returned to his former calling: White slavery.

Although Foucauld was not yet close enough to overhear what the Baron had said, he knew that Madame Darcy would not consent to travel in the company of any man unless her husband was also with her. And he knew that she would resist such familiar handling, if she was in full possession of her faculties. Anne, the latest in a long line of meek and obedient wives, had likewise disembarked from the *Marit Buck* and was trailing her husband along the dock, not quite able to catch up. Etienne was fully focused on the men around the Baron. Foucauld never broke his stride. In one fluid movement, he removed his cape with a dramatic flourish and waved it through the air like the challenge flag it was. He wanted Mrs. Darcy to see it. He did not care who else saw it – and others did.

What Jammin Hard saw was the one man in Hull that knew him on sight and knew Elizabeth Darcy on sight and would very happily testify in a criminal court that he had seen the two of them together. The Baron cursed in a sailor's tongue, took the *Sea Urchin*'s Captain's cutlass, and advanced.

Foucauld kept his gaze steady and drew his blade from its concealment in his cane. He made a mental note to never let his sword go unrepaired ever again.

Seeing that this interloper was clearly overmatched, the *Sea Urchin*'s Captain took possession of the woman and let his lascars join in the fun. When the Captain grabbed her about the waist and hoisted her from the carriage, Elizabeth roused and screamed for help. The Captain boxed her chin, knocking her senseless. He had no difficulty muscling her toward his ship's gangplank.

Etienne's weapon was little more than a dagger with a jagged tip. Since he had no realistic hope of defending himself against a cutlass (of all things!), he resolved to forgo defense altogether and rely completely on the skill of his attack.

The dock was teeming with people, crowded with cargo, and brimming with noise. Darcy cursed Wickham with every breath. Why had he listened? She was probably already in Leeds. How would Elizabeth suffer for his ill-placed reliance on the word of a man they both knew to be so far below contempt?

He did not hear Elizabeth scream.

But the little grey horse pricked its ears, neighed, and spun so quickly that Darcy almost lost his seat. Darcy stood up in his stirrups but saw nothing. *"She must be here!"* He loosed the reins and urged the grey stallion into the crowd. Arabian Moonlight eagerly picked his way around coils of rope, passengers, crates, kegs, and sailors. A constable called to Darcy that he must dismount and lead his horse, and not ride him on the dock. Darcy waved the constable off. Then, Moonlight broke into a gallop. People scattered as the animal hurdled bale and box. The constable blew his whistle, shouted threats of arrest, and chased after the horse and rider.

Unaware of the excitement elsewhere, Anne watched in horror as the sailors closed around her husband. Etienne, however, seemed remarkably calm, even as he whirled and dodged and parried. "He is enjoying himself!" Anne heard herself remark.

Foucauld recognized the Baron's certitude that the heavier cutlass would overwhelm the thinner weaker blade, and so Etienne feinted a panicked retreat until the Baron was maneuvered into putting all his weight into a slashing sweep that Foucauld sidestepped, then (using the tip of his blade perpendicular to the cutlass blade) redirected the cutlass into a cotton bale. While the cutlass was buried up to its hilt, Foucauld plunged the heel of his fist into the bridge of the Baron's nose. The Baron saw popping stars and was limited to trying to regain his senses for several minutes. This gave Foucauld an adequate amount of time to show the undisciplined brawling lascars that brute force was no match for finesse: They were slow, they were off-balance, and they kept getting in each other's way.

And then, in one moment of perfect confluence, Arabian Moonlight sailed over a crate and landed directly before Coxcroft, paused just for a moment, and then bounded over the Baron's head.

After Moonlight's leap scattered the Baron and the lascars, Etienne had a moment to catch his breath. The Baron was the first to recover, and he advanced swinging the heavy cutlass.

Etienne's blade would be ineffective if he tried to parry, so Etienne backed away as the crowd pulled away from him. Etienne dodged. He leapt atop a crate and jumped to a barrel. He rolled underneath the arc of the cutlass blade. He managed to get behind the Baron, and he kicked him in the seat of his pants.

Anne's heart was in her throat; she could not even call out. Her husband was in the midst of three men, all determined to kill him. She felt a hand on her shoulder and heard her mother's voice. "Good choice, Anne. He has courage."

Then Anne saw a flash of a red soldier's coat, and she saw Colonel Fitzwilliam pull one of the lascars away, engaging him in a fair fight. Bingley! He was here, too! He took on the other one, but was less particular about the fairness of his fight. Bingley kicked his quarry directly in his...well, in his bollocks. The man crumbled, and Bingley took his wooden club away from him and bopped him. Once the lascars were eliminated, Foucauld jerked his head in the direction Moonlight had gone. "Madame Darcy! She is in danger!"

The pair hesitated because they both knew that a broken epee could not possibly defend against a cutlass.

"Quickly!" Foucauld commanded.

As she saw Colonel Fitzwilliam and Charles Bingley run off, Lady Catherine repeated, "Tremendous courage." She paused. "No brains, though."

Darcy dismounted at the *Sea Urchin*'s gangplank and rushed toward his wife. The Captain pushed her toward her husband. Raising his open hands above his head, the Captain appeared to be quite willing to surrender the woman if Darcy would break off his attack. As the ship's crew gathered behind their Captain, Darcy swung his fainting wife into his arms.

"Well, Mister," sneered the Captain, "it appears you have your hands full." He poked the shoulder of a very big sailor and told him to "escort our guests to their cabin."

Darcy remembered the pistol he had secreted in his coat. But he could not reach it without dropping Elizabeth, and even then, one pistol would not hold off a dozen men. He cradled his wife closer and considered the efficacy of prayer.

"Planning a voyage, Darcy?"

Prayers answered, Fitzwilliam Darcy smiled with grateful relief. He did not even have to look. Bingley!

"Would you like some company, Cousin?" called Colonel Fitzwilliam. "What say you, Captain? Should we come aboard, or are your guests not staying?" On his short journey along the dock, the Colonel had been joined by some pub-crawling junior officers from another regiment. About six of them. All armed. All a little drunk. And all smiling as they drew their swords.

The Captain surveyed the dock, did some quick addition, and determined that whatever he might be paid for one wench was not worth the cost of replacing an entire crew. "Prepare to set sail," he cried out, turning his back on the lady, the gentlemen, and the wharf-rat that had gotten him into this mess. And had stolen his cutlass!

Elizabeth roused a bit and started to struggle in the firm grasp that held her. She felt herself being carried, and she recognized voices, soothing voices, familiar voices. She was settled into a carriage – it was the de Bourgh coach! Oh. Arabian Moonlight pushed his head in through one of the windows, tearing the sidecurtain, and letting slobber fall on the floor and the velvet seatcushions. The drivers were standing outside the coach, asking if there was anything they could do. She asked for water. And an apple, if they could find one.

By some miracle unknown to the cheering crowd that surrounded them, the Frenchman had held off the pirate for several minutes. In fact, Foucauld turned and twisted so many times that Coxcroft almost lost his footing a time or two and cursed the "bloody, jumping Frog" without pause.

The crowd was so thick that Bingley and Fitzwilliam could not get through. They had to circle around it to join Lady Catherine and Lady Anne. The Baron's cutlass swings were coming closer and closer. Lady Anne gathered her breath to cry out, but Fitzwilliam reached her just in time to cover her mouth with his hand. He whispered in her ear, "You are your husband's most dangerous enemy because you are the only one who can distract him. In a fight like this, one break in his concentration, and he will surely die."

The Baron had the tip of his cutlass at Foucauld's throat. Darcy was on the other side of the crowd, but being a tall man, he was able to see over the people blocking his path. Foucauld was in exactly the same position that he had been in when he and Darcy had fought in the Pemberley library. Darcy reached for his pistol – No. He had left it with the stableboys to ensure Elizabeth's safety.

Anne had heard what the Colonel had said, and she nodded to indicate her understanding of it. She took a deep breath, and then jammed the heel of her shoe onto the toe of Colonel Fitzwilliam's boot as hard as she could. Fitzwilliam cried out in agony. The Baron reflexively jerked around, instinctively looking for the source of this unexpected sound. Madame Foucauld had succeeded in her plan; she had distracted the Baron.

Monsieur Foucauld bent backward, so far backward that the hair on his head brushed the dock beneath his feet as he dropped to both knees, pivoted on one knee, and then the other. Frenchman and Englishman were now facing in the same direction, with the Englishman on his feet and brandishing a cutlass and the Frenchman in a kneeling position inside what would be the arc of that swooping cutlass. The cutlass tip was no longer at the Frenchman's throat; it was pointing at air. Foucauld leaned his head back against the English lord's chest, nestled his French shoulder into an English ribcage, and with his right hand, he rammed his tiny remnant of a sword into the part of the Baron's anatomy that laid between Foucauld's left ear and Foucauld's left shoulder – the spot where human beings store their hearts. Somewhat surprisingly, that is also where the Baron of Coxcroft stored his heart. The surprise being that he had one.

The constable pushed through the crowd and demanded that Etienne surrender his weapon. Foucauld released his grip on his sword immediately and rose to his feet, knocking the Baron's body backward, face up on the dock.

Etienne looked down at the handle of his sword protruding out of the Baron's chest. "My gift to you, Monsieur. You may keep it."

Anne buried her face in her husband's chest, alternately crying and laughing. "When I saw his cutlass at your throat…"

"Ma chere femme, I was in no danger! I am the owner and fencing master at L'Academe Militaire de Boulogne. That is a move I teach all my students." Foucauld caught Darcy's eye and smiled. "On their first day."

A police sergeant presented himself and began to place Foucauld under arrest, but he was interrupted by the constable.

"Sergeant, I was posted in Cornwall before I came here. You say he's a Baron, and that he might be, but I know him beard or no beard. That there is Jammin Hard, and he is wanted for wrecking, for slave-trading, and for murder."

"Slave-trading is not a crime," corrected the sergeant.

"It is the way he done it."

"Jammin Hard?" Foucauld asked the constable. "Are you sure this man is the pirate known as Jammin Hard?"

The constable nodded.

Bingley confirmed it.

Foucauld fixed his eyes on the lifeless body of the man who had ruined Magdeleigne Foucauld, because he wanted to kill him again. The man was not alive, so Foucauld gave him life – he imagined a living, taunting, nimble Jammin Hard skipping just beyond the reach of the tip of Foucauld's blade. One death was not enough! Foucauld was determined to kill him again and again and over again! He would keep this dead man close by him every day…so he could kill him, every day.

"Mister Foucauld. Mister Foucauld?"

Anne tugged at Etienne's sleeve. Mother was trying to get his attention.

Lady Catherine filled her lungs and straightened her back. "I have always hated the French, Monsieur. The war…so many young men, some from my own family. But now, I must choose between hating a man I do not know, and loving my own child." Lady Catherine paused. She gathered both his hands into her own and said, "I choose love."

Foucauld blinked. He was abruptly struck by thoughts of Mrs. Collins' playful teasing on a dancefloor, Darcy's solicitude when Magdeleigne was in need, and the two men who came to fight at his side against their own countrymen (without even knowing what the fight was about!). He exclaimed, "Anne! You did not tell me your mother is *tres romantique!*" He kissed his English mother-in-law on both her cheeks, he kissed her on the top of her head, he winked at her and said (to Anne's astonished horror), "Tell me the truth, Madame! You are French, no?", and then he kissed Lady Catherine on her lips. Lady Catherine made a sound that Anne had never heard from her mother before: Lady Catherine covered her mouth with the tips of her fingers and…giggled.

Etienne Foucauld embraced his English wife, he shook hands with his English friends, and he told his dead English enemy to go to ----.

CHAPTER FORTY-FIVE

Lily of the Valley

Just one-half hour after the noon meal, a servant from GanderGlen arrived at Pemberley with a single sheet of folded notepaper. Mr. and Mrs. Darcy were engaged in their customary afternoon walk and were overtaken at the footbridge. When he read the note, Mr. Darcy lowered it, then read it again.

"Incredible," he said.

Then, he read it a third time.

"Incredible," he repeated.

Mrs. Darcy had become more than a little distressed. "Darcy," she whispered urgently, "is it from Bingley? Is my sister well? Has Peter suffered a relapse?"

Darcy stared at her rather stupidly and gave her the note.

"*Darcy,*

Do you recall how we all laughed at Charlotte Collins' observation that my cousin Ambrose bore some resemblance to the Baron of Coxcroft? I am informed that the resemblance was not coincidental. Indeed, there was a family relationship on their mother's side! Since the late Coxcroft passed on to his (very just) reward without a direct male heir, the estate has devolved to one Mr. Ambrose Terwilliger, who is now the Baron of Coxcroft! My cousin has written me that he expects to be in Derbyshire today and asks that I do all in my power to secure an invitation to Pemberley at the earliest opportunity. He writes as though he believes that you would not welcome him, which I know to be the sheerest nonsense. I anticipate that we will join you at dinner, this night. If I presume on your hospitality, send the servant back to GanderGlen at once. Otherwise, let him rest in your kitchen. He fancies your scullery maid.

Bingley"

After Elizabeth read the message a third and fourth time, she noticed that the Bingley servant was still standing by. When her eyes fell upon him, he turned a bright shade of pink and tried to hide within himself.

"He may fancy the maid, or he may not, but he certainly cannot be trusted with private correspondence," she noted to herself.

"Mr. Darcy," she said, securing her husband's full attention, "do you wish the servant to carry a response to his master?"

Darcy was still somewhat in shock, but Elizabeth's words had encouraged a return of his senses. "No. No message. Take yourself to the kitchen, man, and rest and refresh yourself. The Bingleys are expected here tonight. They will not mind if you tarry a bit."

After the servant had gone, Darcy shook his head and scanned the letter once again.

"Can it be? Ambrose Terwilliger, a peer? A Lord?" Darcy stared at his wife, still gripped by disbelief.

"Were there ever two men, so different?" asked Elizabeth.

"Was there ever one man, so different?" mused Darcy, recalling how he had once observed Terwilliger standing in a meadow, inducing butterflies to light upon the outstretched palm of his hand.

By the time they reached the house, Darcy had reminded Elizabeth that the cook would have to be informed at once, and Elizabeth had reminded Darcy that Georgiana should be told of the change in circumstance experienced by her former piano teacher. At the great door to Pemberley, they parted and prosecuted their separate chores.

As expected, Darcy found his sister in the music room. "Georgiana, the Bingleys are expected for the evening meal."

"Oh, that is good. Will the whole family be together? It would be a great pleasure for Little Fits to have Peter to play with." As was usual, conversation decreased the volume of her playing but did not interrupt it.

Darcy sighed. "Please do not call Fitzgeorge, 'Little Fits.' You know I detest nicknames."

"Eliza." Georgiana said flatly, not looking up.

"That is not a nickname. That is a...a...a...an endearment! Anyway, I believe the whole family will be coming. Steel yourself, Georgiana because Elizabeth's mother, Mrs. Bennet, is visiting. Caroline Bingley will also join the party, I believe, and Sir James. And one other. Also joining us is a guest with whom you may wish to renew your acquaintance: Ambrose Terwilliger." He was watching his sister carefully. Was Elizabeth correct? Would Georgiana betray a partiality?

Georgiana stopped playing but did not look up. "I have no interest in renewing my acquaintance with Mr. Terwilliger."

Darcy remembered the words of Bingley's note, particularly the phrase, *"he believes that you would not welcome him,"* and Darcy became alarmed. "Georgiana, has Mr. Terwilliger affronted you in some way? Elizabeth and I, we thought you liked him!"

She did not answer at once. Then, "Mr. Terwilliger and I have come to a very clear understanding of the nature of our friendship. Mainly, that there never was, and never could be, a friendship of any kind."

Darcy had always been confident that Elizabeth had to be wrong, and certainly this unequivocal statement directly from his sister's own lips confirmed that it was his opinion that was the correct one. Husbandly triumph, while there, was barely in evidence as he continued. "Georgiana, if I had even suspected that such was the case, I never would have consented to his visit here, but now, under the circumstances, with him taking title to Coxcroft Castle…"

"What is that? What did you say?"

Darcy proceeded to explain Mr. Terwilliger's ascent in society and the sudden and mountainous increase in his worth. For some reason, the news seemed to amuse her. She thought of all the balls he would be invited to, all the debutantes he would be introduced to, and all the barmaids he would disappoint. Or not. *"At any rate, he will learn whether he prefers to be dismissed for lack of fortune, or welcomed merely for its glut."*

Georgiana's thoughts returned to the present and to the presence of her brother. "Well, be at ease. I am certain that Mr. Terwilliger will no more seek out my company than I will seek out his. The evening will go very quickly, and he will go just as quickly. I look forward to another of his abrupt departures." She turned back to her music and left Darcy to wonder just exactly why, if it was not to see Miss Darcy, Ambrose Terwilliger would come to Pemberley at all.

That evening, a few minutes after the greetings were made, Darcy received his answer. Terwilliger asked to see Mr. Darcy privately, and Darcy ushered him into the library.

Ambrose pulled an envelope from inside his coat and removed an object from the envelope. It was a single golden ring, encrusted with a *D*iamond surrounded by four smaller stones: An *A*methyst, a *R*uby, a *C*itrine, and a *Y*ellow topaz.

"The authorities sent me the late Baron's personal effects, and this ring was among them. Fortunately, there is a phrase inscribed inside the band. It says, "GD to AF,..."

"Always Love All Ways," completed Darcy. "George Darcy to Anne Fitzwilliam. It is my parent's wedding ring. I gave it to my wife when we married."

Ambrose presented it at once. "Mr. Darcy, I am delighted to return this heirloom to your family!"

Darcy took it and studied it for a moment. "You have questions, sir?" The man had to have questions! Why would a married woman remove her ring? If she did not voluntarily remove it, had it been stolen? If it had been stolen, why had the theft not been reported? How is it that the Baron of Coxcroft, a bachelor, came into possession of an item of such personal significance to a married woman? The whole business with Elizabeth's abduction, her presence at a secluded inn while in the company of two men (neither of whom was her husband) had all been hushed up. Now, exposure was certain. Terwilliger's discretion could not be counted upon, for there was no love lost between these two men, and any influence that Georgiana might have been able to exert...well, she had made it clear that there was no longer any sympathy between them.

"Questions, Mr. Darcy? Of what are we speaking? Please forgive me, for so much has happened recently, I find that I forget my own name most of the time! Well, it is a new name!" Ambrose tittered, then became serious. "I am sorry, sir, but I have completely forgotten the topic of our conversation. Shall we join your other guests?"

Dinner was mildly convivial, although Darcy noted that Georgiana confined her remarks to the guests on her right. The guests on her left had no opportunity to feel slighted by her silence because they received Terwilliger's enthusiastic attention. No one seemed to notice that Georgiana Darcy did not acknowledge the existence of Ambrose Terwilliger, and no one seemed to notice that the Baron of Coxcroft was charming and affable to all at the table – except that one empty chair occupied by the lovely and demure sister of their host.

CHAPTER FORTY-SIX

Camellia

Elizabeth Darcy would spend years puzzling over exactly how her mother had maneuvered every other person out of the sitting room so that the Baron of Coxcroft could have a precious few unnoticed, unchaperoned minutes with Georgiana Darcy. Not only that! In addition, Mrs. Bennet had instigated discussions about the hostile relationship between France and England, and about the scandalous impoverishment of Beau Brummell, and other topics that encouraged excited conversation, so that not even Darcy himself realized that his sister was not among the company.

Unaware of the goings-on in the parlor, Ambrose only noted that the door to the sitting room was closed and was remaining closed. Miss Darcy had her back to him. He had thought that she would never speak to him again. Well, she still had not. But she had not gone to the door. Yet.

"Do you remember Hannah Hill?" he began.

She stiffened. This was the last subject they had quarreled about. "I heard that she is in Manchester."

"Stockport, near Manchester. She has a son. She is engaged to be married to an innkeeper. He is older, a widower. The name she has been using is Widow Buxton."

"Yes. I gathered that from your letter to Mr. Bingley," Georgiana nodded. She wanted to leave the room, but she knew that once she went, she would never be alone with him again. Maybe, for the length of a single dance, at balls. Maybe, at his wedding. Or hers. But never just with him. Never.

Ambrose extracted a second ring from his pocket. He handled it for a moment. What he had to say, he could not say to her back. He circled her, knowing that the last time they had faced each other in conversation, he had said everything imaginable to insult her, and she had ordered him to leave this very house.

"Miss Darcy, some time ago, the Widow Buxton asked me to return this to you." It was a plain band, not even gold. "She would not entrust it to the mails. She said that you told her it was your mother's wedding ring."

Georgiana stared at it. "It was. It is." She reached for it, but Ambrose moved it, keeping it just beyond the edge of her fingertips.

"Your brother just told me that he gave your mother's ring to his wife, on their wedding day, ten years ago."

She swallowed. "You misunderstood him."

Ambrose would have none of this! He knew she was lying, and he suspected he knew why. "Georgiana, this ring is cheap costume jewelry! They sell such things in Gretna Green!"

She snatched the ring from between his fingers. "I regret that its elegance does not impress you. It has value to me!"

"I am certain it does!" Ambrose had raised his voice, and his words had flown out of him. He immediately regretted his temper. He was all gentleness when he asked, "Did you love him?" Then, he shook his head, *"no,"* and became a little more urgent. "What I mean is, do you *still* love him?"

"If I ever did love him, it was only because I believed he loved me." Then, she laughed with rueful disdain. "I was disabused of that notion, very quickly. My brother found us within a day and bought him off."

"Your brother! What right had he to interfere?"

"Every right! Every duty! He was still my guardian. I was fifteen."

Ambrose gasped. He remembered how, when he was fourteen, Jammin Hard had robbed him of his innocence.

Georgiana went on. "My brother destroyed all evidences of the marriage, save two. One was this ring. I kept it because I foolishly believed that our love would survive a temporary separation."

"But the boy. Did he not return?" Ambrose cursed himself for asking, but he had to know where this man was, and most of all, if she was yearning for him.

"The boy, as you put it, was fourteen years my senior. And, yes, he did return. He wanted more money." Georgiana tilted her head and looked at Ambrose full on for the first time that entire night. She had been avoiding him. Truth be told, she was afraid she would dissolve into tears or say something foolish. Now, she no longer cared to obtain his good opinion, not if it could only be had through concealment or deceit. "You see, Baron, you are not the only man who knows my true measure. Without my fortune, I am not worth having. And, if my fortune can be had without having me, so much the better!" She smiled at him triumphantly.

Ambrose wished he could crawl unseen out of the room, preferably by a route that traveled beneath the floorboards. Yet, he feared that when this conversation ended, there would never be another. His thoughts ran about chaotically, searching madly for a subject that would allow him to maintain this dialogue, in the hope that he could find some pathway that would lead to a continued acquaintance.

For Georgiana, however, the time had come to end it. She formed the words of parting in her mind, but before she could utter them, Ambrose spoke.

"What was the second thing?"

She stared at him blankly.

"You said there remained only two evidences of your marriage. The ring…what was the second thing?"

Georgiana turned away from him for a moment, then she turned back, chin out, mouth firm, eyes steady. "Do you remember the last time we spoke? You sought to insult me by describing a girl that carried the proof of her kindness, generosity, and love beneath her heart, until it could have a life of its own. Your rebuke was far sweeter and more comforting than you intended. The second evidence is Peter Bingley. He is my son."

Ambrose's jaw dropped. He stared at her open-mouthed. Not a pretty sight.

Georgiana gathered her skirt and began to leave the room.

"Miss Darcy, I…" Ambrose stopped. He straightened his shoulders. "You must know…"

Georgiana stood at her full height, looking down on him. *"Oh, yes, Baron of Coxcroft. I quite know what you will say. A poor man must accept flaws in a woman with a fortune, but Barons merit virgins. You may dawdle with a dozen barmaids, Ambrose Terwilliger, for you are a man. A woman who has given herself to one man, one time? Soiled. A woman whose marriage was annulled? Beneath you. A woman that the law says was never married and yet bore a child? Go find the door, Baron. Escape! Be done with me, for I am done with you."*

Ambrose threw his hands in the air. "This is idiotic! I am in love with you! I have always been in love with you! If you do not love me, then you are a heartless flirt! Are you going to marry me or not?"

In the silence that followed, Ambrose reflected upon the unlikelihood that many declarations of love included words like "idiotic" and "heartless flirt." The expression on Miss Darcy's face (now, it was her turn to stare at someone with a mouth that hung open and eyes that bulged out) told the Baron that if she were allowed to respond, he would not receive the answer that he wanted to hear.

So, he could not allow her to respond.

"Well," he said cheerfully. "I am glad that is settled." He paused. She was still staring. "We will marry here at Pemberley, in the Spring. Lovely setting. And then, we will live in my castle, in Cornwall. You will like Cornwall, I think. Of course, I expect that the Bingleys will be frequent visitors, for I shall never forget their kindness to me before this title became mine. Should we get Peter his own pony, do you think? Well, we can discuss that later." He approached her, but she leaned away from him, still staring. He bounced up on his toes, kissed her cheek, and said, "Good."

Then, he stepped back. And he waited.

He waited for what felt like forever.

Forever passed him by. He was just now beginning to comprehend the meaning of the word 'eternity.'

Finally, she closed her mouth. She licked her lips. At last, she spoke. "The little frog seems to have lost his silver tongue and replaced it with a steel whip."

She smiled.

She smiled!

Ambrose blushed, hung his head, and nodded. Then, he peeked up at her through a shock of reddish hair, grinned impishly, and said, "The heart is still the same, though. Still gold. Still yours." It was only then that Ambrose Terwilliger, the youngest-ever Baron of Coxcroft, spoke the words of ardent love and complete devotion that are customary on such occasions. The return to social convention was a relief welcomed by both, which they together abandoned immediately, mixing an eager flurry of tiny kisses with an equal number of randy puns and wholly improper innuendoes.

Whether it was a moment later, or an hour gone, they heard a sound at the door. When it opened, they were at opposite sides of the room, their mutual disinterest plain to any observer. Mrs. Bennet's disappointment was clear upon her face. She had been so sure that their diligent avoidance of each other at the dinner table was a symptom of love gone higgledy-piggledy. *"They just need to talk to each other,"* she had thought. But Coxcroft made it abundantly clear that he was delighted to see Mrs. Bennet enter the room because it gave him a creditable opportunity to leave it. He did not even take the time to ask Miss Darcy to excuse his departure!

"Young men today are not what young men were yesterday," harrumphed Mrs. Bennet, more to herself than to Georgiana.

Georgiana merely smiled as she saw her young man go immediately to the library door and knock.

CHAPTER FORTY-SEVEN

Love-in-a-Mist

"What is this about?" wondered Darcy. *"The man spent months refusing the hospitality of my library, and now he insists upon inflicting his company upon me for a second time today. Between this Baron of Coxcroft and the last Baron of Coxcroft, I pray I never host another peer in my home again."*

Ambrose took a very deep breath and spoke the most important sentence of his life. "Mr. Darcy, I have the great honor of requesting your sister's hand in marriage." He flushed with self-congratulations. He had not stumbled over one word. Excellent!

Except...Mr. Darcy was giving no reply. Actually, Mr. Darcy did not seem to be breathing. Finally, Mr. Darcy spoke. "Excuse me, sir? What did you say?"

This was not good. Ambrose could feel himself becoming flustered. "Your your your sisssster, sir. Her hand. Marriage. Marriage." Oh. He had done so well the first time. It had been years since he had stuttered.

Darcy went from straight and tall to straighter and taller. But, then, enlightenment! The last Baron of Coxcroft had obtained Georgiana's hand, so this young fool thought that the

Barony itself was all that was required – any man who called himself a Baron could claim Georgiana Darcy!

Darcy was relieved. Indignant, but relieved, for he knew the correct words to say to – ahem – The Baron. "Sir. You are very courteous to make this offer to my sister. But I assure you that it is unnecessary. She informed me some time past that she had erred in accepting your kinsman's offer and that it was her wish to end the engagement. I assure you that whatever her feelings for him may have been, they were thoroughly extinguished long ago. While she is sensible to your natural inclinations and is undoubtedly sympathetic to your loss, she herself is not grieving. You have no obligation to my sister, Baron." His thoughts continued on, but he did not speak them aloud: *"Now, get out."*

Ambrose had tried to follow what Mr. Darcy had been saying, but it was so obscure. Had Georgiana been engaged to Uncle Benjamin? Her brother apparently thought so. *"She and I have a great deal to discuss, and we will discuss it thoroughly…after the wedding. Well after. Years, perhaps. You are an idiot, Ambrose Terwilliger, and unless you want the corruptions of Jammin Hard in your life forever, you will kick him out right now."*

Ambrose insisted. "Mr. Darcy. We are in love. We wish to marry. Will you give your permission?" Well, surprisingly, that was very easy. The stutter was gone! Ambrose inhaled and relaxed.

"Excuse me, Baron, but do you mean to say that you have approached my sister about this matter?"

Ambrose vigorously nodded assent, while his thoughts started to make war on his composure. *"What is wrong with this man? Of course, I spoke to his sister. Does he think I would be asking for her hand if she had not indicated genuine delight?"*

What Mr. Darcy said was, "And...she accepted?" but what he thought was, *"They did not exchange so much as a glance at dinner, let alone a word!"*

"Yes! Of course!" Ambrose insisted.

"When?" was what Mr. Darcy asked with undisguised incredulity, while he was thinking to himself, *" 'Never was a friendship of any kind,' she said that to me just this afternoon. She said, 'Never could be a friendship of any kind.' Those were her exact words."*

"Just now," came the Baron's immediate and somewhat baffled reply.

Title or no title, Ambrose Terwilliger was still six inches shorter than Georgiana Darcy, still more than four years younger, and...he was...so nondescript that furniture exuded more personality than he did. Blank walls inspired more admiration! There was absolutely nothing about him that could attract anyone, man or woman, let alone someone as beautiful, as refined, and as tall as Georgiana Darcy. *"This man is delusional. Raving mad. I have got to get him out of the house before he starts foaming at the lips."* Mr. Darcy drew in his breath and spoke. "Baron, you are most patient. I love my sister dearly. If she wishes to be your wife, then this marriage is my profound desire. Please accept my heartiest congratulations. And ask my sister to come to the library."

Ambrose shook hands with his future brother – what a fraternal pairing that promises to be! – and then went immediately to Georgiana's side.

"Darcy asks that you join him in the library," Ambrose whispered in her ear, turning his attentions to the other ladies seated in the parlor. Georgiana smiled, for Ambrose's use of the familiar "Darcy" in place of the more reverent "Mr. Darcy" meant that her brother's approval had been secured. She left the room and went to the library, contemplating lullabies. And nocturnes.

As she was just about to knock on the door, it opened. Her brother stepped aside to let her enter, then shut the door securely. He could not control his tongue another moment.

"Have you lost your senses to be accepting this man?"

Georgiana drew herself up and was silent. Her head was bowed, so the expression on her face was therefore concealed.

Darcy did not know what to do. He paced. He fumed. He looked at her again and again, remembering the time that Wickham chucked chestnuts at her pony. The pony shied, she fell, and Darcy had laughed at her. His little sister chased him forever, and when she caught him, she pushed him into the trout stream. She was six, Darcy eighteen, and she was glorious!

Where had she gone?

Darcy's energy flagged. He had to accept the truth. Wickham had triumphed. Georgiana had been stripped of her childhood, her virtue, and her self-respect. A brother's devoted love was not enough to make her whole again. Her acceptance of this puny piano player told Fitzwilliam Darcy that his sister was determined to settle for a life of material convenience and to insulate herself forever from all emotion. She would never know the pleasure of being truly esteemed by a man worthy of her love, nor would she ever experience the pride of being a source of joy to her lover.

More to himself than to her, he said, "How can you be so enamored of a title?"

Darcy saw his sister's eyes for the first time in many years, and he saw fire.

"How dare you?" she demanded. "How dare you speak as though I should be ashamed of my love for him?"

Darcy's jaw dropped. He stuttered something incoherent. She advanced. He retreated.

"You love him? How can you love him? He does not hunt, he does not fish, he does not ride…"

"What of it? Neither do I! I want a companion for myself, Fitzwilliam Darcy, not a companion for you!" And with that, she backed him into the library's sofa. He tumbled backward, plopping down with an ungentlemanly lack of grace, and stared up at her, mouth open, eyes wide.

"Georgiana," he entreated, "please do not push me into the trout stream again."

"What?"

Darcy could not answer her. He had started to laugh. Georgiana shook her finger at him, and she stamped her foot, and she made every other show of anger that she could think of, but he would not stop laughing. He laughed so hard, tears began to roll down his cheeks. Georgiana could not help but smile at how foolish he looked, and once she smiled, could not keep from laughing. She sat on his lap, and hugged him, and kissed his cheek, and confided the depth of her love for the man of her dreams. Darcy took her chin between his thumb and forefinger, and told her that he had once described Ambrose as a leprechaun, and, "I must have been right because…" he looked into the depth of her eyes and smiled wistfully, "…I see magic there."

Georgiana beamed, kissed him once more, and went to find her love.

Not too many minutes later, Elizabeth slipped into the library. Darcy did not rise; instead, he adjusted the position of his leg, so that his wife could have a comfortable seat upon his lap.

"A glass of wine, shall I get you?" She poured two small glasses of sherry, but did not bring them to the sofa until she had first locked the library's door, to assure their complete privacy. He raised an eyebrow and smiled. With his wife on his lap and sherry in hand, he declaimed on the wonders that he had just experienced. He praised the Baron of Coxcroft. He boasted of his sister's marvelous tantrum! He speculated on the many forms of happiness that the young couple would experience in Cornwall. As Elizabeth kissed his cheek, he pronounced the words that she had been waiting to hear (for she knew they would come, eventually): "I thank heaven that I have but one son and no daughters."

Elizabeth, very gently and very firmly, explained that those particular sentiments would not remain valid too much longer.

"Such is the price of love!" exulted Darcy, as he took full advantage of the opportunity afforded by a locked door…and a library sofa…and a love that will burn through the pages of a book, forever.

ABOUT THE AUTHOR

Linda Marie Mako Kendrick is a graduate of John Marshall High School in Cleveland, Ohio. She has pursued her education at Ohio University (AA, Journalism) at Athens, Ohio; Mountain Empire Community College at Wise, Virginia; Florida State University (BS, Business) at Tallahassee, Florida; and, Case Western Reserve University, School of Law (JD, Law) at Cleveland, Ohio. She has worked in the coal-mining industry (Virginia/Appalachia), the entertainment industry (Hollywood), and the mortgage business (Hawaii), but the bulk of her professional career has been spent as a Federal Contracting Officer at NASA, in her home town of Cleveland, Ohio. She is an avid fan of the Florida State Seminoles NCAA Football Team, but she lives and dies with the fortunes of the Cleveland Indians, Cleveland Cavaliers, and of course (being a native-born Clevelander) The Browns.

Made in the USA
Columbia, SC
24 December 2018